Love Finds You™

IN

Amana

IOWA

Love Finds You™
IN
Amana
IOWA

BY MELANIE DOBSON

summerside
PRESS™

Summerside Press™
Minneapolis 55438
www.summersidepress.com

Love Finds You in Amana, Iowa
© 2011 by Melanie Dobson

ISBN 978-1-60936-135-8

A Scripture references, unless otherwise indicated, are from the Holy Bible, King James Version (KJV). Scripture references marked niv are from The Holy Bible, New International Version®, NIV®. Copyright © 1973, 1978, 1984 by Biblica, Inc.™ Used by permission of Zondervan. All rights reserved worldwide.

The town depicted in this book is a real place, but all characters are fictional. Any resemblances to actual people or events are purely coincidental.

All epigraphs used with permission from the Amana Church Society. Translated from the German Psalter-Spiel (Amana Church Hymnal).

Cover Design by Koechel Peterson & Associates | www.kpadesign.com

Interior design by Müllerhaus Publishing Group | www.mullerhaus.net

Map of the Amana Colonies by Kristin Chambers, PaperWasp Studio | paperwaspinvites.com

Back cover and interior photos of Amana, Iowa, provided by Melanie Dobson.

Summerside Press™ is an inspirational publisher offering fresh, irresistible books to uplift the heart and engage the mind.

Printed in USA.

Dedicated to my daughter Kinzel Shae

....

Your love and sweet laughter fill my heart with joy.
You are my treasure.

A glimmer of pity washed through his eyes. "There's danger all around us, Miss Wiese."

Her aching shoulders stiffened at the urgency in his words. And the condescension.

The villages of Ebenezer weren't as isolated as the new Kolonie, but they'd been sheltered from most of the evils in the world. The crimes she'd heard rumored about in the cities never touched their community. But now, even though they traveled as one, they were no longer separated from evil. The western world, like the Ohio trail, was full of ruts and thorns threatening to ensnare them. People and problems she didn't understand.

She sniffed the smoky air and stepped back from Mr. Faust.

The world didn't frighten her—at least, not as much as her fear of how she would survive if she were thrown into it. The untamed wilderness was not her friend. She belonged in her neat kitchen, managing her assistants, feeding her people. In her world, she could ward off danger with her tongue.

"Amalie!" Mr. Faust demanded, and she snapped back to him. She would have reprimanded him for the use of her given name, but his hazel eyes had turned as dark as the night sky, piercing her with their intensity. It wasn't the time to confront him or dwell on her fears about the world. It was time to stop the danger here from infecting all of them.

"I need you to take charge," he said.

Instead of waiting to give commands to Brother John or Niklas or one of the other men, he steered his horse toward the fire and rode off.

Amalie patted the ox beside her one more time, trying to assimilate her scattered thoughts. She had no problem being in charge, but she wasn't sure how the men would respond to her. Though if Mr. Faust were able to ride toward the danger instead of away from it, she supposed she could organize the group as well as any of the men on this journey.

Karoline nudged her arm. "What can I do?"

She took a deep breath. "Go get the men at the back of the train and bring them here."

As Karoline scurried off, Amalie turned to the wagon in front of her. "Brother Niklas!" she shouted. "Brother John!"

Twenty-two-year-old Niklas Keller and his father rushed to her side.

Niklas rubbed his hands together. His eyes were on the black smoke funneling into the sky, his voice passionate. "Someone needs our help."

She shook her head. "Mr. Faust said there might be danger."

He skimmed the forest line and glanced at the wagons behind them. "I see no danger."

"He said we should group together and wait for him."

Niklas leaned back against the rear of the wagon. The elders had put Mr. Faust in authority over them for this trip. If he said to wait, they would all wait. But the minutes crept past and Mr. Faust didn't return.

A low rumble echoed through the tangled forest on the left side of their train, like the roar of hooves in a stampede. Amalie squinted into the shadows of the foliage and shuddered.

Maybe it *was* a stampede.

The men and Karoline thronged around Amalie's wagon. Peace filled each of their eyes, a peace that passed understanding, and she wondered if she was the only one whose heart raced.

"We will pray," Brother John announced, and he began petitioning their Lord for wisdom and for His hand of protection.

The roar drew closer, and her heart beat even faster.

What were they supposed to do? Christian Metz spoke regular testimonies to them in Ebenezer, inspired words from the Spirit to give them direction, but Brother Metz wasn't with them on this journey.

She glanced up at the sky, as if God would write His direction for them in the clouds, but God was silent for the moment.

1863
IA

A gunshot blasted through the trees, the sound echoing around them. She looked into the faces surrounding her. Fear flickered in some of their eyes. Questions. Several of the men had shotguns to hunt game, but they would never use a gun on their fellow man. They had only one choice.

Amalie steadied her voice, pointing toward the trees. "We need to run. Hide."

A second shot rang out and the people around her didn't hesitate this time. Karoline vanished into the forest along with most of the men standing around Amalie.

She looked at her wagon one last time, at the pots and kettles she'd spent hours cleaning and polishing and preparing for this trip. Kettles that were supposed to feed her brothers and sisters in the new kitchen.

Niklas pressed his hand on her shoulder. "Run, Amalie."

She looked back at the wagon one last time. And then she ran.

Love, which overcame and conquered
my perverse and wayward heart;
Love, by which I'm bound and anchored
that from Thee I would not part.
Johannes Scheffler

Chapter Two

Friedrich Vinzenz swiped the curved blade of his scythe through the alfalfa and flung the fresh grass over his shoulder, into a mound by the wagon. The other field hands were supposed to stack the alfalfa and toss it into the wagon, but he didn't turn around to see if they were doing their jobs. Here in the Amanas, one man had to rely on another. Trust one another. Wilhelm Hauser, the farm baas, ensured the work was done correctly, but he rarely had to make sure the men were doing their jobs. In an intricate, precise rhythm, they worked together to harvest the grass for the animals to eat over the winter.

Friedrich was a clockmaker by trade, but he hadn't built many clocks since he moved to the new Kolonie. The elders assigned him and most of the other men in the Amanas to build, plant, and harvest for their community. They would work wherever they were needed most, under the leadership of their great God and the elders He had put in authority over them. Friedrich liked the variety of the summer work. It kept him focused on the task at hand instead of feeding the wanderlust that sometimes crept into his mind and rooted itself into his soul when he was tinkering with a clock.

Behind them, in the village of Amana, he could hear the echo of hammers pounding against nails with a steady beat, inspiring all of them to work hard for the day, work unto God instead of man. The carpenters were building an addition to the woolen mill and a new barn that Friedrich and the other field workers would fill with the harvested hay. And the masons were building two homes for the colonists who were supposed to arrive from New York in about three weeks.

He tossed another bundle of grass behind him and smiled at the thought of Amalie finally coming to Amana. Beautiful and determined Amalie.

She'd caught his eye while they were still in Lehrschule. He'd had to fight to get her attention, and there was nothing Friedrich liked better than a good challenge. Amalie Wiess challenged him in so many ways.

He was almost twenty-six now. The minimum age for the men in their Kolonie to marry was twenty-four, and if the *Grosse Bruderrath*— Great Council of the Brethren—permitted it, he and Amalie would wed. Then he planned to spend the rest of his life trying to teach his wife, the newest and probably most efficient *Küchebaas* in the community, how to enjoy life as well.

The challenge exhilarated him, almost as much as the thought of seeing Amalie again. They would be together every night after evening prayers and in the early hours of the morning before she would leave to prepare the food that would fuel their community for the day. After a lifetime of being brother and sister in Christ, they would be husband and wife.

"O we ain't gonna thresh no more, no more," one of the men started singing, and Friedrich joined him with his baritone voice. "We ain't a gonna thresh no more."

The work out here was monotonous—and hard—and the elders didn't mind if they broke up the threshing work with a bit of song. It kept the men alert and focused on their job. And it kept them from dozing off in the afternoon hours when their bodies were begging for sleep.

Life would be different when Amalie arrived. Different but good. One day they would have children, and even if Amalie never joined him for singing, he would teach their children to sing. They would be a family who loved each other. A family who enjoyed each other. Just like the family he'd left behind in Ebenezer.

This autumn his mother and father and his younger sister would be joining them in Amana, when his father was no longer needed to supervise the last harvest of their fields in New York. Then he would have Amalie and his parents alongside him.

Amalie's parents wouldn't come to the Kolonie for a year or two, when the final group traveled here. He and Amalie would start their lives together long before her parents arrived, and they would thrive.

"What's that?" one of the men said, stopping the song, and Friedrich's eyes traveled across the field, toward the banks of the Iowa River.

Two men were riding toward them on horseback, both of them dressed in the steely blue uniform of the Union Army. Yellow stripes lined their trousers, and the gold buttons on their uniforms gleamed like the eyes of an opossum caught in a lantern's light. Friedrich glanced around for their baas, but he didn't see Wilhelm among the workers in the field.

As the horses trotted toward the workers, Friedrich glanced at the men surrounding him, but no one volunteered to meet the soldiers.

One of the men nodded toward him. "You speak with them."

Grasping the wooden handle of his scythe, Friedrich carried it alongside him as he approached the soldiers, curious about why these men were visiting their Kolonie.

The buttons of the man riding on the first horse bulged around his midsection, and his frock coat displayed a red patch in the shape of a shield along with three other badges across his left breast. His white beard was trimmed; his boots looked spit-and-polished.

The other man was a few decades younger than his companion. He had dark skin and a crooked nose. Friedrich had seen only a handful of Negros in his life, and those had been strung together like fish after they'd been trying to escape across the border to Canada. He would never forget those slaves, just like he would probably never forget the black soldier in front of him.

"We are representatives of the U.S. government," the older man said.

Friedrich sighed. They'd moved all the way from Ebenezer to escape the intrusion of the government and battles over the property rights of their land.

He swept his hand across the fields and trees. "We are the rightful owners of this valley."

"I don't doubt your ownership of the land, son, but I do question your service to our great Union."

Friedrich's back stiffened. He prided himself in his service to God, his community, and to his country. "I've never been disloyal to the Union."

"Loyalty means you fight when you are needed."

"No one has asked me to fight."

The man leaned down toward him and tapped one of the bronze pins on his chest. "Do you know what this badge means?"

Friedrich stared at the engraving of a soldier shaking hands with a sailor. The award probably meant the man was important by worldly standards, but Friedrich had no idea about the scale of importance.

"Abraham Lincoln himself gave it to me, for gallant conduct in this bloody war. It was made from a cannon we took from those blasted Rebels."

AMANA
1863
IA

He nudged the horse to the right, and Friedrich looked down at the man's trouser leg, dangling over the barrel of the horse. Friedrich's stomach rolled when he realized the man was missing the bottom half of his leg.

"Now they've got me back here recruiting instead of soldiering, but it doesn't mean I'm any less loyal to the war." He slipped a roll of paper from a burlap bag. "My job in *I-o-way* is to find other able-bodied men like yourself to fight for freedom, since they won't let those of us who were wounded fight any longer."

Friedrich glanced back over his shoulder, wondering where Wilhelm had gone, but all he saw were his fellow brothers, who had returned to their work harvesting the grass.

The soldier hopped down from the horse and balanced himself with a wooden cane. He was inches shorter than Friedrich, but his very presence demanded respect.

Friedrich's fingers twitched, and he felt like he should salute the man or something. Worldly men saluted each other, honoring their fellowman instead of God, but he wasn't sure if a salute would show proper respect to their government or if it would esteem one man more than another.

He kept his arms at his sides.

"You think those Confederates are going to let you keep your valley if they make it to Iowa?"

Friedrich didn't reply. The Southern rebellion seemed so far removed from their peaceful Kolonie; he couldn't imagine Confederate troops marching on their land.

"With prime property like this," the soldier said as he glanced over the field, "they'd probably burn all your pretty new buildings and take over your land."

Friedrich bowed his head slightly. "Our plans are not always the plan of God."

"You think God might want to destroy this?" When Friedrich didn't respond, the soldier continued. "Would you stand by while the Rebels burned your village?"

He shook his head, confused. "I don't know what I would do."

"My name is Colonel Liam O'Neill." The man unrolled the brown scroll in his hands. "What is your name?"

"Friedrich," he replied. "Friedrich Vinzenz."

"And you're one of the inspirational people?"

"Inspirationists," Friedrich corrected him. "We belong to the Community of True Inspiration."

Colonel O'Neill glanced down the piece of paper, repeating "Vinzenz" over and over again until he flicked the paper. "That's what I thought."

Friedrich looked over the top of the paper at the long list of names. "What is it?"

"We are forming a new regiment from the boys here in Iowa County." He reached in his pocket and withdrew a small stack of envelopes. He thumbed through them and then handed one of them to Friedrich. "You've been conscripted to serve as a soldier to fight for the Union Army. In the 28th Iowa Infantry."

The rhythm of the hammers faded behind him, his mind racing. The government had passed a new law earlier this year, requiring every man in the North to be ready to serve in the military if he was called. Some of the men in the Amanas and over in Ebenezer had already been conscripted, but he didn't know who had been called to fight. Each time someone was called, the Bruderrath paid commutation fees to excuse them from service.

"We are conscientious objectors," Friedrich said, the envelope weighing heavy in his hands. "Our faith doesn't permit us to fight."

The colonel limped forward, his eyes on Friedrich's face. The intensity in his green eyes unnerved him. "Do you have children, Friedrich?"

AMANA
1863
IA

"No."

The man's bushy eyebrows arched. "Surely you are married then."

"Not yet."

"But you're willing to send another man to fight in your place. A man with a wife and children."

Friedrich stabbed the blade of his scythe into the ground. "I don't want anyone to fight this war."

Colonel O'Neill clucked his tongue, the lines of his face drawn tightly toward his beard. "Do you even know what this war is about?"

Friedrich's gaze dropped to his boots for a moment. How could he admit to this man, decorated in awards from the president of their great country, that he didn't know much of what happened outside the Amanas? His work was to make clocks and harvest the crops to feed their people and help build their new community. There was no need for him to know what was happening outside their Kolonie.

"It is an unholy war among brothers," Friedrich said, repeating what he'd heard their head elder Brother Schaube and the other elders tell the people in their community.

"Unholy?" The man's voice was incredulous.

"Men are fighting for pride's sake when they should be seeking peace."

Colonel O'Neill shook his head, and in a voice so low Friedrich could barely hear him, he said one word. "Joseph."

The Negro prompted his horse forward, his dark eyes focused on the horse's mane.

"Would you kindly show this gentleman your arm?"

When Joseph looked up, Friedrich saw the humiliation in the man's eyes. Pity ballooned inside him, and he waved his hands to stop the man. "I don't need to see anything."

In spite of Friedrich's protests, Joseph pushed up his long sleeve, and Friedrich saw swollen patches of pink on his dark skin. Skin that had been torn with a knife or a whip. The wounds had woven them-selves together in healing, but the scars would be permanent.

"Do you need to see his back as well?" the colonel asked.

"No, thank you."

"Joseph was born in Georgia. He never knew his father, and he hasn't seen his mother since he was a child, when she was sold to another plantation. As a young man he was beaten many times for seeking the freedoms you and I enjoy every day."

"How did you escape?" Friedrich asked the man.

Joseph glanced at the colonel, who responded with a nod. "Go ahead, Joseph, tell him."

Joseph's gaze remained fixed on his saddle horn. "The massa's son and I—we was friends when we just boys. Phillip was afraid to stand up against his papa, and I cain't blame him—his papa was a mean ol' codger. But one night, while the massa was out travelin', Phillip help sneak me away."

Friedrich could feel Colonel O'Neill's intense gaze on him as Joseph fell silent.

"Phillip might have been disowned or even killed for helping a slave escape," the colonel said. "But he did what was right, and his sac-rifice, like the sacrifices of our Union soldiers today, was far greater than a thousand words spoken out against slavery."

"But it is an unholy war—" Friedrich repeated.

Colonel O'Neill interrupted him. "Some of us believe it is a holy war, fighting for our brothers and sisters like Joseph who cannot fight for themselves."

Friedrich tried to think of a response. Even though Joseph had cov-ered his mutilated arm, he could still see the twisted, discolored scars in his mind. It didn't matter the color of one's skin. What kind of man did that to another man? To a brother in God's eyes?

"It's been two weeks since the battle at Gettysburg." The colonel drummed the stack of envelopes in his hands. "You have heard about Gettysburg, haven't you?"

"No..."

Colonel O'Neill sighed, and Friedrich fidgeted with the handle of the scythe. The man didn't understand their way of life. He and the men and women who lived in the Kolonie weren't stupid. They chose to separate themselves, and in their isolation, they worshipped and served God instead of concerning themselves with the worries of this world.

Even so, Friedrich was curious about the outside world.

"How many people do you have living in your towns here?" the colonel asked.

"Almost a thousand."

Colonel O'Neill drew closer, his voice gruff. "We lost twenty-three thousand of our soldiers when the Rebels attacked our army in Pennsylvania."

Twenty-three thousand. The number was too staggering to comprehend.

"What—what happened to them?"

"Some of them were lost or wounded. Some were captured." He paused. "And at least four thousand of them died on behalf of the rest of us."

Friedrich ground the tip of the scythe's blade in the dirt. He hadn't asked these soldiers to fight in his place. He didn't want anyone to die for him.

"We need to replace these soldiers," Colonel O'Neill continued. "To protect our people and to stop those who beat and kill men like Joseph because they believe people of color are meant to be their slaves."

Friedrich swallowed hard, the man's words warring in his mind. Even though he believed there were better ways to resolve conflict than battling one another, he couldn't help but admire men who stood up for what was right. What would it be like to go into a battle to fight for those who couldn't fight for themselves?

Even as his mind churned with questions, something began to stir in his heart.

Colonel O'Neill thumbed through the envelopes and pulled one from the stack. "Your address is in Amana."

The colonel lifted another envelope from the stack, reading the name. "Do you know a Matthias Roemig?"

"I do," he said. He didn't tell Colonel O'Neill that Matthias was his best friend.

The colonel handed him two envelopes. "Will you deliver his letter to him?"

Friedrich nodded as he took the envelopes.

Colonel O'Neill climbed back on his horse, flung his pant leg onto the other side, and tucked his cane into the saddle in front of him. "Five more of the inspirational men in Middle and South Amana have been conscripted to join the Iowa regiment as well. Unless you decide to hire someone else to take your place, you are required by law to report to the enlistment office in Marengo on Monday morning."

The colonel turned his horse toward Middle Amana. "I would encourage you and Mr. Roemig and the other men of your colony to come fight for your brothers like the rest of us. Fight to save men like Joseph from the abuse of men who call themselves Christians but hurt their fellow man."

Friedrich watched as Joseph turned his own horse around and followed the colonel. The men galloped away.

What would it be like to wear the pressed uniform of a soldier, ride with a company of other men who fought with integrity and passion? Men who fought together for what was right.

He stuffed the envelopes into his pockets, then pulled his scythe out of the dirt and twisted it in his hands. What would it be like to fire a shotgun at a person instead of an animal?

His stomach turned like the tool in his fingers and then he swung the blade through the alfalfa. With the soldiers gone, the men around him returned to their singing, but the lyrics lodged in Friedrich's throat.

In an hour, over supper, he would give Matthias the conscription letter. He knew exactly what Matthias would say, but this time, he wasn't sure he would agree with his friend.

Though devils all the world should fill, all eager to devour us,
We tremble not, we fear no ill, they shall not overpower us.
Martin Luther

Chapter Three
....

Tree limbs snagged Amalie's dress as she raced through the trees. The sharp branches struck her bonnet, cut her face, and her heels tangled in the overgrowth. She yanked her boots forward, trying to flee the gunshots, but it seemed like the entire forest was conspiring against her.

A man called out, yelling for her to stop, but she kept running. She didn't even look back, at the man or the road or her friends or the precious pots and pans she left in her wagon.

She could hear the horses now, panting behind her, trying to stop her. In seconds they would overtake her and she wouldn't be able to divert them, but until they stopped her, she continued to run, praying for God's mercy on her life. Praying that if it were time for her to go home, He would take her quickly to Him.

Beside her, a black horse pushed through the overgrowth, and seconds later, four horses surrounded her. She stopped, struggling for breath as she turned to face her pursuers with confidence.

The confidence faded as she looked at the riders. They were the most unkempt, the most motley group of men she'd ever seen. Even more rugged than Mr. Faust or the men who came to their colony in search of work. Their cotton shirts were tattered and stained. Their trousers faded. She couldn't tell if their uniforms were blue or gray, but since they were traveling through Ohio, she assumed they were Yankees. The Confederates, she'd been told, were much farther south in Kentucky and Virginia.

She leaned back against the tree, trying to breathe before she spoke. "Why are you chasing me?"

The soldiers looked over her shoulder, and she turned to face a tall man with an arrowhead-shaped beard on his chin and a mustache that curled up on both ends. Even with the summer heat, he wore a gray jacket, the collar encircled in stars.

"We are chasing you—" he started, and then he laughed. "We are chasing you, miss, because you are running."

"But—"

"Allow me to introduce myself," he interrupted. "I'm General John Hunt Morgan of the Confederate Army, and these are my men."

"The Confederate Army?" A wave of nausea swept over her. She hoped the rest of her brothers and sisters had run far away from these soldiers, a place where they were safe.

The edges of his lips peaked upward to his mustache. "Have you not heard of me?"

"I have not."

The general laughed again, seemingly pleased by her lack of knowledge about him. "The Yanks calls us savage beasts."

Beasts. She cringed at the word and the crassness in his tone.

"But we think of ourselves more like troublemakers."

"There's—there's not supposed to be any fighting in Ohio."

He laughed again. "Well, there's no time to educate you at this moment. We have people chasing us as well."

He glanced back toward the trail and then motioned his men to ride around them. She didn't know how many horses to expect, but it seemed like there were hundreds. "Your Yankee friends can tell you the stories about me and my fine men though."

She clung to the tree as the horses stomped by her. "I don't have any Yankee friends."

His eyebrows slid up. "You should be grateful for that. A Yank will say he's your friend, and then he'll shoot you in the back."

She tried to stand taller. "Aren't you supposed to be in the South?"

His grin grew even wider. "Our orders are to wreak havoc across the North, and I must say, we are quite good at it."

"You're burning things?"

"Ah," he said. "You saw our handiwork firsthand."

"We saw the smoke from it."

"Are you traveling to Lisbon?"

She nodded. "For the night."

"I'm sorry to say it, but the loss of the bridge will lengthen your journey."

Hope sprang up inside her. Perhaps he would release her to continue her journey.

His horse stomped on the ground, and he inched back the reins. "We had to stop the men chasing us, you understand, but even with the fire, some of them will make it across the water. I think they take pleasure in chasing us, almost as much as we enjoy raiding their land."

She marveled at how he could smile in spite of the danger, or perhaps because of it.

"You and your friends best keep moving along the trail," he said. "It isn't safe in these parts right now."

"Nor will it be if you don't stop wreaking your havoc."

He laughed one last time, and then clucked his tongue. She ducked behind a sheath of leaves as General Morgan and the rest of his solders ran past her. As the general predicted, another band of men and their horses raced through the forest behind him minutes later.

Through the leaves, she saw their fine uniforms made of blue, but thankfully, they didn't seem to see her hidden in the trees. She prayed the Union soldiers would be as genteel to her brothers and sisters as the company from the Confederacy had been to her.

Even when the soldiers were gone, she didn't move. There could be more men behind this wave, trailing the Union men. As the minutes passed, the clamor of shouting and gunshots and the pounding of horses' hooves were replaced by the soft brush of leaves dancing in the breeze.

Quickly she moved back toward the trail. None of the other Inspirationists had returned, but the ox teams remained at the side of the path, eating grass along the trail. None of their animals or wagons appeared harmed.

She breathed another prayer of thanks that the general hadn't wreaked havoc on their wagon train.

She climbed into the back of her wagon and cinched the cord to block out the sunrays. Running her hands over a wrought iron kettle, she hoped they could all celebrate together the Lord's provision for them. Tonight they would rejoice as a community. The meal would be simple, biscuits and stew, but it would still be a celebration.

She waited inside the wagon until she heard the galloping of a solitary horse. Peeking out the front, she saw Mr. Faust ride up, and she climbed off the wagon.

He jumped off his horse when he saw her. "You are safe?"

She nodded.

He glanced around the wagons, like her friends might be hiding inside as well. "And the others?"

"I pray they are waiting in the forest."

Mr. Faust reached back into his leather bag and took out a horn.

The bugle blast rattled the pots hanging behind her, and she put her hands over her ears until the sound died out.

"The Rebels burnt the bridge to Lisbon," Mr. Faust said, his voice grim. "There's no other place for us to cross in miles."

She didn't tell him about General Morgan and how, in his pride, the man had laughed at the destruction. Or how the general seemed charming in spite of his actions. That's how Satan himself would be, she guessed, if she ever met him. Charming and destructive. He would take as much pleasure in stealing and destroying as the general did.

One by one, men clad in flannel shirts and trousers slipped out of the forest, onto the trail. Her heart leapt at the sight of each face, and she counted them as they joined her and Mr. Faust by the wagons.

Nine. Ten. Eleven men.

Mosquitoes swarmed around her bonnet, and she brushed them away as she squinted into the trees, looking for Karoline. They had left Ebenezer with twenty-five people, and they would arrive in Iowa with the same number.

Minutes crept past, and the number of people walking out of the trees trickled.

She counted sixteen now. Seventeen.

Eight people were still out there, and she prayed silently that they weren't lost in the woods.

One of the brothers gathered the travelers into a circle. Mr. Faust stood on the outside as they beseeched the Lord for the people still in the woods. She didn't close her eyes during the prayers, watching instead for Brother Niklas and his father. For Karoline Baumer.

The days of all of their lives were numbered, but she didn't want to lose a single one of their members. Not today.

One of the men began singing a hymn, the words and tune memorized from the *Psalter-Spiel*.

When my God brought upon me terror
And the danger has gone by,
Then I will bring offerings of thanks
And sing with mighty voice.

Amalie didn't sing, but in her heart she offered her thanks for those who had returned. And she prayed again for those who had not.

From the corner of her eye, she saw another face in the trees, and Karoline Baumer stumbled out to the trail. Her sunbonnet was gone, and her golden hair fell tangled across her shoulders.

"Karoline!" Amalie ran to her. Blood matted the girl's hair, and there was a gash near her ear. She put her arm around Karoline's shoulders. "Did the soldiers hurt you?"

Karoline shook her head. "There was a horse, running toward me. I tried to get out of its way."

Amalie shuddered. "Its hooves—"

"I fell." Karoline put her hand to her head, touching the wound. "And I hit my head on something, a tree or maybe a rock on the ground. I don't know. Something sharp."

Gently Amalie directed the younger woman toward the kitchen wagon. "I will clean your wound."

Karoline stared down at the red on her fingers. "I didn't know I was bleeding."

The women passed by Brother Niklas and John as they walked out of the forest.

Twenty-three and twenty-four.

The singing grew louder behind them. Only one more person left to return from the woods, and they would all be together again.

Amalie lifted several sacks out of the kitchen wagon to make room for Karoline and unrolled her canvas bed sack on the wooden floor. She removed her pillow, comforter, and several blankets from the roll and she smoothed the comforter on the floor. Two of the men helped Karoline step up into the back of the wagon.

Karoline leaned her head back against the roll of blankets, and as Amalie dabbed her friend's forehead with a cloth to clean the wound, she thought Karoline would murmur with the pain, but she was silent instead.

The doctor in Ebenezer had provided Amalie with a medical kit and instructions on how to use the different remedies in case someone was hurt on the trail. She took out a bottle of ointment from her trunk, rubbed the ointment onto a piece of fabric, and tied the cotton material around Karoline's head. Hidden in the bottom of the trunk was a tincture of cannabis for the pain, and she spooned the medicine into her friend's mouth.

Amalie smiled. "You're almost as good as new."

Karoline closed her eyes. "I don't feel new."

Even with the summer heat, her friend shivered, and Amalie pulled a blanket up to her shoulders.

"You rest now," she told her. "We'll find a doctor in Lisbon to look at your head."

She didn't want to think how long it would take them to get to Lisbon.

"I don't feel the pain anymore," Karoline said.

"Good." Amalie closed the trunk. "I'll make you some soup to eat tonight, and you'll be well again soon."

Karoline opened her eyes, staring up at the canvas wagon top. "Do you see the stars?"

Amalie glanced up and then looked back at her friend. "It's still light, Karoline."

"But I see stars."

Amalie squeezed her hand. "You need to rest now."

Karoline muttered something else, but Amalie couldn't understand her. She patted her friend's hand gently until Karoline's breathing indicated she was sleeping, and then she climbed back out of the wagon.

Niklas was waiting for her outside. "Is she going to be all right?"

"I pray so," she said. "But she needs to see a physician."

"Faust will get us to Lisbon as soon as he can."

She glanced across the heads of the men loitering in front of the wagon, waiting to move on. "Did the last person come out of the forest?"

"Everyone is accounted for."

Her eyes grew wide. "But I only counted twenty-four people."

Niklas silently counted the heads around them and then smiled. "I believe you've neglected to count yourself, Sister Amalie."

She thought back over her counting and then sighed with relief. He was right—she had forgotten to include herself.

As she and Niklas walked toward the rest of their community, Mr. Faust lit his pipe and smoke rolled from his lips. When he reached the circle of men he began speaking.

"The bridge to Lisbon has been destroyed." He lifted his hat and raked his fingers through his dark hair. "We will supper at the banks of the river tonight, and then tomorrow we will have to ford the water."

Amalie stepped forward. "Sister Karoline is not well."

Mr. Faust contemplated her words for a moment. "We can send one of the men ahead tonight to get a doctor from Lisbon."

She sighed with relief.

He looked up at the sky. "We have at least two hours left of light tonight so we best be moving."

They all dispersed to travel alongside their appointed wagons, and Amalie walked slowly back to hers. Her stomach rumbled, ready for the supper meal. When they stopped, she would make soup for Karoline and stew for the rest of them from dried meat and their remaining vegetables.

Her mind wandered back to Ebenezer and then forward to Amana. Friedrich and the others were sitting down for their meal now. The baas and her assistants were probably scrambling to place slices of roasted, warm meat on the platters and pour milk into pitchers for the diners. She would give just about anything for a cold glass of water or milk.

In a few weeks she would be back in the familiarity of a kitchen. Her own kitchen. Since the time she was fourteen, she had spent almost every day cooking and cleaning. She'd spent her summers canning and the winters creating new recipes from their bounty. Some women felt confined inside a kitchen house, but she thrived in it. Sometimes, when her baas was gone for the day, she imagined herself to be a queen, reigning over the kettles and pots in her kingdom. She would never tell any of her friends about her imagined queenship—they would be right to accuse her of being proud instead of humble, even in her imagination—but it was a game she played nonetheless.

Mounted on the side of her wagon was an oak barrel, and she ladled the water from it into a tin cup. The water had been baked by the sun, more hot than tepid in temperature, but as she sipped it, she pretended it was a glass of milk.

In three weeks she would be in her new kitchen…and she would be with Friedrich. Was he as nervous about seeing her as she was to see him?

As the months and then years went by, his letters became less frequent though they were always signed with his undying love for her. Over the years she'd wondered if he would wait for her, worried that by the time she arrived in Amana he would already have given his heart to someone else. Sometimes she even wondered if the years apart would sever the relationship they'd once enjoyed.

Friedrich had always been passionate, even as a child. Instead of weighing every consequence like she did, he made his decisions on a whim; often she wished he would just sit down and think for five minutes before he made a choice that would affect his—and now her—life.

The elders had given Friedrich the choice to come to Amana three years ago or wait for her. He'd chosen to come to the new Kolonie. Not because he didn't love her, he said, but because he thought waiting together in Ebenezer until he was twenty-four would be torture. But now he was two years older than the age required to marry, and she hoped they were both mature enough to rationally think through their decisions instead of act upon their emotions.

Even though his letters weren't as frequent as they used to be, every time Friedrich wrote he said he was faithful to his promise to her, that he waited for her. Her heart remained true to him as well. Never once did she even consider marrying one of the other men who remained behind in Ebenezer. For more than a decade, she'd believed that she and Friedrich were meant to be together.

Still, she had changed over the past three years, and he must have changed as well. And the moment she saw him, she believed she would know if she would become his wife.

Lifting her skirt, she climbed into the back of the wagon, beside Karoline. The younger woman was sleeping on the comforter, breathing softly. There wasn't much room among the stacked crates and trunks and barrels, but Amalie tucked her knees close to her chest and leaned her head back against a trunk. Until they left Ebenezer, she hadn't realized how important the seemingly simplest comforts were to her. A bed. A bathtub. A clean place to wash her clothes.

Mr. Faust shouted, and the wagon lurched forward.

Turning, she reached into the chest and pulled out a small, hand-carved box Friedrich crafted for her before he left New York. It was made of dark walnut wood and polished until it almost glowed. She opened it slowly and looked at the rose petals inside, from the flowers Friedrich had given to her to remind her of his love for her while they were apart.

She sniffed the rose petals, hoping for even the slightest scent to remind her of his love, but they'd long since lost their aroma. Closing the lid, she clutched the box in her lap. It was a very small sacrifice to leave the comforts of Ebenezer for their journey west. It would all be worth it when they arrived in Amana.

Her eyes drooped, and she tried to open them again, but they wouldn't obey her. The wagon hit a hole, and everything around her and Karoline shook, but the clanging didn't awaken her friend. Amalie reached behind her, placed her precious box back into the trunk, and rested beside Karoline.

When the wagon stopped again, Amalie rubbed her eyes and squinted outside at the fading sunlight. A river reflected a brilliant scarlet color from the setting sun, and she pulled herself to her feet to begin supper before the darkness engulfed them. Karoline was still asleep, but maybe Niklas or one of the other men could help her prepare the meal tonight. Even with two of them working hard, it would take a good hour to finish the biscuits and the stew for twenty-five of them, but if they were as hungry as she was, they would complete it as quickly as they could.

She stood on her toes, trying not to wake Karoline as she lifted a pan off its hook. Then she took a burlap bag filled with potatoes off the heap of supplies. She'd wanted to conserve them, but they were almost to Lisbon now. The boiled potatoes would help fill their bellies tonight along with the stew.

She started to climb over Karoline, and then she stopped. Karoline was quiet. Too quiet.

Amalie dropped the potatoes on the floor and knelt down by her friend, dropping her cheek to her chest.

"Karoline," she said, quietly at first. Her voice trembled when she said her name again. "Karoline!"

When she shook her, Karoline didn't respond.

"Niklas!" she screamed as she ripped open the canvas. "John!"

Seconds later both men were at her side.

Watch against thyself, my soul, see thou do not stifle
Grace that should thy thoughts control, nor with mercy trifle.
Johann B. Freistein

Chapter Four
....

Friedrich wiped the cloth napkin over his mouth and paused before he took another bite of the tender roast pork and red cabbage. Forks clanged against the ceramic plates as forty men and women ate the roast and vegetables prepared by Henriette Koch and her assistants. No one spoke except to ask for the salt or to pass the basket of rolls. Conversation was reserved for time away from work and meals and their daily services in prayer and worship.

He lifted another bite to his mouth, but then he set his fork down, pushing away his plate of food. How could he eat when men like Joseph were getting beaten tonight? When they were being starved? He spent his days harvesting food for animals while there were men who were fighting and dying for what was right.

Loyalty means you fight...

Colonel O'Neill's words played over and over again in his mind, and he couldn't seem to rid himself of the burden of guilt that entangled him. By not participating in this war, was he being disloyal to the government God had placed over him? Was he a coward?

Sophia Paul stopped at his table with two pitchers of milk in her hands. Lifting Friedrich's glass, she slowly filled it. Friedrich didn't look at her, but he could feel her presence as she lingered beside him, filling the glasses of the men on each side.

When he glanced over at her, Sophia giggled, and he refocused his eyes on Matthias, across the table. One of Matthias's eyebrows rose, and Friedrich's eyes narrowed at the grin on his friend's face. Matthias's smile grew even bigger, and Friedrich wished he could reach across the table and wipe the smirk off his face.

Matthias knew Friedrich was planning to marry Amalie Wiese, and no matter how many times Sophia refilled his glass or brought him and the men in the fields baked goods for their lunch, he wouldn't change his mind.

Sophia moved to the women's table and placed one of her pitchers on it. Friedrich noticed she neglected to fill any of their glasses.

The man sitting next to Friedrich elbowed him and whispered, "Won't be long before Amalie's making supper for you."

Friedrich nodded. Amalie's cooking was renowned across the community. When her baas was ill in Ebenezer, Amalie developed a reputation as someone who demanded those under her to work hard, but all of their hard work paid off during meal times. Most of the brothers hoped they would be selected to eat in her new dining room, but as Amalie's husband, Friedrich would be guaranteed a place at one of the tables.

Amalie wasn't silly like Sophia or some of the other young women who giggled around the men. She was serious and determined and dedicated to their community. There was no finer single woman among the Inspirationists than Amalie, and she was going to be his wife.

But tonight, instead of excitement about her arrival and their subsequent marriage, an eerie sense of dread settled over Friedrich's heart. In weeks, he would become one of the married men the colonel talked about, and in a year's time, he could be a father as well.

He wanted to marry Amalie, and he especially wanted to have

children, two or maybe even three. But how could he live with himself, knowing he didn't fight for his brother? His children would never respect him, not if he didn't respect himself. And how could he, if he knew people were suffering in their country, and he covered his ears and his eyes to their pain?

Maybe the timing wasn't right to marry Amalie or begin a family. Maybe he should fight first and then return to her.

When he looked up again, Matthias was watching him, but this time Matthias didn't mock him with his smile. Instead he nodded at Friedrich's half-eaten plate.

"Are you ill?" his friend whispered.

He shrugged his shoulders. He couldn't whisper back all that had happened this afternoon or the thoughts raging in his head. Lifting his fork again, he pushed the remaining cabbage and potatoes around his plate. The thought of taking even one more bite made his stomach roll so instead of eating, he guzzled down his glass of milk and then slid off the bench before Brother Schaube closed the meal with prayer.

The dining room door slammed behind him, echoing through the silence, but he didn't care. How could any of them fill their bellies in silence when so many of their countrymen were dying? It seemed wrong now, so much peace here when a war raged in their country.

He marched forward on the narrow pathway that wove through the houses and gardens in Amana. He had to get away from the others, to a place where he could clear his mind.

Ahead was the stone residence where they met each night for prayer. Beside it was a grove of plum trees, lined in neat rows in a procession out to the cornfield. In the midst of the quiet trees was a wooden bench, and he sat down on it, resting his chin in his hands.

There was no fighting in their community. No battles among their people. Amana and the surrounding villages were about as close as one could come to experiencing a bit of heaven on this earth. The community members worshipped God together. Ate together. Encouraged and consoled one another.

Would God have him leave this peaceful world and the people who had loved him since he was born to go out to a place where people hated one another? Where a man wounded and sometimes killed his brother?

He pulled the envelope from his pocket and opened it. The letter was brief, but it was exactly what Colonel O'Neill had said. The government was mustering him to fight for the state of Iowa, for their union. And they wanted him to report for duty on Monday.

He flicked his fingernail against the paper. He hadn't started this war, but something continued to stir inside him, something that urged him to fight.

Since he was a boy, he'd been the one to fight for the underdog. He'd even fought for Amalie when they were in school, stopping the boys who teased her when she excelled above all of them in their studies. He'd never tried to fight for his own good, only for the good of those around him, but he'd suffered the consequences for the fight that swelled within him, suffered under the switch of their schoolmaster and his father's paddle.

His father often said that Friedrich reminded him of Otto Vinzenz, Friedrich's grandfather. His grandfather had fought against Napoleon Bonaparte's army fifty years ago and was one of many who defeated the tyrant in the Battle of Waterloo. A war hero. His father rarely talked about Otto Vinzenz, but Friedrich used to pepper his mother with questions about him when he was a child.

When his parents joined the Community of True Inspiration and moved to the United States, God had placed a new government over them, and now the same government that had provided freedom for them from oppression in German called him to duty to fight against the oppression of slaves.

Their leader, Christian Metz, spoke often of the war and sometimes about slavery. He didn't think slavery was right, but he and the other elders believed that this evil would one day be eliminated by God, like other evils in their society.

Friedrich shook his head. What if God ordained this war to eliminate slavery? He wouldn't join the infantry if he lived in the Confederacy, but the Union was fighting for freedom. How could he turn his back on men like Joseph who had been sold and beaten because of their skin color?

Matthias sat down beside him. "You never leave food on your plate, Friedrich."

"I wasn't hungry."

Matthias leaned back, crossing one leg over the other. "I never thought I'd hear those words come out of your mouth."

Friedrich didn't respond.

"Is it Amalie?" Matthias asked.

"Partly."

"Have you changed your mind?"

He shook his head. "Neither my mind nor my heart have changed."

"She'll make a good wife for you."

"You don't even like Amalie."

"That's not true," Matthias protested.

"You said she's too impertinent for me."

"When she was sixteen!"

Friedrich managed a smile. "So you've changed your opinion."

"People change over the years—"

"It doesn't matter anyway," Friedrich interrupted. "Amalie isn't the problem."

"So there is a problem—"

Two sisters walked by them, and Friedrich waited to speak. More than a thousand Inspirationists had arrived from New York now, which made privacy in Amana almost impossible. Each member had their own room in which to sleep, but they worked and worshipped together. And sometimes they talked about each other like they were a giant family as well.

The two women slipped into the stone house, and Friedrich glanced back down the path. No one else was coming toward them. "Two men visited us today in the fields."

"Vagabonds?"

He shook his head. "Soldiers."

Matthias frowned. "What were they doing here?"

"Recruiting."

"Metz said none of our men would be going to war."

"The man was a colonel," Friedrich said. "And he played a powerful argument."

"It doesn't matter how powerful an argument. It matters what is right." Matthias's voice was strong, determined, but Friedrich barely heard his words.

"There was a colored man with the colonel," Friedrich said. "He was beaten by his owner in Georgia."

"Slavery is a terrible, terrible evil."

"An evil that should be stopped."

"This isn't our war," Matthias said.

"Why not?" he probed. "This is our country. I can't understand why this isn't our war as well."

"Slavery is wrong," Matthias agreed. "But instead of brothers battling each other, the slaves should flee to safety, like our people did when we left Germany."

"There is no place for the slaves to flee."

"They can run north. To freedom."

Friedrich fidgeted on his seat. "But what if they can't run?"

"The colonel is playing with your emotions, Friedrich, so you'll follow him instead of following what God has ordained for our community."

His thoughts raced. "What is God's plan for us?"

Matthias was quiet for a moment. They'd both heard the same words, the inspired testimonies from their *Werkzeuge*—the men and women God used to communicate to their society. Brother Metz had begged the leaders in Washington to cast themselves down in the dust of humility so that peace would be preserved, instead of stirring up brothers to war against each other. His words went unheeded.

"We need to pray for peace," Matthias said.

Friedrich shook his head. "It's too late for peace."

"It's never too late—"

"The Confederate Army just killed four thousand men in Pennsylvania."

"Four thousand—" Matthias's voice faded away as he looked across the street, toward grapevines that had entwined itself around the trellis. Brother Schaube walked by them with his wife and son. He tipped his hat, but Matthias didn't seem to notice.

Seconds passed, the number of casualties walled between them. Matthias's eyes stayed on the grapevines, his voice low. "How many Confederates did the Union soldiers kill?"

"I don't know."

"It is happening just as Brother Metz said it would. Instead of seeking peace, the brothers are fighting themselves. Killing each other."

"For their fellow man."

"*Ach*," Matthias snapped. "For the pride in their Union."

The bell tolled from the tower, announcing their evening prayers, but Friedrich didn't stand up. He held Matthias's letter out to him.

"They want us to fight."

"We are not to fight," Matthias said as he stood. "We are to pray."

Friedrich remained on the bench, still holding the letter out to Matthias. "We're supposed to report to the enlistment office in Marengo on Monday."

Matthias sighed as he took the envelope, but he didn't open it up. "They cannot make us fight, my friend. The Bruderrath will hire substitutes for us and we will continue to build our Kolonie, where God has called us."

As the chiming faded away, Friedrich stood up and followed Matthias to the stone house. His friend opened the door for a woman whose shoulders and head were covered with her shawl, and then the two of them entered the large sitting room. The woman walked to the left, and both men sat on a pine bench on the right.

Brother Schaube led them in prayer for their country and for the men and women traveling west to them tonight. Friedrich dropped his head in his hands and prayed like he'd never prayed before.

Should this night prove the last for me in this dark vale of tears,
Then lead me, Lord, in heaven to Thee and my elect compeers.
Dr. Johann Herzog

Chapter Five

. . . .

Amalie wouldn't release Karoline's limp hand. Niklas brought cold water from the river, wiping it across Karoline's forehead, but all Amalie could do was cling to her friend's fingers. She felt so powerless. Her friend was breathing, barely, but there was nothing Amalie could do. Karoline wouldn't wake up, no matter how cold the water.

The sliver of the crescent moon was out tonight, its light spilling over the coolness of the evening and across the wagons in their campsite. Karoline was unconscious in the night air, stretched across the canvas Niklas had spread to protect her from the ground.

Amalie tucked a quilt tight around her friend's shoulders, and Karoline moaned, tossing her head as Niklas dipped the washcloth back into the pail and dampened her forehead again.

It was her fault Karoline wouldn't waken. She shouldn't have given Karoline the cannabis nor should she have let her sleep. And she should have insisted that Mr. Faust ride toward Lisbon immediately when they realized Karoline was injured instead of waiting for the cumbersome wagon train to plod toward the river.

"Sister Amalie," Brother John whispered. "The men need to eat something for supper."

She looked up at him, dazed. "Supper?"

"Nothing fancy," he insisted. "Just something to get us by for the night."

Amalie took the washcloth from Niklas and dabbed Karoline's head again. Then she stood up. "I have to start a fire."

"We already started it," John said, and she turned to see several campfires glowing along the riverbank. "You tell us what to do and we'll cook tonight."

"I will help you."

He shook his head. "You tend to Karoline tonight. We'll make do."

She considered his words for a moment. "Can you boil potatoes?"

"I believe I could if you would tell me how."

"Remove the iron kettle from my wagon and two of the coffee tins," she instructed. "Fill them with water."

When John moved toward her wagon, she explained to another man how to light the camp stove for the coffee and prepare the beans with her grinder. Niklas heated the kettle water for potatoes while the coffee brewed. John cut up pieces of beef jerky with his knife. When he was done, the men could mix the pieces with the potatoes to add flavor to the bland meal.

Amalie stroked Karoline's hair while the men cooked, and prayed that God would allow her friend to stay on this earth with them a little longer. She couldn't greet Karoline's mother in Amana with the message that her daughter had died on the trail. The very thought wrenched her heart, but she blinked back her tears. Not since childhood had Amalie allowed anyone to see her cry. Her parents had taught her well that tears were a sign of weakness. She had never once seen either of them cry, not even when their only daughter left Ebenezer for Iowa.

Karoline's mother reminded her of Louise Vinzenz, Friedrich's mother. Both of them would do just about anything for their children.

Minutes later John returned to her side with a steaming tin cup outstretched in his hand.

"Thank you," Amalie said as she sniffed its aroma. Then she sipped the heavy liquid. Her stomach growled, and for the first time that night, she realized she was hungry as well.

A horse neighed, and there was a splash across the river. She looked up to see Mr. Faust gallop into their camp. As he pulled back his reins, his horse sprayed water down on her and Karoline. She cringed, brushing Karoline's face off with the washcloth, and then she tried to search the darkness behind Mr. Faust. The fires and lantern light blocked her view of the river.

"Where is the doctor?" she asked.

He thumbed over his shoulder. "He's waiting for her in his carriage, across the river."

She stared into the black space beyond their camp, trying to see the outline of a carriage, but she couldn't even see how far it was across the river. "Where is he going to take her?"

"To Lisbon."

She stood. "I need to go with her."

Mr. Faust shook his head. "We need you here to make breakfast."

She stared at the stripes lining his flannel shirt, trying to capture the bitter words in her throat before they spewed all over him.

Was he speaking out of selfishness for his own belly or for the benefit of her people? Or was it selfish for her to go to town with Karoline and leave the men without someone to cook in the morning?

She couldn't begin to question her motives now. Instead she stood up beside Mr. Faust as he dismounted from his horse.

"Someone needs to go with her," she said.

Niklas was beside her again. "We can make breakfast without Amalie."

Mr. Faust laughed. "Are you planning to cook?"

Niklas didn't return the laughter. "We managed to boil potatoes tonight. I think we can cook oatmeal over the fire."

Amalie held up her tin cup. "And they made coffee tonight as well."

Mr. Faust glanced back and forth between them and then down at Karoline. Without another argument, he began barking orders to the men, telling them how they were going to transport Karoline across the water in the wagon, to the doctor's carriage.

Amalie looked over at Niklas, and he shrugged his shoulders. Faust hadn't told either of them who would be traveling with Karoline, so she sat back down beside her sleeping friend and waited.

At Mr. Faust's command, the men set down their plates and moved toward her wagon. Two of them climbed into the back and began rolling the heavy barrels of flour and sugar to the men below. Then they picked up her grandmother's trunk, and she held her breath as they lifted it over the back of the wagon and put it safely on the ground.

Mr. Faust turned toward John and appointed him to be a footman. "Take off your boots and roll up your trousers."

Amalie heard him explain how they would prod the riverbed in the darkness, searching for the firmest possible ground, so that Amalie's wagon wouldn't get stuck in the soft mud. They would mark the chosen path with sticks.

Minutes later, the grass around her was strewn with burlap bags, barrels, pans, and her massive trunk. Mr. Faust and John secured the long sticks under their arms and each carried a lantern. As they waded into the current, they seemed to vanish in the blackness.

Niklas rehitched the oxen to the wagon, but there was nothing for Amalie to do except sit quietly beside Karoline and pray her friend would make it safely to Lisbon.

For the briefest of moments, Amalie entertained the thought of crossing the river like the men, but then her mind flashed to the feeling of mud oozing up between her toes. Slime clinging to her ankles. She shivered. The mud would swallow her feet if she stepped into the river.

And what if she slipped on a rock and soaked her dress? The water might pull her under the current. It didn't matter how fast or slow the water was running. She didn't know how to swim. Maybe it would be better if she stayed here to cook for the men in the morning. Someone who knew how to swim could escort Karoline in the darkness.

A whistle traveled across the river, and Niklas rushed back to her.

"Mr. Faust wants you to travel with Karoline."

She brushed her skirt off, taking a deep breath as she stood up. "I can't make it across the river."

"You'll be riding in the wagon," he said

The men carefully lifted Karoline into the wagon. Amalie plucked up the satchel with her clothing from the ground, eyeing the remaining trunk, barrels, and all of her cookware. Surely the men would take care loading and carrying her belongings across the river.

Well, there was no use worrying about it now.

She climbed into the back of the wagon and settled in beside Karoline. Her stomach growled again and she wished she had eaten one of the boiled potatoes. It was ironic, an hour ago this wagon was filled with food, and now she was hungry with nothing around her to eat.

Mr. Faust whistled, and the wagon bumped as Charlie guided the oxen forward. The wagon dipped down toward the river, shifting Amalie and Karoline forward. Water sprayed the sides of the canvas.

In the dim light, Amalie scanned the wooden wagon floor and then breathed with relief. As far as she could see, no water bubbled through the tar that was supposed to seal the cracks.

The wagon rocked and she clung to the side with one hand, trying to secure Karoline with the other, as the wheels bumped over rocks and tree limbs hidden under the surface.

Only one time had Amalie been on a boat before, and that was on the steamer she and her parents had taken from Germany to New York when she was five. She didn't remember much about the trip except she'd spent part of it playing on the deck with Matthias and part of it below with a chamber pot in her lap, unable to keep food in her stomach. Friedrich had spent almost the entire trip in his family's cabin, sick from the wicked reeling of the waves.

The water didn't reel tonight. It lapped against the sides of the wagon as the team lurched forward again. Then the wagon jerked to a stop. Mr. Faust shouted, and she heard the crack of the whip, but the wagon didn't budge.

Slowly she crawled to the front of the wagon and edged back the canvas. She could barely see the outline of the oxen's thick frames, but she heard their pants, straining against the hitches to pull the wagon through the water and the mud.

"Come on," she whispered, wiping sweat off her face. The animals had to get them across to the doctor.

Karoline stirred and Amalie crawled back to stroke her arm.

"Don't worry," she whispered. "The doctor is waiting for you."

Mr. Faust waded by the wagon, shouting at the oxen to move. Karoline thrashed her head back and forth at the sound of his voice, and Amalie tried to secure Karoline's head in her lap. She heard him whip their backs, trying to force them forward

Light from a lantern stole through the back of the wagon, sending shadows across the floor. Then Mr. Faust leaned in through the canvas.

"The wagon's stuck," he announced.

She brushed her fingers over Karoline's head again. Before she spoke, she had to soften the panic swelling in her throat. "What are you going to do?" she finally asked.

"I don't think I can do anything."

"But Karoline needs to get across the river."

After another shout at the oxen, Mr. Faust leaned into the wagon again. "The animals are tired."

"Maybe you should let them rest."

"They won't rest as long as your wagon's hitched to them," he said with a shake of his head. "They'll keep trying to pull."

"Can't you unhitch them?"

"Not if you want to take your things to Iowa with you. Once the oxen reach the other side, I'm afraid they won't come back for the wagon."

Karoline groaned again.

"What can we do?" Amalie asked.

"We need to lessen the load on the wagon and try again."

With a quick glance around the barren wagon, Amalie reached for the only items left—her and Karoline's satchels. She held them out to Mr. Faust, but instead of taking them, he just stared. "That's not going to—"

She pushed the bags toward him. He needed to try. He mumbled something she didn't understand, but he took the satchels from her and transported them to the river bank.

When the oxen pulled again, the wheels moved a few inches closer to the bank.

Mr. Faust nudged his head into the wagon again, his long hair falling into his eyes. "We need to get rid of some more weight."

"But the men already took everything else out of it."

His eyebrows slid up. "We can't take Karoline out of the wagon."

She eyed the water and slid back from the door. "I can't get out."

"Amalie—" he started.

"My name is Miss Wiese," she barked at him. "And I'm not getting on that horse with you."

"We don't have another choice."

Amalie whipped the canvas curtain shut. They had to get Karoline to Lisbon, and they couldn't do it if Amalie remained in the wagon. She wasn't getting on that horse with Mr. Faust.

Amalie groaned as she pulled her feet close, unlaced her boots, and yanked them off. If she didn't ride the horse, she had no other choice but to walk through the water. She rolled down her stockings and tucked them inside her boots, listening as she did so for the sounds outside. The splash of the horse and panting of the oxen. She kept hoping they would suddenly lurch forward, pushing through whatever obstacle had gotten in their way, but the wagon didn't move.

"I'm not leaving you for long," she told Karoline, hoping the younger woman could hear in her sleep. "I'll see you on the other side of the river."

Standing up, she uncinched the canvas on the back of the wagon and hid her toes under her dress, feeling half-naked standing there without her stockings or boots. Mr. Faust coaxed his horse forward and offered her his arm to step onto the narrow ledge on the back of the wagon. She shook her head, keeping one of her hands on the canvas to balance herself and the other clenched around her skirt to try to cover the bareness of her feet from the man's eyes.

And he didn't even have the courtesy to look away, not when she climbed onto the ledge nor when she dipped her toes into the silvery water.

The chill stunned her for an instant. A shock of cold flared up her spine, and she almost hopped back into the wagon. But Mr. Faust was watching and so were the others. She wouldn't let them see how weak she really was. Or that she was a coward.

She wasn't doing this for herself anyway. She was doing it to help Karoline.

Closing her eyes, she pulled her skirt above her knees and slid her leg down into the water. The river climbed above her knee and wrapped around her thigh the moment her foot oozed into the mud. She tried not to think about the frogs in the river. Or the snakes.

Her stomach rolled again, and she was glad she hadn't eaten supper.

Her head seemed to swim along with the current, but she refused to let her emotions control her body. Her dress floated like a sail behind her, the current spilling over her skin, and she skimmed her hand across the water. The ripples slid through her fingers, and she tried to focus on the top of the water instead of what was underneath.

With both hands, she tugged the hem of her skirt up to the surface and tied it in a knot above her knees. Then she stepped forward. If she kept pretending her boots were protecting her feet and she was walking on dry land, she would make it to the other side.

But the water that soaked her skirt weighed her down, and she struggled to take another step. In the midst of her struggle, she watched with a mix of gladness and horror as the ox team pulled her wagon away from her, leaving her behind. The current rushed over her waist, and she teetered.

"Take my arm," Mr. Faust insisted.

She wouldn't touch him. Not unless she absolutely had to. Instead her hands splashed beside her then in front of her as she struggled to stay above the water.

When she tried to step again, she tilted to the side, and Mr. Faust reached out to straighten her and her heavy skirt.

She thanked him and then shook his grasp away. She would make it across the river by herself and help take Karoline to Lisbon.

Left to ourselves, we shall but stray;
Oh, lead us on the narrow way.
M. Michael Schirmer

Chapter Six

....

Friedrich hooked an earthworm with the sliver of metal, and from the tree stump he tossed his line into the Iowa River. The hook fell with a soft swoop inside the curved rock walls that Indians had built more than a hundred years ago, presumably to catch fish as well.

The river was peaceful down here by the Indian Dam. The water loped around a curve that nature had carved into her grassy banks before it continued on its path east. A piling of rocks in the shallow water had become a gathering place for walleye and catfish and black bass.

The draft letter was still in his pocket and its plea for help begged for an answer. He'd spent much of last night in earnest prayer, trying to convince himself that staying in the community, submitting to the leadership and the words spoken through them, was the right thing to do. But no matter how hard he tried to convince himself to stay, peace eluded him.

He'd learned long ago that his desires were not always what God wanted of him. He'd fought his flesh since he was a boy. Sometimes he won the battle; sometimes he lost. But this time he didn't know what or whom he was supposed to fight.

Friedrich had been in one of the evening prayer meetings when Brother Metz began shaking in front of the room, overcome with God's Spirit. That night their leader delivered a powerful testimony, words Friedrich would never forget. Words that were then delivered by letter to the president of the United States and the Senate and House of Representatives.

And if ye do not hearken to the spirit of grace, the true peace-maker, then it will come to pass that innumerable voices will cry pain and woe upon you, because ye have torn and destroyed one another through your dissension and discord.

Metz's warning proved to be prophetic. People across their great country were now crying out in pain. They were destroying each other instead of seeking peace.

In his heart, Friedrich wanted peace within their nation. He didn't want them to fight. But if their leaders had sought peace and it didn't bring freedom, perhaps they had to fight.

Down the pathway, he heard Matthias's whistle, and he looked up to see his friend strolling toward him, a fishing pole resting over his shoulder. The villages were quiet on Sunday afternoon, many of their people napping or reading, but the river called to him and Matthias during these long summer days. If they caught anything, they took it back to the kitchen, but fishing wasn't work for them. It was pure rest for their bodies and their souls.

Matthias opened the cover on his tin pail and removed a worm. When he threw his line into the water, it bobbed in the slow current and he began to reel it slowly back toward him.

"I spoke to Brother Schaube this morning," Matthias said, his eyes on the water as he talked. "He said he will go to Marengo tomorrow and pay the commutation fees at the enlistment office."

"You're not going to enlist?"

His friend shook his head. "Neither of us are going to."

A hawk flew through the trees and soared above the river, free to go where he wanted. Friedrich watched the hawk with envy. If only he wouldn't hurt so many people by leaving the Amanas. Amalie. Matthias. His mother and father and sister.

The elders would be disappointed with his decision to leave, but they would welcome him back into the community at the end of the war. His family would welcome him back as well, but what would Amalie do?

"They need your letter," Matthias said as he trolled along the bank. "Before tomorrow."

Friedrich brushed his fingers over the crumpled paper in his pocket. "How can you be so certain you've made the right decision?"

"It's not my decision to make."

"You can't believe that, Matthias."

"How could I believe otherwise?" Matthias asked. "I've never heard the Spirit of God speak, except through our leaders. And the elders have clearly told us not to fight."

"But your heart," Friedrich insisted. "What does your heart say?"

"Our hearts can be deceitful," Matthias said, quoting the words from the prophet Jeremiah.

"Not always, Matthias."

His friend shook his head. "I never trust my heart."

Something tugged on Friedrich's fishing line, and he slowly reeled the hook toward him.

That was the difference between the two of them. Matthias was as loyal as anyone he knew, loyal to their friendship and Friedrich's family and to the entire society of Inspirationists. Friedrich's heart betrayed him at times, but even though he couldn't always trust it, he couldn't ignore it either.

He wouldn't do anything against the Spirit of God, at least not willingly, but he wasn't as convinced as Matthias that every word from their elders was delivered from the Lord. Testimonies were weighed against the Word of God, every word tested to see if it lined up with the nature of God. But still the testimonies were sometimes colored by human weakness, the Werkzeug's desires and views mixed in with prophetic words and the heart of their Lord.

Even after he prayed for absolution from this war, his heart called him to the battle, tugged within him to fight for those who were being abused. If he couldn't trust every testimony from the Werkzeuge, if he couldn't trust his own heart, then what could he trust?

He blinked into the sunlight and he knew the only thing he could trust. He had faith that when he asked, God's Spirit would direct him to do the right thing. He would have to search for God's truth and embrace it.

Something hooked on his line, and he reeled it in. The black bass fought in his hands until Friedrich removed it from his line and re-hooked the fish onto their stringer. They would clean it later for Henriette's kitchen.

"You need to wait for Amalie to arrive," Matthias said, "so the two of you can decide together."

He shook his head. If he waited for Amalie, his heart would most certainly decide for him, and it wouldn't be the right decision.

His friend stepped over and clasped his hand on Friedrich's shoulder. "Don't leave us," he said simply.

Friedrich shook his head, his heart heavy. "I don't know what I'm supposed to do."

* * * * *

The aroma of fresh bread breezed through Libson's streets like warm tufts of ribbon. Amalie relished the scent as she strolled alone down Market Street. Karoline was resting quietly in the doctor's office as they waited for the other wagons to arrive.

Last night's river crossing was a blessed blur in her memory. With Mr. Faust's assistance, she'd made it across the river without tumbling and ridden into the town with the doctor and Karoline. Karoline had awakened in the back of the carriage last night, crying out for her mother. Amalie had tried to soothe her as best she could, but she was grateful that Karoline was able to cry out even if she was in pain.

The doctor had given Karoline another medication and she slept peacefully through the night. Amalie spent the night in the guest room of the kind doctor and his wife. Not only had they given her a fine feather bed to rest on, the doctor's wife asked their house servant to draw a hot bath for her and she spent a good half hour soaking in the warm water to clean the grime off her skin. The servant made her a hot cup of chamomile before bed, and she slept better last night than she had her entire trip.

This morning Amalie had breakfast with the doctor and his wife, and she couldn't remember the last time she'd had a meal that she hadn't been responsible to help prepare. Then the doctor insisted Amalie go outside and refresh herself in the morning air. At first she told him that she'd had plenty of fresh air the past two weeks, but she didn't protest for long. She was curious about the worldly village.

Twenty-four years ago she'd been born in a German *Dorf*, but she barely remembered the village where she'd spent her childhood. Her family immigrated to Ebenezer the summer before her sixth birthday, and she hadn't visited another town since their move. She knew their community was different than others, based on stories the visitors who came to their colony told and on the vivid descriptions of those

Inspirationists who'd been to Buffalo. She had often wondered what it would be like to visit another town.

As she walked this morning, past a row of brick buildings, her hands fidgeted beside her. She wasn't used to being alone nor was she used to being idle. Traveling alongside the wagons had occupied her for the past two weeks, but before that, her work in the kitchen kept her in constant motion with long hours of cooking, baking, and cleaning. She thrived in the midst of the busyness.

Lisbon's businesses were all closed for Sunday, and the streets were quiet. Too quiet. The few people on the wooden sidewalks looked at her oddly, silently critiquing her plain dress, but she held her head high and ignored them. That was one of the many reasons she loved the villages of her community. No woman was singled out by her fine dress or her lack of gay attire. All the women looked the same, and they were content in their sameness.

Turning the corner, Amalie strolled past a funeral parlor and a store with musical instruments. On the grassy lawn to her right, dozens of people poured out of a white building with a narrow steeple that towered over them. A sign by the arched front doors read First Congregational Church.

The churchwomen all wore fancy dresses that reminded her of the colorful gourds the Inspirationists harvested every autumn, narrow in the center and then puffed out from their waists to the ground. Many of the men who flooded through the church doors wore full beards and stovepipe hats, tall and grand. Some of them strolled away from the churchyard while others climbed into carriages or wagons and rode up the street.

They talked and laughed as they walked. Two boys ran across the lawn with a shriek before they catapulted over a row of petunias. She watched the boys with curiosity.

AMANA
1863
IA

Why didn't anyone stop their antics? The adults in her community would never let the children trample flowers. Inspirationist children played in their village, silly games like "The Cutest Pig in the Parlor," but their play was never rough or loud like this. Boys and girls alike learned to quietly read and write and knit, and at a very early age, the children learned to respect older people. They also learned to respect each other in the established, orderly world of their community.

Did the children and their parents know how close danger had been to them, just yesterday? Surely they knew about the burnt bridge to their east and how close General Morgan and his troops had come to warring against their village. If they were aware of these dangers, she couldn't tell.

She rested beside the steps of the church, mesmerized by the many colors that radiated from the stain on its windows. The bright colors of glass blended together to form a lion on one side of the window and a lamb on the other. An arched window in the center of the others depicted a picture of Christ on the cross, His eyes pleading with the heavens. Her breath was stolen away from her as she contemplated the horror of His death. And the beauty of His sacrifice.

The summer rays warmed her skin, and she pulled her sunbonnet closer to her face.

Christ had given His life for her, for all the people in this town and across their country, for sweet souls like Karoline Baumer and even for those like General Morgan, who were intent on following the path to destruction. Christ's sacrifice offered her and all of them the free grace they desperately needed to eradicate their sins, and her heart filled with a renewal of gratefulness for all He had done for her. She didn't need anything except His love and grace.

Did the people in this church live like they believed this provoking portrayal of their Christ? Did they know how much He loved them? She prayed they did.

Even with God's grace, she still struggled daily to follow what He wanted her to do. And even to know what He would have her do.

Most of the congregation had dispersed as she continued her walk through the village, turning onto High Street. There were more storefronts before her, and she stopped to gaze into their windows. In one store, a beautiful woman stood in the display window arrayed in a pink and yellow dress. Amalie stared for a moment, waiting for the woman to move, but when the woman didn't even blink, Amalie realized she wasn't real at all. The woman was a giant doll, molded to look like a person.

Embarrassed, Amalie backed away from the display before anyone realized she thought the doll was real. Hurrying down the street, she glanced into the other windows. One store was filled with crockery and hand-painted pieces of china. Another window displayed a spinning wheel and yards of colorful fabric.

Amalie had never seen so many items for sale. In the colony at Ebenezer, they had only a small general store where the Inspirationists could obtain anything they needed for their basic needs—writing paper and shoes and even candy for treats. Since they didn't have money, every member of their society received a credit at the beginning of each year for purchases at the store, and the storekeeper kept track of what they'd purchased in their credit-book.

At the window of the next store, Amalie rolled her fingers over the warm glass. The sign said it was a mercantile, and she could see the barrels and shelves filled with many different items. Shiny copper pots, glasses, candles, tin cookie cutters. And there were books—stacks and stacks of them beyond the window. What did one do with so many things?

As she was trying to read the titles of the books, she saw something move behind the display. When she lifted her eyes, a man with a bushy brown beard and wiry glasses was looking back at her. At first, she thought he too was a giant doll. When he waved, she gasped and her hands froze on the window as he motioned for her to come inside.

The store in Ebenezer was closed on Sunday, but she didn't know how people acted outside Ebenezer. Were they allowed to shop on the Sabbath? She reached for the doorknob, but she didn't step forward.

There wasn't any harm in looking at his inventory, was there? She couldn't buy anything, of course, but maybe the shopkeeper wouldn't mind if she opened the covers of the books and peeked inside. Then she would go back to check on Karoline.

A bell chimed overhead when she pushed the door, startling her, and she almost ran back outside like a spooked rabbit. Before she ran, though, the man stepped forward and introduced himself as the owner of the shop.

"How can I help you?" he asked in a soothing tone that helped calm her fears.

She pushed her sunbonnet off her hair, revealing the small black cap she wore underneath. The sunbonnet rested on her shoulders as she glanced around the room, overwhelmed and strangely exhilarated by all the merchandise in the store. "Are you open?"

"Not officially," he said, a twinkle in his eyes. "But I'd never turn away a customer in need."

She shook her head. "Oh, I don't need anything."

The twinkle dimmed a bit. "Well, I'm just cleaning up a bit. You are welcome to look around if you'd like."

She glanced over the kitchenware and hats and shoes. Her eyes rested on the shelves at the far corner of the store. "Can I look at the books?"

"Certainly."

Amalie walked over, and her fingers reverently rolled over the dozens of hardcovers on the shelf. She'd only read a handful of books in her life. The Bible and the book of inspired testimonies from their Werkzeuge. The only fictional book she'd ever read was *Pilgrim's Progress*, and every word of the pilgrim's journey delighted her. When Christian arrived at the Celestial City, she celebrated with him.

She'd longed to read another story like *Pilgrim's Progress*, but most works of fiction were idle pleasure. If only she could find another story that encouraged Christians on their journey instead of distracted them from it.

She carefully picked a book off the shelf and then replaced it seconds later without even opening the cover. There were too many books to look at. She didn't know where to start.

Her gaze rolled over the titles, resting on a bright blue cover. She reached for it and stared at the silver foil on the front, a man and several children playing near a log home of sorts. She smoothed her fingers over the cloth binding, reading the author's name. A woman wrote the book. A woman named Harriet Beecher Stowe.

She turned and looked back toward the counter, holding the cover up so the man could see it. "What is this book about?"

He glanced up from the ledger in his hands and set his glasses on top of it. "You've never heard of *Uncle Tom's Cabin*?"

"No."

He shook his head. "Some people call it the book that began this darn war."

She turned it over in her hands. How could a book possibly begin a war?

"Is your husband fighting for us?" he asked

She shook her head. "I'm an Inspirationist."

One of his eyebrows slid up. "A what?"

"Our community believes that the United States should pray for peace instead of fight for it."

"Oh—"

She held up *Uncle Tom's Cabin*. She didn't want to talk about her community's views of peace or the fact that she didn't have a husband. "Is it a book about a Christian?"

He tapped on his ledger for a moment, thinking. "It's more of a book about Christ."

About Christ? Then maybe it would be a story she'd enjoy.

"You should read it," he continued.

She looked down at the cover again, the silver gleaming in the light. "I would like to."

"I'll sell it to you for two dollars," he said.

"Oh, no." She quickly placed the book back on the shelf and backed away from it. She hadn't meant to give him reason to think she would purchase it.

He paused for a minute. "I suppose I could go down to a dollar seventy-five. You won't be able to find it any cheaper than that."

She stepped back, toward the door. "I can't buy it."

She could feel him critiquing her dress, her hair pinned neatly behind her head.

"Why not?" he asked.

"I—I don't have any money."

He paused for an instant, like he wasn't sure if he believed her. "You don't have any money?"

Amalie tapped her tongue against her teeth, trying to find a way to explain to him the way they lived, in words he could understand. "I live in a colony," she said. "We don't need any money because everything is provided for us."

His eyebrow shot up again. "Everything except books."

"We have books," she said, wanting him to understand. "Just not novels."

He closed his ledger on the counter and sighed. "Well, you have to read this book."

She backed toward the door. What would she say to the others if she brought a novel to Amana with her? A novel that started a war. "I should probably be going."

The man scooted around the counter and marched toward the shelves. He plucked the blue book from the mass of browns and reds and held it out to her. "It's a story that will change your life."

"I don't want my life to be changed."

"Aah," he said as he pulled the book back. "You are satisfied with your life."

"I am."

"Smug?"

"Oh, no," she stopped him. "Nothing like that. I'm just content."

"And is the world content around you?"

She thought back to General Morgan and the smirk on his face as he told her what he was doing to the people in the North. There was a reason the Inspirationists chose not to live in the world. It was partly to stay away from people who chose to pursue worldly passions and desires more than their journey with Christ.

Even when General Morgan succeeded in burning the bridge in Lisbon, he longed for more destruction. Lust is what the Bible would call it. Without God, there was no contentment in worldly pursuits. Why should she care about the world?

"We choose to live apart from the world."

The man took the book to the counter and began to wrap it in brown paper. "Someday the world will come to you, whether or not you want it to. You might want to know why so many people have chosen to give up their farms and their families to fight in this war."

"I'm on my way to Iowa," she told him. "Our new community is separated from the rest of the world."

"No matter how hard you try, you and your people will never be able to completely separate yourself from the world."

A protest bubbled on her lips, but she choked it back down. There was no use disagreeing with him. People on the outside could never understand the tight bond of the Inspirationists or their pursuit of righteousness. They couldn't seem to understand how her community could be content living away from the luxuries of a town, but she and the others had everything she needed in her village. And their focus wasn't on things. It was on following God.

The man handed the package to her. "Please take this."

She looked at the brown paper, her hands unmoving. "I don't have any money," she repeated.

"Consider it a gift," he replied, and then he pulled it back. "But only on one condition."

"What is it?"

"That you read it."

She considered his offer for a moment. She didn't know when she could read it, certainly not while she was on the trail. There were too many people watching her, watching each other. But perhaps she could read it when she got to Iowa. If the man were wrong, if the story was corrupt, she would dispose of it.

"Is the story truly a picture of Christ?"

When he nodded, she reached out. "Then I will read it."

He slipped the package into her hands. "Your heart will never be the same."

Chapter Seven

....

Candlelight flickered along Friedrich's wall as he huddled over his desk. Before he lit the candle, he drew the green muslin curtain over his window so the night watchman wouldn't see the flame in his room and come knocking to check for a fire. The clock on his bureau read 3 a.m. and while most of the Inspirationists were early risers, no one besides him and the night watchman should be awake. And he didn't want the watchman checking on him.

He dipped his pen into the inkwell and wrote another line on Amalie's letter, but the words sounded too crass. He wanted Amalie to know how much he cared for her. How he didn't want to leave her or their Kolonie. How he didn't want to leave, but he knew he had to go.

Something smoldered within him like the flame of the candle. A small voice that told him he was supposed to fight. Whether it was God's Spirit or not, he wasn't certain, but there was no peace in his heart at the thought of paying his way out of the army, nor could he allow his blood to be on another man's hands. His government had conscripted him and he would fight.

He didn't want to hurt Amalie, but he didn't know the right words to write in the letter, not without wounding her.

Frustrated, he held the paper over the candle and let his words burn before he opened the stove's door and threw the letter onto the smoldering ashes.

How could he communicate all he was feeling to Amalie and to his parents? And to Matthias?

They would think that Friedrich had abandoned them, without even saying good-bye. He had no desire to abandon any of them, but if he waited a month to see Amalie or until the autumn when his parents arrived, he knew he wouldn't leave for war. They would talk him out of it, or he would talk himself out of it. And he would never forgive himself if he didn't go.

He slid another piece of paper onto his writing desk to begin a third letter to Amalie. There wasn't much time left now. An hour at the most. He would have to leave under the cloak of darkness to avoid the questions, before even the baker began making bread for the day.

He dipped his pen into the inkwell again and words began to flow from within him. He told Amalie that his heart was hers, but he couldn't respect himself nor could he ever expect her to respect him if he didn't fight for those who were enslaved. He told her about Joseph and the scars on the man's arms. And he wrote about the wrenching in his heart, the powerful pull to fight for the wounded like David had written in the book of Psalms.

Deliver the poor and needy: rid them out of the hand of the wicked.

But even as he scribbled his thoughts onto paper, the words seemed hollow. No amount of words nor the structure of them could make her understand why he had to join the Union forces. Amalie believed the shedding of blood was wrong, for any reason, and like Matthias, she probably believed God would right the wrong of slavery through a peaceful resolution. Only those who chose not to wait on God were drawn into the fight. Or at least, that was what she and Matthias and his family thought.

With a loud sigh, he leaned back in his chair and reached for a yellowed envelope he kept at the edge of his desk. Opening it, he slid out the lock of hair Amalie cut for him in secret before he left Ebenezer, hours after he asked her to marry him when she moved to Amana. He rubbed her hair gently between his fingers. He had no likeness of her on paper, but even after three years, he could still envision the sculpting of her beautiful face in his mind, the vibrancy and strength in her eyes. He longed to see her face again, touch her skin, but he couldn't let his desires thwart his determination to do what he believed to be right.

Amalie Wiese was strong. She would be able to weather this season without him, like she'd done the past three years, and with God's help, he would be able to weather it as well.

He tucked the envelope with the lock of her hair into his pocket, and then he picked his pen back up and asked Amalie to wait longer for him. When the war was over, he wanted to marry her. He wrote about their future together, about their children, and as he wrote, he dreamed about the many years ahead that they would spend as man and wife.

But in case something happened, in case he didn't return in the next year or two like he planned, he wrote that he wanted her to live a life of dedication in the Amanas without him. And a life with love. He didn't want her to be alone.

After he sealed the letter with glue, he wrote her name on the back and then he wrote a letter to Matthias and one to his parents and placed them beside the one to Amalie.

When the clock chimed four times, he blew out the candle. Ashes sprinkled over his hand as he brushed them into the stove. He strung his burlap bag over his shoulder, packed with a blanket, a change of clothes to wear until he received his uniform, the Gospel of John, and his coat.

Leaning down, he kissed Amalie's letter one last time. Then he placed his straw hat on his head and walked out the door.

* * * * *

Matthias Roemig tossed on his pillow, trying to force himself to sleep a few more minutes before the morning bells rang. His mind wouldn't let him rest. It skipped across the bits of conversation he had with Friedrich yesterday. The questions Friedrich had about fighting in the war.

The pull for Friedrich to fight was strong; he could hear it in his friend's voice and see it in his face. The passion that burned in Friedrich often challenged Matthias, and sometimes even changed his perspective, but this time it was his turn to influence Friedrich and make him understand that this war wasn't his burden to carry. Their responsibility was to help build their community and pray that the war, along with slavery, would end soon.

Kneeling beside his bed, Matthias prayed for God's blessing on his day, and he prayed that God would work in Friedrich's heart to give him the peace he sought. Each person in the Kolonie was on a journey to follow after their Lord, but Friedrich seemed to search more than any of them, trying to balance the desires in his heart with the will of the Lord.

He understood why Friedrich felt like he should fight. The thought of slavery sickened Matthias, along with the stories tourists told of children being sold on auction blocks and owners who treated people like property. He didn't know enough, though, to separate truth from propaganda. Some of the stories seemed to be generated by a government that needed men to fight its war.

His hands resting on his comforter, his head bowed in humility, Matthias begged God for the wisdom he needed to speak to Friedrich. Wisdom to help his friend realize he didn't need to feel guilty because he chose to stand for peace instead of fight. The burden of this war should be dropped at the foot of the cross and left there.

He knelt in the stillness of the morning for another five minutes, until the bells began to toll, and then he slowly rose from the hard floor and brushed off his knees. It felt as if God's Spirit of peace stole into his room along with the morning sunlight. Today the elders would pay fees to relieve him and Friedrich from their obligation to go into battle or hire substitutes to fight in their place. They needed to keep their focus on building the villages and supplying food for their people instead of on the worries of the world far away from them.

His hand traveled over his bedpost. He didn't have to choose a side in this awful war to know that God loved the slaves and the soldiers and even the slave owners.

For a moment, he wondered what it would be like to fight in a battle. The comforts of Amana he could live without, but he couldn't fathom hunting down his fellow man like a deer or a wild turkey. It must break God's heart to see His children killing each other.

Matthias put on his hat and reached for the door. The wickedness of slavery made him tremble in his core. But thousands upon thousands of people who didn't own slaves were dying as a result of this conflict between the states. If only the leaders of both the North and South would seek God's face, like Brother Metz entreated of them. If only they sought peace while seeking freedom for the slaves, the war could end without another battle.

Stepping into the hallway, Matthias glanced at the closed door across from his room. Usually his friend was waiting for him in the hall by the cedar wardrobe, ready to begin his day, but Friedrich wasn't waiting today. Perhaps he was still in prayer, asking for help, like Matthias had done this morning.

Matthias hesitated beside the closed door, but when Friedrich still didn't come out for breakfast, he knocked. If they didn't hurry to the kitchen house, they wouldn't be able to eat before their long day of work began—and neither he nor Friedrich ever missed a meal.

"Are you ready?" he called out.

Silence met his call.

"Friedrich?" he called again as he turned the knob.

The dark purple quilt on Friedrich's bed was neatly made, his curtain closed. For a moment, Matthias thought Friedrich had left for breakfast without him, but before he slipped back into the hallway, he saw the envelopes set on the desk. There were three of them, neatly placed across the wooden top.

Even though he saw the envelopes, seconds passed before Matthias began to comprehend what Friedrich had done. He knew what was in the envelopes, knew Friedrich had left him, but he didn't want to acknowledge the truth.

As he stepped to the desk, he saw a letter for Amalie and one for Friedrich's parents. He left both of those on the desk, but he took the envelope addressed with his name and hid it in his pocket. He wouldn't read the words Friedrich had written to him. Instead he would go to Marengo right away, and he would stop Friedrich before he made this foolish choice. He'd stop him and hand back his envelope without reading a word.

Racing down the steps two at a time, he pushed open the front door and burst out into the morning air.

It wasn't too late to stop his friend. The conscription letters said they were to report to Marengo at eight thirty, two hours from now. Brother Schaube was planning to meet the colonel this morning to negotiate the commutation fees for seven Amana men. Together they would stop Friedrich from joining the regiment, and then they would bring him home before anyone knew he had tried to leave.

He found Brother Schaube in the kitchen house, eating sausage and pancakes. Matthias didn't waste precious seconds greeting his other brothers as he shuffled around the benches and tables to the elder's side.

Guten Morgen," the head elder whispered as Matthias scooted into the seat beside him.

Matthias leaned close to him, speaking low as well so the others couldn't hear. "He's gone."

Brother Schaube's eyes widened with alarm. "Friedrich?"

Matthias nodded.

"When did he leave?"

"I don't know. I was just in his room, and he left letters for Amalie and his parents." He didn't mention the one in his pocket—those words were written for him.

Brother Schaube wiped his mouth on a cloth napkin and stood. "We must go to Marengo at once."

The others watched them leave before breakfast was finished, before Sophia served second cups of coffee or they closed in prayer. A hundred questions must be swirling through the minds of the men and women, but if they retrieved Friedrich before supper, no one needed to know he almost left them.

At the stable, Matthias and Brother Schaube each saddled a horse, and within a half hour, they were riding west. Two miles outside Amana, they rode through the village of Middle Amana and then they passed though High and West Amana. People waved to them, but they didn't stop to greet their brothers and sisters like they normally would. The property of the Inspirationists ended after South Amana, and they followed the dirt road for six more miles until they arrived in the county seat of Marengo.

Matthias had only been to the town once, earlier this year when all the men in Iowa County were required to have a physical in case the government mustered them to service in the military. He didn't remember where the enlistment office was located, but Brother Schaube directed them toward the courthouse. They hitched their horses a full half hour before the newly drafted men were supposed to arrive.

Brother Schaube went straight to the enlistment office on the bottom floor, past the line of almost twenty men standing outside the office with an assortment of suitcases and bags in their hands. Some of the men wore tattered clothes while others were dressed in as fine of suits as Matthias had ever seen.

Matthias searched their faces, but he didn't see Friedrich among them. Could he have been wrong about Friedrich's letters? Perhaps his friend wasn't coming to join this regiment. Perhaps he was running away from Amana.

His fingers slipped over the letter in his pocket. Friedrich had too much honor in him to flee from this situation, certainly when the elders were willing to pay for someone else to take his place in the infantry. But even if the elders didn't pay the commutation fees, he couldn't imagine Friedrich running away.

When Brother Schaube didn't see Friedrich among the group of waiting men, he marched to the front of the line and knocked on the door of the enlistment office.

"We'll be ready in a half hour," someone barked on the other side.

Brother Schaube leaned toward the wood, his voice firm. "I need to speak with you right away."

The door whisked open, and on the other side stood an older gentleman with white hair and a trimmed beard. When he saw Brother Schaube, his voice hardened even more. "The government requested seven of your men to join our regiment."

Brother Schaube held out a leather satchel toward him. "I am here to pay their fees."

The officer swore, lifting the hand that was wrapped around his cane. "I form regiments. I don't take blood money."

Brother Schaube lowered the satchel. "But I need to pay for their exemption."

"I'm sure someone in Des Moines will be glad to take your money," the officer said. "But you'll only have to pay the fees for six exemptions."

"Seven of them were conscripted," Brother Schaube insisted.

The officer stood a bit straighter, a tinge of pride coloring the harshness in his voice. "One of your men has chosen to serve with us."

Matthias could hear people talking behind the officer. He looked over the man's wide shoulders to see who else was in the office, but he couldn't see anyone.

"We are here to get Friedrich Vinzenz." Brother Schaube held out an official-looking notice. "This letter is from Governor Samuel Kirkwood, and it says if we choose not to fight because of religious reasons, we can pay for our men to be released from duty."

"Private Vinzenz has the ability to choose on his own whether or not he wants to join us."

"Friedrich is not a private," the elder said. "He is our brother."

With a shrug, the colonel began to push the door shut with his cane. Matthias stepped forward, stopping him. "Please let me speak with him one last time. Just to tell him good-bye."

"I'm sorry. Private Vinzenz has been removed to a different location to await his orders."

Standing in the crowded hallway, Matthias felt like his chest was about to erupt. Friedrich was there, behind that door. He couldn't see him, but he knew Friedrich was there. Still his friend didn't speak up.

Friedrich had never turned him away before. But now, on the eve of going to war against an unknown enemy, he didn't even have the courage to say good-bye to those who loved him.

"Tell him not to do this," Matthias said.

"I will tell him no such thing."

"Then tell him that he better come back home to us as soon as he can."

When the colonel slammed the door shut, Matthias prayed Friedrich had heard his words and that he would harbor them. His friend must come back to the Kolonie when this war was done.

He and Brother Schaube moved back down the long corridor, past all the men waiting to join the new regiment. Frustration burned within Matthias. He couldn't imagine why anyone would want to leave the Society, for any reason.

"We can't let him join the army."

Brother Schaube bowed his head, his voice sad. "This is his choice, Matthias. We cannot force him to stay."

"Friedrich doesn't know what he is doing," Matthias insisted. "He doesn't know what awaits him out there."

"I wouldn't be so certain."

Matthias wanted to believe Friedrich didn't have any idea how much his decision would hurt all those around him, because if he knew...

If he knew, how could he leave them?

"Go home," Brother Schaube instructed. "I have business I must attend to before I return."

In a daze, Matthias stumbled out of the courthouse. Somehow he managed to mount his horse again, and as he rounded the block, he looked back at the courthouse one last time. He hadn't cried since he was five years old—the day his mother left him—but the tears came now unbidden. For a moment, he felt like that five-year-old again. Abandoned and alone.

The tears flowed harder now. He wanted to make them stop, but he couldn't control himself. How could his closest friend—his brother— abandon him? Friedrich knew how much Matthias hated people leaving him, especially with no good-bye.

He and Friedrich had been the best of friends since that day his mother left him at the estate in Hesse-Darmstadt and never returned. He traveled the long journey with Friedrich's family from Germany to New York when he and Friedrich were both seven, and for almost twenty years, they had eaten every meal together, worked together, fished together, prayed together.

He wiped the back of his sleeve over his face, hoping at first that the townspeople would think his cheeks itched, but then he realized he didn't care. He dared anyone to say he didn't have a right to his tears.

In three weeks, the wagon train would arrive from New York. What was he going to say to Amalie? Friedrich had been faithful to her over the past three years, he could assure her of that, but she would probably blame him for Friedrich leaving, and he wouldn't stop her.

He should have talked more with Friedrich. Prayed more. Now his friend was gone, and he had no idea when, or if, he would come back.

Whichever way my eyes are turning, Thy wondrous
works I can behold.
I bow my head in adoration to see Thy majesties untold.
Author Unknown

Chapter Eight

....

August 1863

Mist draped over the Iowa River and swept through a grove of cedar trees. Pink mantled the horizon in front of the wagon train as the darkness welcomed dawn. Long before the sun began to warm the day, Amalie and the other travelers from Ebenezer had awakened to begin their final trek. After more than a month of traveling, they would finally be home.

Karoline had rested for much of the journey, recovering slowly from her injury, but she refused to remain inside the wagon for their arrival. She walked alongside Amalie, leading the wagon train as they traveled through the valley.

Amalie's hands tingled and her heart quickened with anxiety and excitement. On the other side of the forest, Friedrich Vinzenz would be waiting for her. Not with open arms in front of the other brothers and sisters, but she hoped there were would be a smile on his face, a promise of things to come.

Never again would she have to hover over a camping stove to cook.

Nor would she have to sleep in a tent or unload her kitchen supplies each night from her wagon and then load them up the next morning after breakfast. By day's end tomorrow, if she wanted, she and Karoline would be able to work the stove in their own kitchen.

With Amana just a few miles in front of them, it felt like the wagons were barely crawling toward their destination. She wanted nothing more than to run all the way to the village, even if she ran by herself. But they'd traveled for five weeks as a community, and with the exception of the two men Mr. Faust had sent ahead last night as messengers, they would all arrive together.

Men waved their hats at them from the fields, and as they passed through the small village of Homestead, several women ran out to them with fresh fruit. The women squeezed their hands and welcomed them home. Their group didn't stop in Homestead, but the warm greeting empowered all of them. They moved even faster toward Amana.

Next, they crossed railroad tracks and slowly hiked along a path in the forest. The sun broke through the leaves and the fog, and Amalie stepped out of the trees into the grass and shaded her eyes as the yellow light flooded her with warmth.

A windmill towered in the distance, above clusters of homes that reminded her of Ebenezer. Smoke wisped gracefully into the air—not black smoke like the burning bridge in Ohio but gentle puffs of white from the chimney of the kitchen house, preparing for the noon meal.

Friedrich was in one of those buildings this morning, waiting for her.

As they drew closer to the entrance of the village, Karoline took a deep breath beside her, but she didn't slow her pace. Amalie turned toward her and whispered, "Do you need to rest?"

"Oh, no." Karoline shook her head. "I have to see their faces."

"Your mother?"

She smiled. "I want to see everyone, but I especially want to see Friedrich when he catches his first glimpse of you."

Amalie couldn't help but smile back as she smoothed the hair hidden under her sunbonnet. She'd brushed her long hair for a good ten minutes last night and even bathed in a creek near where they slept. After three years of waiting, she didn't want Friedrich to be disappointed at the sight of her.

She almost wished he were in the fields instead of the village this morning. She could slip away in the crowd before she saw him and at least change into the calico dress she'd kept clean in her trunk and brush the remaining trail dust out of her hair. Maybe she could even wash her face again before she greeted him.

But with the messengers sent ahead last night, Friedrich would know the caravan was on its way. Even though she would like to change before she saw him, she'd be more disappointed if he wasn't there waiting for her, as excited and even as nervous to see her as she was to see him.

She would know, the moment she saw Friedrich, if he was glad to see her or if he was disappointed in her. She would pretend, if she must, that she couldn't see his disappointment.

As they drew closer to the village, Mr. Faust rode up beside her and Karoline and slid from his horse.

"Amalie from Amana," he sung. "You were named for this place."

"My parents didn't know anything about Amana when they named me."

"You sure you won't change your mind, Miss Wiese?" he asked again, his eyes teasing her. "Before it's too late—"

Amalie started to rebuke him, but her heart felt so light this morning. She'd spent the entire trip protesting this man's advances, but now they were close to the end of their journey. Maybe she could tease him back.

She tilted her head. "Are you asking me to marry you, Mr. Faust?"

Panic replaced the cockiness in his eyes. "I—I might ask if you hadn't promised to marry another."

"Maybe she can unpromise," Karoline said. A giggle burst out of her lips when Mr. Faust's lower lip dropped.

Ahead of them, Amalie saw the strength and beauty of the sandstone and brick buildings that lined the streets of Amana, the heritage already steeped into the homes and kitchen houses. The wooden buildings were left unpainted, but even in its newness, the weathered wood gave the village a sense of permanence far beyond its eight years.

Gardens flourished at the edge of the village, vibrant beds of reds, purples, and yellows, and behind the gardens were acres and acres filled with alfalfa and corn and orchards of fruit trees. Breathing deeply, she inhaled the warm summer scents of grass and cattle and life in abundance.

Friedrich was right. This was paradise.

She turned to Mr. Faust. "I'm sure the elders could find a nice job for you in Amana, caring for the sheep maybe or harvesting the grain."

The wagon master's face whitened a shade, and he hopped back on his horse to ride beside them as they entered the village. Amana was paradise for them, but it would be hellish for a man like Mr. Faust. He could never conform to the strict lifestyle and devotion of the Inspirationists, just as she could never imagine living a life outside.

Her heart skipped when bells tolled, ringing out across the valley. Dear brothers and sisters swarmed out of the buildings and surrounded them. Excitement punctuated the air as the men and women rushed forward to shake her hand, kiss her cheek.

People crowded around her, but in the midst of the crowds, she searched for Friedrich's face. There would be no private reunion today for her and Friedrich. The crowd would be watching them more than the others, but even with all of the people, she would be happy just to be close to Friedrich. To see him again.

She hoped, though, that he wouldn't touch even her hand until they were alone. She wanted to relish his first touch, to enjoy every moment of being close to him. She would cherish it for the rest of her life.

A woman shouted, and when Karoline saw the wave of her mother's arms, she ran to her. Sister Baumer embraced her daughter, and Amalie smiled at their reunion. Sister Baumer had been called early to the Kolonie because the colonists requested a good mother to guide and care for them as they built the villages. The elders needed Karoline to stay working in the Ebenezer kitchen for several more years, but now that the mother and daughter were reunited, they would never have to part again.

Amalie was so very glad she didn't have to deliver the news of Karoline's death to this sweet woman. Instead of mourning, it was a day for rejoicing. A good day for all of them to reunite.

In the midst of her search for Friedrich, Amalie found Matthias Roemig instead. He was staring at her from the outskirts of the crowd, his brown eyes prominent in the sea of so many blue eyes.

There was no welcome smile on Matthias's lips, but she shrugged off the animosity in his gaze, trying to ignore him as she scanned the faces of the men around him, certain Friedrich would be nearby. She looked along the wooden sidewalk and searched the doorways and windows, but she didn't see the face she longed to see.

Someone reached for her again. Rosa Schaube. The sister shook her hand but then faded back into the crowd. In that moment, Amalie realized people were talking all around her, greeting the travelers, but no one seemed to want to speak with her.

"Sister Baumer." She called out to Karoline's mother, and the woman turned toward her. Amalie leaned down to whisper in her ear. "Where is Friedrich?"

Worry flashed across Sister Baumer's face. Or was it fear? Instead of answering, the woman patted Amalie's arm and then nudged Karoline forward. Karoline turned around to mouth an apology, but Amalie waved her on. It should be a time of celebration for Karoline and her mother.

Amalie glanced around again, certain Friedrich must be near. Her arms started trembling when she still couldn't find him.

Had he changed his mind and promised his hand to someone else? Maybe he hadn't wanted to write her with the news, but now that she was here, he would be forced to admit the truth. Perhaps it was easier to hide than face her.

She wrapped her hands across her elbows in an attempt to stop her shaking. Who had won his attention in Amana? Did it happen in the past few weeks, while she was on the trail even?

She'd heard whispers about Sophia Paul. The woman was only a year or two out of Lehrschule when she traveled here, and everyone knew she wanted to marry Friedrich. But Friedrich had assured Amalie over and over that he wasn't interested in Sophia. He said he was waiting for her.

Her hands secured over her elbows, Amalie controlled the shaking in her arms, but then her legs began to tremble under her long skirt.

People were watching her, and she inched her chin a little higher. Even if Friedrich jilted her, she would not be humiliated by his actions. At least she wouldn't act like she was humiliated around the others. She was an expert at keeping her emotions dammed up inside her until she was alone in her room, the only place where she allowed the floodgates to open.

She had been faithful to Friedrich since he left for Iowa, and the two years prior. There was no reason for her to cower in front of the others.

As the brothers and sisters turned back to the buildings, Matthias stepped forward. His eyes were focused sharply upon her, like two arrows intent on their prey. She wanted to flee from his scrutiny, but she refused to cower. If Friedrich had changed his mind, if he'd decided to marry another, she prayed Matthias wouldn't be the one to tell her. She'd never be able to hide her humiliation from him.

And it would take a lifetime for her to forgive Friedrich for asking his best friend to bear his sin.

Matthias stood over her now, his dark hair tucked back under his hat. His arms and his eyes were as strong as the rest of his features, like they'd been since he turned fourteen and began working with Carl Vinzenz in the carpentry shop. Neither his strength nor the intensity in his eyes intimidated her like it did other women, though.

She met his stare and locked it. In his eyes was a mixture of pity and dislike. He didn't have to pretend that he liked her or that he was glad to see her. If only he would lean down and whisper that Friedrich was waiting someplace private for their reunion. Waiting to surprise her.

Her heart tangled in the chaos of her mind.

"Who is that man?" Matthias quizzed, his voice an eerie calm.

She glanced behind her and saw Mr. Faust beside his horse, watching her. A small group of people was still greeting those in the last wagons with stiff hugs and warm smiles. The others had gone into the kitchen house for their meal.

"Our wagon master."

"You were awfully friendly with him."

Anger welled up inside her. How dare he insinuate she'd been the least bit unfaithful to Friedrich? She kept her chin high in the air. It didn't matter what Matthias thought or said. She didn't have to answer to him.

"Where is Friedrich?" she demanded.

"Amalie—" He tried to prod her forward, away from the crowd, but she didn't move. Instead, she looked him straight in the eye.

"Has he changed his mind about our marriage?"

Matthias shook his head, and her shoulders fell a notch. "Then where is he, Matthias?"

He pointed her to a dirt road, off the main street, but she didn't want to skulk away with him. She wanted answers.

"Where is—" she started again, but her voice trailed off. "What happened to him?"

When he still didn't answer, a shadow crossed over her mind and filled her with dread. For a moment, she was back in the wagon, pleading with Karoline to wake up. She'd almost lost her friend on the trail, but she hadn't thought once about the possibility of losing Friedrich. He was too young and much too spirited to pass into eternity.

The ground felt like it tilted under her, and she reached out for the side of the wagon to steady herself.

"Is Friedrich ill?"

When Matthias took her arm again, she allowed him to guide her away from the chaos of the crowd. With every step, her feet ached, and the pain surprised her. She'd been so excited to arrive that she hadn't even felt the blisters on her heels in a week. Now the pain rushed back to her, and she felt tired and much older than her twenty-four years.

On the other side of a long sandstone building, away from the throng of people, Matthias released her elbow. She stepped away from him.

"He's left us," Matthias said simply.

Amalie looked into Matthias's dark eyes flecked with yellow, and she saw the hurt in them. And she felt his pain before she could even begin to process how she felt, before she even understood what happened.

Some people had left the Community of True Inspiration over the years, but most members remained their entire life. She couldn't imagine any of the Vinzenz family leaving the community, especially not Friedrich.

Her voice trembled in spite of her intent to control it. "Tell me where he went, Matthias."

He shifted on his feet, his words low. "He went off to war."

"What?"

"He left the Society to fight in the war."

Left the Society. War.

She tried to fit the words together, but she couldn't seem to comprehend what he was saying.

"Where did he go?" she asked again, as if this time her question might change the answer.

"Friedrich joined the Union army."

She fell back against a tree.

"Amalie?" Matthias said, both hands in front of him as if he could capture her if she toppled.

She pushed his hands away. She didn't want him to touch her. "When did he leave?"

His lips moved, but no words came out.

She stood up, willing her strength to come from within her and support her body. "When, Matthias?"

"Three weeks ago."

Several people walked around the corner, but their faces were a blur to her. She didn't care if they were watching her or what they thought. She had every right to her anger, to ask whatever questions she wanted.

She'd spent the past five weeks trekking across the rugged trails of this country. She'd waded across a river, cooked and slept in the wild. She'd been dirty and tired and blistered from the sun and her shoes, but it had all been worth it to see her future husband before the other Inspirationists came in the fall. Instead of waiting to greet her, though, or to even say good-bye, the man she planned to marry was gone.

She tried to keep her chin held high, pretending that she was a queen again instead of a woman jilted by the man she loved.

"Where is my kitchen?" she asked.

Matthias stepped back, his hands in the air. "Your kitchen?"

"Yes, my kitchen," she snapped. "I—I want to start unloading my things."

Matthias's mouth dropped. "You're unbelievable, Amalie."

Didn't he understand? If she stayed here, out on the street, she would crumble and then he would have to pick up all the pieces.

But he continued to stare at her like she was Judas Iscariot. A betrayer. He didn't understand, and right now she didn't care what he thought, what any of them thought. She had to get busy in her new kitchen, or she would collapse.

Later, when she was alone, she would think about the repercussions of Friedrich leaving, but this morning she would fall back on the best cure for any ailment of the heart or the head. Or at least the best distraction. Hard work in the kitchen house would distract anyone from their pain.

She asked Matthias again about her kitchen. When he refused to answer, she picked up her skirts and brushed by him. If he wouldn't assist her, she would find someone else who would.

From the corner of her eye, she saw Mr. Faust approach them. She didn't want to talk to the man nor did she want to tell him that Friedrich was gone.

With a quick swivel on her heels, she marched back toward the main street. Matthias could say what he wanted to Mr. Faust. She needed to start unloading her supplies into her new kitchen house. She had planned to wait a day or two before she began cooking again, but there was no reason to wait now. Her responsibility was to cook for the people in Amana, and she would start right away.

Sorrow and doubt leave me fearful and shaken;
Oh, who will help me when nobody can?
Christian Metz

Chapter Nine
....

Matthias kicked the rock in front of him and watched it fly down the road. As the stone rolled away from him, it pushed away everything that was in its path. Just like Amalie Helene Wiese.

He kicked another rock, venting his own anger under his breath. The woman didn't look back as she fled around the meetinghouse, running away from her problems. Like ignoring her anger or sadness would make it better.

For a moment there, he thought Amalie might actually grieve Friedrich's decision like the rest of them. Or at least express her anger. But if she cared for Friedrich, the feeling was buried so deep within herself that she might never be able to express it. All she cared about was her kitchen. Her stupid, sterile kitchen where the only pain she might feel was a flesh wound from the cut of a knife or burn from the stove. Nothing that would wound her heart or soul.

He'd hoped for Friedrich's sake that Amalie had grown above the self-centeredness that plagued her most of her life. But apparently her coldness was going to be a permanent trait, just like her father. And her mother.

Congratulations, Amalie. If she couldn't have Friedrich, at least she would have her kitchen.

He kicked one last stone and watched it roll far away from him.

Maybe it was good that Friedrich had gone off to war before he married Amalie. When he returned, he would discover what she was really like, and he would change his mind. Maybe he would marry Sophia Paul or another woman instead.

Stuffing his hands into his pockets, Matthias stepped away from the tree and saw the wagon master at the end of the street, watching him.

Matthias's shoulders stiffened as he eyed the man.

What if Friedrich had been waiting for Amalie in the village? He would have been devastated to watch the woman he'd pledged his life to laughing with another man, a man clearly enamored by her.

The wagon master took the six or so steps over to Matthias. "My name's Faust."

Matthias reached out his hand for a firm shake before he folded his arms over his chest.

"Did you two quarrel already?" Faust asked.

"Amalie and I always quarrel," he blurted, and then he wished he hadn't spoken. It was none of this man's business whom he fought with or why.

"I wouldn't let her be angry too long," Faust said. "She might start looking to marry someone else."

Matthias almost said that was fine with him, but that would have been an outright lie. His relationship with Amalie was too complicated for him to understand, much less explain to a stranger.

"Amalie can marry whom she pleases," he replied.

Faust's eyebrows climbed with disbelief. "You better be careful, my friend. You might lose her."

"She's not mine to lose," he muttered as he turned away from the man.

The bell rang for the noon meal, but instead of swarming to the kitchen house with the others, Matthias stole through the back streets of the village. He didn't want to see Amalie again, nor did he want to answer any questions about her kitchen.

Some of the men would spend the rest of their day visiting with those who'd arrived, listening to news from Ebenezer and of their travels. But most of the people Matthias loved wouldn't arrive in the Kolonie until next month, so there was nothing else for him to do except return to the woolen mill.

It took less than ten minutes for him to reach the mill. Inside he climbed the ladder to the second floor of the structure and walked to his tool chest at the side of the room—a gift crafted by Friedrich's *Vater* and given to Matthias when he turned sixteen.

He reached under the top drawers and dug through the planes and joiners until he found his jack plane. As families reunited across their village, as Friedrich was off someplace fighting this war, Matthias pressed out his frustration across a floorboard until it was smooth. Then he moved to the next piece of wood.

At least he had plenty of work to do in the mill. Someone else would have to build Amalie Wiese her new kitchen.

* * * * *

The moment Amalie rounded the corner, she bent over, grasping herself around the waist. A sharp pain bludgeoned her belly and shot through her entire body as she struggled to breathe. Friedrich Vinzenz had left her. Instead of waiting to marry her, or even waiting to say good-bye, he had gone off to war.

Amalie collapsed back against a stone wall as she tried—and failed—to steady her breathing.

How could Friedrich have done this to her? He said he would be here, waiting for her when she arrived from New York. He had to know the news of his departure would devastate her.

She wrapped her arms around her chest, forcing herself to breath more slowly. In and out.

Could it be that the thought of marrying her was so bad, the only way he could get away was by joining the infantry? Perhaps he left all of them because of her. Because he didn't want her as a wife. He'd run away before she arrived, left her behind, and given his best friend the job of telling her he was gone.

As a woman turned the corner toward her, Amalie pushed away from the wall to tug her sunbonnet low over her face. If the villagers didn't recognize her, maybe they would stop welcoming her to Amana and stop watching for her reaction about Friedrich's decision.

The bell rang out again, and she forced her legs to start walking toward the kitchen house. She would find one of the elders and ask where her new kitchen was located. As long as her hands stayed busy, she wouldn't have to think about her loss or her future.

As she climbed the steps to the dining room, she pushed her sunbonnet back over her shoulders and walked through the narrow door with her head held high. People filled the dining room, and before them was a meal of salami and cheese spread out on platters, fresh blueberries piled high in communal bowls.

To her left was the kitchen, and she saw the graying hair of the older sister, Henriette Koch, bent over the stove. Back in Ebenezer, when she was a teenager, Amalie had worked for four very long years in Henriette's kitchen.

Brother Schaube was on her right, preparing to sit down on a bench, and she moved toward him. When he saw her, he looked like he might slip away like the rest of them, but instead he stepped forward to greet her. His eyes were hidden under his thick spectacles, his smile as solemn as the figures on the stained glass she'd seen in Lisbon.

"We tried to stop him—" he began, but she stopped his apology before he finished. She didn't want to talk about Friedrich's choice with him or anyone else.

"I wanted to speak with you about my new kitchen."

"Your kitchen?" he repeated as if he was as stumped as Matthias by her question.

"You wrote to me," she reminded him. "You and the other elders asked me to start a new kitchen house in Amana."

"Indeed," he replied, sounding relieved that she didn't want to speak about Friedrich. "The kitchen will be completed soon."

"Soon?" Her voice escalated with indignation. "It was supposed to be ready when I arrived."

"There was work to be done on the woolen mill before we could complete the new kitchen."

"Where will everyone eat—"

"There are three kitchen houses in Amana." He took a seat and reached for a pitcher of *Hinbeerensaft*. Raspberry juice. "It might be crowded, but we have enough seats for everyone until the next group arrives in September."

She couldn't wait until September to begin working in her kitchen. She needed to start today.

He took a long sip of the juice and then began stacking meat and cheese on his plate.

"All I need is a stove," she said.

He scooped up a bite of meat on his fork and held it in front of him. "We've ordered one from Cedar Rapids, but it won't arrive for another month."

In spite of all the people crowded in the room, it was silent. She should wait to talk again, until after the elder was finished eating, but she'd traveled almost eight hundred miles to reach this valley. Now the man she was planning to marry had deserted her and she didn't even have a kitchen to work in. There was no place for her to run now. No place for her to hide.

She didn't want to speak with Brother Schaube about her marriage, but he could at least tell her about her kitchen.

"What still needs to be finished?" she pressed.

He lowered his fork. "The cellar is complete."

"Only the cellar?"

"We're building a strong structure, Sister Amalie. Your kitchen will be standing a hundred years from now."

She took a step back. At this moment she didn't care if the kitchen lasted a thousand years. She needed it right now.

He pointed at the food in front of him. "Join us for a meal," he directed, but she shook her head. She didn't think she could eat.

"Do you have a room ready for me?"

He took a deep breath, apparently relieved that she didn't press him further about her kitchen.

"We have a temporary room where you can stay until the kitchen house is built."

She glanced over to the next table, at Brother Schaube's wife. Rosa Schaube was a small woman but a strong one. Sister Schaube would understand.

"I need something to do with my hands," Amalie said. "Just until the kitchen house is complete."

"There is plenty of work for you here," he agreed. "We have already assigned you a place."

"Where?"

He tilted his head down, his words barely audible. "Here, in Sister Henriette's kitchen."

She stared at him.

"That won't be a problem, will it?" he asked, looking up at her again.

She hesitated. Her years working for Henriette had been challenging on the best days, devastating on the worst ones. But it didn't matter right now. As long as there was a job for her to do, she would try to be content.

"Karoline Baumer came from Ebenezer to work with me."

He nodded. "The kitchen in Middle Amana has requested her services until the new kitchen is complete."

She took a step back. For so long she'd been looking forward to arriving in Amana, but nothing was as she had planned. She needed to get out of the dining room, away from all the eyes.

"I need to go to my room," she muttered.

Sister Schaube slipped off her bench, reaching for Amalie's arm. "I will show you the way, dear."

Comfortless Thy soul did languish
Me to comfort in my anguish.
Ernst C. Homburg

Chapter Ten

.... •

Rain sprinkled on the canvas tent and trickled in through the leaks in the roof. Friedrich brushed a splatter of rain off his face, but the shower didn't stop him from packing his things this morning. He placed the trousers and shirt he had brought from Amana into his knapsack and the one extra cartridge box the army provided for him.

After using one piece of stationery to write Amalie yesterday, he had two pieces of paper along with two envelopes to keep in his knapsack. Once he received his first month's wages, he would buy postage and more supplies to write her again along with Matthias and his parents.

Around him the soldiers were dressed in their new blue uniforms and caps. They worked efficiently, joking with each other as they folded their woolen blankets and the oiled ground cloth they would sleep on in the field. Friedrich was tucking his sewing kit into his sack when one of the soldiers grabbed the kit out of his hands.

"Whatcha got there, Fred?" Private Earl Smith held the kit high above his head. "You gonna knit some socks down in Tennessee?"

"I can mend mine if they need it. Or I can mend yours."

He tossed the kit back on Friedrich's cot. "You hear that, boys? Freddy here is gonna stitch up all our socks."

He could make socks too if he needed to do it, but he didn't mention that to Private Smith. He had never felt uncomfortable around the other men in Amana, his brothers, but here he couldn't seem to understand the joviality of these men, nor did they understand him. They laughed in the face of the sacred, trivialized what should have frightened them.

But even if he couldn't feel joviality for the battle ahead, his blood still rushed in excitement as they prepared for their journey. He didn't know what lay before them. He didn't know about these other men, but the Spirit of God traveled with him wherever he went, even into the enemy's camps.

In his haversack, Friedrich packed a fork, tin plate, and the canteen he'd already filled with water. And he placed a small burlap bag inside with the salt beef and hardtack the army provided, rations to last him for the next four days.

"You got your Bible in there?" Earl asked.

Friedrich picked up his Gospel of John and quietly placed it in his knapsack. The men around him snickered, but he didn't acknowledge their mockery of him. This feeling of loneliness—it was foreign to him. He'd spent his life surrounded by his family and friends, and he thought he would like being in the company of the soldiers as well. But even with all the men in the tent this early morning, he was still alone.

"Maybe you should preach to us, Freddy. Tell us about the good Lord and all that before we go out there and fight."

"You're not going absent without leave on us, are you, Fred?" another voice asked. "Stitchin' up socks back at camp while we're all fighting for you."

"I hear the man don't believe in fighting."

"He ain't gonna run," someone else said. "Sergeant said he'll shoot deserters, and Freddy here don't wanna be shot. He'll probably turn traitor instead."

"Or be taken prisoner. That's what happens to boys who don't know a lick about fighting."

Friedrich clenched his fists, cringing at the accusations in their voices. He wanted to show all of them that he did know a thing about fighting, but it would only prove that he was just like the rest of them. And he wasn't anything like them.

Someone let out a blood-curdling yell behind him, and he ducked to the ground. The other men laughed.

"You better get used to that, Fred. Them Rebels like their yellin'."

Breathing deeply, Friedrich stood up and slung the haversack over his shoulder, the string wrapped across his chest. He was supposed to fight alongside these men, not fight with them. But if God wanted him to be here, God would have to give him strength to make it through this.

Someone spat a curse word, and Friedrich cringed again. All he wanted to do now was march in silence through the hills in Tennessee, away from some of these men.

If only Matthias had joined the army with him. He could still hear his friend's voice outside in the hallway down at the courthouse, begging to say good-bye to him. Everything within him had wanted to leap up and shake his friend's hand one last time, so Matthias would know he hadn't abandoned him. And that one day, Lord willing, he would return to the Kolonie.

What he would give to have Matthias with him now, to march on the Rebels beside his best friend instead of these men, who took the name of their Lord in vain instead of blessing the very name that created each one of them.

"Leave him alone, Smith," one of the soldiers commanded.

Friedrich nodded at Jonah Henson in appreciation. Maybe he wasn't as alone as he thought.

Jonah was from Iowa County like him. Before he joined their

regiment, Jonah was a clerk at a dry goods store in Marengo. He'd told the other men that he'd never even hunted in his life, but he seemed to serve willingly like the rest of them. The other men respected him, even feared him a little. Much more than they respected Friedrich.

"Don't worry about Earl." Jonah spoke to Friedrich in German.

Friedrich stepped back in surprise. "You speak German?"

"A little," he replied. "My grandfather insisted on teaching me when I was a child."

Friedrich hung a cap pouch and bayonet scabbard from his leather belt as they talked. It was good to hear the familiar language of his family and his community.

Jonah pointed at Earl. "His uncle was some famous general in the last war, and he thinks he's too good to be a private."

"I will pray for him."

Jonah gave him an odd look and then smiled. "You can pray for me too."

Friedrich nodded as he picked up his shotgun. They would all need prayer. The sergeant said there were skirmishes across the state of Tennessee right now, but most of the Federals in Tennessee were fighting to take over the small river port of Chattanooga. There wasn't time to continue training the new infantrymen. They needed soldiers to join the battle, no matter how green. He and the others from Iowa's 28th would support the men already fighting there.

They marched hard all day during their training, and then he collapsed on his cloth in exhaustion, Amalie in his mind. Most nights, right before he sank into sleep, he wondered if she had read his letter and if she knew yet that he wasn't waiting in Amana for her.

Any day she would walk into their village and discover that he was gone. He hoped she would find it in her heart to forgive him for leaving, hoped God would provide her peace as she waited for him, and he dearly hoped she would wait. He couldn't imagine returning to Amana and finding her promised—or even married—to someone else.

He wished he could have been enough of a man to ask the colonel for a few weeks longer to say good-bye to her, but one look at her pretty blue eyes, one soft touch of her hands, and he never would have left Iowa.

He and Jonah were the first ones out of the tent, ready to get on the open wagons that would transport the men from Camp Pope to the train station. As they walked toward the wagons, Jonah lifted a letter out of his haversack and dropped it into a barrel that would take the mail to the local postmaster.

Jonah turned back toward him. "You have something to mail, Vinzenz?"

"I'm waiting to buy a stamp in Tennessee."

"Why didn't you buy one from the post office?"

He hesitated. "Because I didn't have any money to bring with me."

Jonah gave him an odd look. "Where are you sending it?"

"Back to Amana."

"I've heard about your colony." Jonah paused. "I think I'd like to visit one day."

"You are always welcome," Friedrich said.

Jonah dug in his sack and pulled out a stamp. He handed it to Friedrich.

Friedrich eyed it for a moment. "Are you certain?"

Jonah smiled. "You can repay me in Chattanooga."

He borrowed Jonah's glue as well, and with the stamp on the envelope, Friedrich dropped it into the barrel.

An hour later the men packed into the seats on the train, and Friedrich waved good-bye to the lush grass and hills of Iowa and to Amalie and Matthias and the entire community west of the camp.

He didn't know what would be waiting for him in Tennessee, or what the enemy looked like, but he was ready as he could be for the journey.

* * * * *

An afternoon storm turned Amana's main street into a stream of sticky mud. Water soaked through Matthias's straw hat and his work clothes as he trudged through the mess, back to his room. The other workers left the mill an hour ago for supper, but he kept sawing and smoothing the lumber for the floor. He was plenty hungry, but not hungry enough to be in the same room as Amalie.

He walked along Price Creek, swollen from the rain, and passed by the stone soap factory and the wooden windmill set back in an orchard. A smaller stone building housed the bakery at the corner and next to it was the shop where he and the other carpenters built and sometimes fixed broken furniture. Beside the carpentry shop was the cellar of the new kitchen house, awaiting its frame.

His stomach rumbled, and he stepped off the muddy street to the orchard along the side. While the others were eating meat and some sort of potatoes, he would attempt to satisfy his hunger with fruit tonight, and then tomorrow he would ask one of the elders if he could begin taking his meals at another kitchen house.

He ate the plum so fast that he barely tasted it and then he picked another one for his pocket. The elders would excuse him from eating supper, but not from evening prayers. Hopefully the fruit would keep his stomach quiet as they prayed.

When he reached his room, he threw his soaked clothes onto a heap on the floor and dried himself with a towel.

Amalie might be living in Amana now, but it didn't mean he had to acknowledge her presence. He would ignore her, like he had done before he left Ebenezer. And like she had done to him.

He threw the towel against the blue wall and watched it slide down.

He couldn't avoid every meal nor could he skip the services in the meetinghouse or their evening prayers. Maybe he could talk to the elders and they could assign Amalie to a job someplace far away, like South Amana. He might never see her again if she lived there, or at least he wouldn't see her until she and Friedrich were married.

He dug through the heap of wet clothes to find the other plum and ate it quickly before he pulled on a pair of dry trousers and a clean shirt.

If only that colonel hadn't come to Amana. If only Friedrich hadn't felt compelled to follow him. Friedrich and Amalie would marry this fall, and Matthias would marry soon as well.

On the table in front of him were the letters from his friend. He'd yet to open the one that Friedrich had written to him. When Friedrich returned, he might open it, just to see what his friend had said, but he couldn't do it now. He was afraid that Friedrich might say he never planned to come back.

Three weeks ago he'd mailed the other letter to Friedrich's parents with a short letter of his own. He'd told them how sorry he was, that he'd tried to talk Friedrich out of leaving Amana. He couldn't imagine how devastated they must be at the news. And embarrassed. None of the community's sons had gone to fight in the war between the states, but now the son of a respected elder had defied the leadership of their community and gone to war.

Next to the envelope with his name was the letter Friedrich had written to Amalie. The last letter he would have to deliver for Friedrich.

Lightning flashed across the sky as Matthias walked back outside. The letter was tucked under his slicker and he shoved his hat down on his forehead before he rushed down two buildings to swing open the door to Henriette's kitchen.

As he stomped his feet on the rug by the door, he considered giving the letter to Sophia or one of the other girls to deliver to Amalie if she wasn't there, but then he felt ridiculous. Friedrich would expect Matthias to be the one to give her the letter, and he could certainly control his emotions long enough to simply hand it off to her and leave. There was nothing else for them to talk about.

From the dining room, he could see Amalie in the kitchen scrubbing a pot in the wooden sink. She was so full of herself and her abilities that she didn't have time for anyone else. Even without her kitchen complete, she had found work in Henriette's, because work was everything to her. More important than any of the people in her life.

He clutched his fists together, welcoming back the anger. He would remain angry at her until Friedrich came home, and then the two of them could iron out their differences.

"Matthias!" He recognized the lilt in Sophia's voice before he looked back at the kitchen.

He didn't see Amalie, but Sophia smiled wide at him as she glided into the room. Her pale face was flawless, no hint of the sweat that drenched most kitchen workers after a long meal.

"Hello, Sister Sophia," he said with a slight bow of his head.

If Amalie heard him, she didn't come to the doorway to greet him.

Sophia crossed the room toward him, accusing and teasing him at the same time. "You missed supper."

"I wasn't hungry."

"You're such a hard-working man, Brother Matthias. It's a shame for you not to be hungry."

He was a wretched man, torn between his desires and what he

knew to be right. He knew Sophia was only flirting with him, like she did with every unmarried man now that Friedrich was gone, but still in some way, her praise seemed to soothe the frustrations within him. "You've worked a long day yourself."

"I don't do it for myself," she said softly. Her eyes widened in open admiration. "I do it for men like you who are working so hard to build our town."

He cleared his throat. "And we appreciate it."

"There's some sausage left over and potato salad," she whispered. "I'll fetch it for you."

"You don't have to—" he started, but sausage sounded mighty good to him right now.

"Sophia!" Sister Henriette called from the kitchen.

Sophia glanced over her shoulder, but before she left, she flashed one last grin at him.

He pitied the man who eventually married her. She needed more attention than any one man could give. A woman like Amalie was confident without a man's attention, without anyone's attention. He'd seen proof of that this very day, when she reacted to the news of Friedrich's leaving by asking for her kitchen house. Amalie needed her kitchen more than she needed a man.

Henriette shot him a stern look when he stepped into her kitchen, but she didn't ask him to leave. Amalie was arched over the sink scrubbing a stack of pans. And she ignored him.

He nodded toward her. "I need to speak with Sister Amalie."

Henriette hesitated at his request. Unmarried men and women were not supposed to socialize in their community.

She motioned him back to the doorway and stepped beside him. "Why must you talk to her?"

"I have something to give her," he whispered. "From Friedrich."

She held out her hand. "I will give it to her."

It was what he wanted, for someone else to deliver it, but still his fingers clutched the envelope. Friedrich would want him to give it to her himself.

"If you allow me to speak with her today, I will not disturb her again."

Her hand dropped to her side. "You must stay in the dining room."

"We will."

With a wave of her arms, Henriette shooed Amalie from the kitchen. Amalie wiped her hands on a towel, and he stood back to let her pass into the dining room. Instead of stopping to speak with him, though, she hurried to one of the tables and began stacking the plates.

"Amalie—" he started.

"Supper finished a half hour ago."

"I'm not here to eat."

She picked up another plate and wiped it clean with her rag before adding it to the others. "Sophia is certainly glad to see you."

He started to protest her words but thought better of it before the denial escaped his lips.

"It's too bad," Amalie continued. "Hilga Vinzenz might think you've been unfaithful."

"I'm not the one who was unfaithful."

She stopped her busy hands and faced him. "If you are implying that I've done something wrong, Matthias, you are mistaken."

The familiar anger surged in him again. "Everyone is always wrong except you."

"I haven't done anything—" she began, but he shrugged her off. Friedrich was the one required to listen to her arguments, not him.

He pulled the letter from his pocket, and when he held it out to her, she stared at it like it was a copperhead posed to strike.

"Friedrich left this for you."

Her gaze remained frozen on the envelope. "What did he say?"

"I didn't read your letter."

She looked up, meeting his gaze, and for a moment the innocence in her eyes reminded him of the girl she once was. "But what did he say to you, when he left?"

"He left without saying good-bye, to me or to anyone else."

Reaching out, she took the envelope from his hands, and when she did, it felt like she'd taken a load from his shoulders. He backed toward the door.

"I have been faithful, Matthias," she repeated, like she had to convince him that she had done the right thing. "I hope you have as well."

As she turned, he tried to shrug off her words, but the burden returned heavy on his shoulders. Louise Vinzenz had spent the prime years of her life teaching him and Friedrich and Hilga about the value of faithfulness and love as well as grace. He would never do anything to hurt anyone in her family.

"Good-bye, Amalie."

When he walked out the door, Sophia was waiting for him outside with a wrapping of brown paper. He could smell the spicy aroma of the sausage inside.

"*Danke schön*," he said before he rushed away to evening prayer.

He'd done what was required of him. He'd told Amalie about Friedrich's decision and his departure, and he'd delivered the letter to her as well. Now his duty was done. Henriette wouldn't have to worry about him speaking to Amalie again.

Now that the night has passed away and its dark shadows wane,
All who were weary yesterday have been revived again.

Christian Metz

Chapter Eleven
....

For the first time in a very long while, Amalie was alone. The feather tick and pillows enveloped her when she sat on the narrow bed, but she hardly noticed the softness of it.

Light from the kerosene lantern glowed orange on the stand beside her, flickering light across the deep blue color on the plastered walls. Friedrich's letter lay beside the lantern, unopened. She'd waited to read his words in the privacy of her new room, but now that she was alone, she was afraid of what he might say.

Leaning back against the headboard, she glanced around her new room. There were windows on two of the walls, the glass covered by brown muslin curtains to keep out the night air. A clock sat on the walnut bureau across from her bed, and her trunk rested on the scrubbed pine floor beside a stove. Near the far window was a washstand, but she'd visited the bathhouse instead of using the washbowl and pitcher tonight.

Her skin was clean, but her heart ached in her chest. She was supposed to be elated tonight, fresh from her reunion with Friedrich. They were supposed to begin their new life together right away in this beautiful place, but nothing was as she had planned.

On the trail she'd longed for a bed and bath, but these luxuries didn't comfort her like she'd imagined. Even with the sturdy roof over her head and feather pillows underneath, she wished she were back on the trail for the night. The anticipation of seeing Friedrich had been so sweet as she counted the days and then hours until their reunion.

Karoline was leaving for Middle Amana in the morning to live in the room next to her mother until the new kitchen house was complete. Amalie had already said good-bye to her this evening, after the prayer meeting. There was no one else for her to confide in here in Amana, about her frustration or her anger or the pain that had entwined itself around her heart today. It would take time for her to build trust with the other women, trust that they wouldn't share what was in her heart.

Tears filled her eyes and began to stream down her cheeks.

How she wished Friedrich were in Amana. She'd been strong for so long, intent on the day they would be reunited. But now she didn't know when she would see him again.

She reached for the envelope and held it to her chest. There was so much for her to sort out now, so much to consider. Would Friedrich come back to Amana after the war? Would he come back to her? And if he did, would he be the same person she'd loved for so many years?

War would have to change Friedrich. People would be dying around him, and he might even be required to kill someone himself, the blood staining his soul. When he returned, he would be different than the Amana man she'd known for so long, since the weeks that they had traveled together across the Atlantic as *kinder*.

Friedrich would be accountable to God for His actions, and she prayed he would consider in earnest before he took up arms in this war. He'd always been a man who acted before he thought of the consequences. And sometimes he didn't even consider the consequences well after he acted. But what he saw in the battle, and what he did, would affect him—and her—the rest of their lives.

She would be faithful to her promise to Friedrich, but what if, after his months outside their colony, he decided the world held more of a promise for his future without their community or without her?

She slid her fingernail under the lip of the envelope to open it and pulled out two pieces of stationery. Wiping her tears off with her sleeve, she focused her eyes on Friedrich's familiar handwriting and began to read his words to her

My dearest Amalie, he began.

She took another deep breath before she continued.

By now you know that I am gone, and I am deeply saddened to think of not being in Amana when you arrive. I do not mean to hurt you, Amalie, and I can't even explain to you exactly why I must go. I agree with Brother Metz and the elders, this war would best be resolved through peace and prayer, but our government has chosen to fight and I feel I must fight alongside my brothers for those who cannot fight for themselves.

I wanted to say good-bye to you before I left, but if I had looked into your eyes, even one glimpse, I never would have left. And I never could have lived with myself for ignoring this call that I believe comes from God.

In the next paragraphs, Friedrich described a black man by the name of Joseph who had once been enslaved by a master who whipped him, and he quoted King David's psalm about helping the poor and needy.

No matter how long I am gone, I will remain true to you, Amalie. I want to marry you. I want to see our children's faces one day, and I want to grow old with you at my side.

I pray that you will wait for me as well, but if I don't return, my desire is that you will live a life of dedication in the Kolonie. And that you will find love.

When I return, if you will have me, my heart will be...
Forever yours,
Friedrich

Amalie clutched the letter to her chest like she held a piece of the man she would marry. Friedrich Vinzenz hadn't run away from his promise to her. He still loved her and he was planning to return one day to marry her.

The promise was still there, the hope of their future together. She might be weak, but God was strong, much stronger than she was. He would give her the strength she needed to build her new life in Amana and be ready when Friedrich returned.

She lifted the letter, written by the only man she had ever loved, and read it one more time.

If God's Spirit was truly tugging on Friedrich's heart, he must follow, but she still didn't understand why God would require him to go to war. There was so much to lose in this war, especially when they were fighting against men like General Morgan, who viewed destruction as entertainment. It was as if he and his men enjoyed the conquest and even the blood.

Instead of waiting on God, Friedrich often fought against what he believed to be wrong, but she couldn't fathom his killing someone. There was too much kindness in his soul to wound a brother.

Her thoughts traveled back to her day in Lisbon, to the shopkeeper who had given her the book that he said started the war.

She glanced over at the trunk again along her wall. Hidden deep inside was the copy of *Uncle Tom's Cabin*. Perhaps the book would answer some of her questions. If she could understand why these men were fighting, perhaps she could understand why Friedrich felt God wanted him to go.

Amalie tiptoed over to the trunk and dug through the blankets and clothing. She removed the house blessing she'd stitched for her and Friedrich's room and placed it on the bureau. Then she found the novel stowed underneath more clothing.

When she returned to her bed, she opened the book to the first chapter and began reading about a slave woman named Eliza and a Kentucky gentleman who was about to sell Eliza's son.

Seven hours later, Amalie rolled over on her bed and rubbed her eyes in the darkness. Someone was pounding pans or something else outside the tent, but she didn't hear the oxen stirring yet. She pulled the cover over her shoulders, trying to block out the annoyance of the noise, but it didn't stop.

She sat up in her bed and gazed wildly around the room for Karoline until she realized they were no longer on the trail. Their group had arrived in Amana, and she was alone in her room. She had stayed up way too late reading. Sometime during the night she had finally blown out the lamp, succumbing to sleep, but the story lingered in her mind.

Someone knocked again, and she jumped up from her bed, wrapping the quilt around her shoulders before she cracked open the door. Henriette Koch was on the other side.

The woman's lips were pressed together, and the familiar annoyance rushed through Amalie at the woman's disapproval.

"You're not living in Ebenezer anymore, Amalie."

Amalie rubbed her eyes. "We get up early in Ebenezer."

"With all the new arrivals, we have fifty people to feed this morning," Henriette barked. "Twenty minutes from now."

The bells of the bakery cart rang on the street below as Amalie backed into her room. "I need to dress."

"Well, do it quickly."

After closing the door, Amalie rushed back into the room and pulled her dress off a hook. This morning she hoped the elders and the other kitchen workers would excuse her tardiness, thinking she needed to rest after her long journey, but she would have to be careful about her rest from now on. If she didn't prove faithful in this job, Brother Schaube would never let her oversee her own kitchen.

As she pulled on her stockings, she glanced over at the book on the nightstand, tempting her to read just one more page.

She'd meant to read only a few pages last night, but she couldn't seem to break herself from the story. The plight of Eliza and little Harry captured her heart, and she rushed through the words, and then the pages, like a thirsty traveler in search of a stream.

She wanted to know what happened to Eliza and Harry and Tom.

And she wanted answers to the call on Friedrich's life.

She tucked the book back into her trunk and rushed down to the dining hall.

Men and women alike streamed into the dining room, minutes before the bell tolled. There was no time to think about Friedrich or the book.

Karoline was on one of the benches this morning, beside her mother, and Matthias sat with the other men. Amalie smiled at Karoline, ignored Matthias Roemig. And she pretended she was a queen, reigning over her little kingdom.

* * * * *

Bowls of sliced strawberries brightened the plain breakfast table along with silver pots of steaming coffee. Matthias spooned strawberries onto his oatmeal and quickly ate the food. Then he gulped down the coffee and stood up before Sophia tried to pour him a second cup.

As he pushed through the dining room, he didn't even glance toward the kitchen. He thought it would be easy for him to ignore

Amalie, especially when she hid herself away in the kitchen, but he knew she was there. Her very presence unnerved him.

This morning he would ask Brother Schaube if he could begin eating at one of the other kitchens. He wished he could think of a reason to convince the elders to send Amalie to another village to work or convince them to send him away instead, but they would ask questions, and he couldn't share the animosity in his heart with them.

The other six villages were all expanding like Amana—most of them probably needed carpenters even more than the main village. With Friedrich gone now, there was no reason for him to stay here. After Hilga and her parents arrived, maybe the elders could send the entire Vinzenz family to West or South Amana. The farther away he was from Amalie, the better it would be for all of them.

During their meeting this morning with Brother Schaube, he would volunteer to work outside Amana.

Swinging open the door from the dining room, he hurried toward the woolen mill. The sun glowed a vibrant red on the horizon.

Hilga would arrive in Amana within the month, and he needed to focus his mind and his prayers on what to do about their future together.

Carl and Louise expected Matthias to ask for their daughter's hand in marriage this fall. He didn't know what Hilga thought about marrying him. Neither of them wrote many letters, perhaps because neither of them knew what to say. They hadn't talked much while they were in Ebenezer, and their communication had been even more limited since he and Friedrich came to Iowa.

Before Friedrich left for the war, he kept Matthias informed about what was happening in his family, always hinting at the future. Sister Louise often wrote Matthias directly as well, with breezy stories and encouragement for him. There was no blood line connecting Matthias to the Vinzenz family, but he'd thought of Sister Louise and Carl

Vinzenz as his parents since he was a child. He would always be grateful to the Vinzenz family for welcoming him into their home and asking him to call them Mama and Papa.

Matthias turned off the main street, moving quickly toward the hum of mill machinery and the hiss of steam, steady sounds that inspired the entire village to work hard at whatever task was assigned them.

As he approached the mill, he recalled the excitement in Friedrich's eyes whenever he talked about Amalie. Ever since the elders received the telegram that Amalie left Ebenezer, Friedrich had been counting down the days, and sometimes hours, until her arrival. With the exception of his service to God, there was nothing more that Friedrich wanted than to see his future wife.

Matthias wasn't like that about Hilga. Instead of counting the days in anticipation, he dreaded the passing of each day. He didn't know what he was supposed to do when she arrived. He couldn't imagine himself married to her—she was six years younger than him, born the year after he arrived in the Vinzenz home.

Just as Friedrich had been like a brother to him, Hilga had been his sister, and he regarded her not only as a sister in Christ but like a blood sister whom he loved and teased. But he would do just about anything for any of the Vinzenz family, even if it meant marrying Hilga if she wanted to marry him.

And if he married, perhaps it would stop the conflict in his heart.

Matthias stepped into the addition on the woolen mill and took a smaller plane out of his tool chest to work on the lumber for the floor. He began smoothing it across the piece of oak, slowly but firmly scraping it into conformity with the others.

This floor was almost finished, and when he was done, he would begin working on the floor upstairs. Carpentry was engrained in him like the fibers in wood. He couldn't explain it, but the work was part of who he was. Making things fit together, smoothing the pieces of wood from the sawmill, and fitting the tongues and grooves together like a giant jigsaw puzzle gave him peace. And that's what he needed today. Peace.

The door opened, and a small crew of workers walked into the large room with Brother Schaube and two other elders. Matthias stood up and joined the group of men to hear about their tasks for the day. The elders had created a detailed plan for the village, and he and the other workers felt privileged to be able to use their skills to create buildings for their fellow brethren to work and worship and rest their heads.

He'd hoped to be able to speak to Brother Schaube in private, but perhaps it would be better to ask his questions with the others around.

"You men have worked hard and well this summer," Brother Schaube said with a pleasant smile. The man always seemed to be smiling, and sometimes Matthias found himself jealous of the joy that seemed to envelop him. "The addition to the woolen mill is almost complete, and we need to begin assigning some of you to new projects."

Brother Schaube unfolded a piece of paper. "We need to begin the bakery in West Amana," he said, and then assigned two masons to set the sandstone.

Next he called one of the newly arrived men forward—John Keller—and assigned him and another man to begin building a hotel in the village of Homestead for the visitors that came by train to purchase wool or flour or calico from their mill or just to experience a taste of communal living.

Matthias stepped forward, waving his hand at Brother Schaube. "I would be glad to go to Homestead as well."

Brother Schaube glanced down at the paper and then looked back at him. "I already have an assignment for you, Matthias."

His heart beat faster. "Is it in Homestead?'

Brother Schaube shook his head.

"But there is nothing to keep me in Amana," Matthias said. "I can take an assignment in any of the other villages."

Brother Schaube raised his eyebrows. "I appreciate your willingness to go, Matthias, but we need you here."

"Perhaps I could work on the new hotel in Homestead when the addition on the woolen mill is complete."

Brother Schaube shook his head. "We no longer need you working on the woolen mill."

Matthias didn't move. He prayed that Brother Schaube assigned him to work on the blacksmith shop or a new barn. Anything but—

"The elders and I need you and Niklas Keller to work on the new kitchen house."

Matthias's fingers clenched the wooden plane in his hand. He wanted to run out of this building, all the way to South Amana or Marengo or even back to Ebenezer. He could work any place, except on Amalie's kitchen.

"We should finish the woolen mill before we start a new project," Matthias persisted, ignoring the gazes of the men around him. Volunteering to take another's assignment was respectable, but it was unacceptable to persist in questioning an assignment, especially for an unmarried man who wasn't trying to work close to his wife or children.

At this moment, he didn't care much about protocol. He might not be able to leave the colony like Friedrich did, but he could find a way to avoid Amalie.

"Without your carpentry work, Matthias, we won't have enough room to feed all the new arrivals from Ebenezer."

Matthias pointed at one of the other men. "Gottlieb would do a better job than I would."

Brother Schaube eyed him for a moment before he assigned Gottlieb and two other men the work of completing the woolen mill.

AMANA
1863
IA

Matthias stepped backward, away from the others, as he tried to rid himself of the feelings that raged within him every time he thought about Amalie. Even when he was angry at her. It only made it worse knowing he might pass her along the street or see her at their meal or evening prayers.

If Brother Schaube knew what was happening inside him, he would send him away or he would relocate Amalie to a kitchen outside Amana. How could he tell this man that he didn't trust himself to be near Amalie Wiese? Or that he was hopelessly in love with his best friend's future wife?

He had loved her since he was fourteen and he hated himself for it. He thought he had outgrown his ridiculous schoolboy feelings, but his mind was battling once again against his heart. He couldn't let her—or Brother Schaube—know of his struggle.

Brother Schaube dismissed the men, but as Matthias reached his tool chest, the man called out to him. The two of them walked outside the building and sat on a bench.

"You are troubled," Brother Schaube started.

The elder had a keen ear to the heart and mind of God. If only Matthias could mask his heart so the man couldn't peer inside and see the wickedness that permeated it.

"I miss Friedrich," he said.

"*Ja*," he replied. "It is hard for all of us, but I need you working in Amana right now."

Matthias wanted to protest again, but he had no good reason to avoid this responsibility. "Could I make a request?"

"Certainly."

"I would like to eat at one of the other kitchen houses instead of Sister Henriette's."

The elder's eyebrows slid up again. Matthias knew the request was irregular—kitchen houses were assigned to each member—but he was fighting to keep himself intact.

"I realize Sister Henriette is not the best cook in Amana, but her food is tolerable," Brother Schaube said.

"It's not because of her cooking."

"Then what is it?"

"I—" he started and wished he had thought through a better excuse before he approached the elder. "Eating there reminds me of Friedrich."

"That is a good memory, I hope."

He nodded, but he wanted to shake himself. This wasn't going at all how he planned.

"You can't run away from your problems, Matthias. Eating at a new kitchen won't make you miss him any less."

Eating at a different kitchen might not make him miss Friedrich any less, but it would help him control his mind.

"But—"

The elder stopped him. "People will think you are switching because of Sister Henriette's food, and we can't have people changing dining rooms because they don't enjoy the meals."

He sighed. "When do you want me to start working on the new kitchen?"

"This morning," Brother Schaube said. "It must be ready when the others arrive."

Matthias stuck his hands in his pockets and walked back toward the building.

How was he supposed to avoid Amalie Wiese if he was required to spend the next month eating at Henriette's…and building Amalie her own kitchen?

In our earthly tribulation, as well as at triumphant goal,
We praise Thee, Lord of all creation, with
all our mind and heart and soul.
Eberhard Ludwig Gruber

Chapter Twelve
....

Amalie slipped the bread loaf into the folds of calico that lined a willow basket. Then she took another basket off a hook and filled it with bottles of homemade brew. On the wooden table were two blocks of hand cheese wrapped in brown paper, and the moment she reached for one, Henriette called over her shoulder.

"Don't forget to pack the *Handkäse.*"

Amalie bit her tongue as she placed the cheese into the basket. She'd spent almost ten years working in a communal kitchen; she knew how to put together a basket for the snack they served every morning between breakfast and the midday meal. Her tongue fought against her, wanting to retort, but she couldn't risk Henriette complaining to the elders about her insubordination.

"I've got everything in the baskets," Amalie responded as politely as she could muster.

Henriette scooted toward her, her wide hips bumping Amalie aside. But she remained close to the baskets as Henriette unfolded the calico and counted the items Amalie had placed inside. Then she added another bottle of beer to the five Amalie already packed.

"Good enough," Henriette said with a clap.

Amalie sighed as the woman placed water onto the stove so she could boil potatoes for the noon meal. The brethren wouldn't arrive for three more hours to eat, but with three meals and two snacks to prepare each day, there was very little time for the kitchen workers to rest or to eat. It was a continual cycle of cooking and cleaning and then time to begin cooking again.

Sophia tapped her fingers on the table, and Amalie pushed both baskets toward her. The girl looped the handles over her arms.

"I'll be back in a bit," Sophia said.

Henriette reached out and grabbed the girl's arm. "Not today, Sophia. I want Amalie to deliver the baskets."

"Oh, no—" Amalie protested.

Henriette turned Sophia's shoulders toward the sink. "I need you to help with the dishes."

Sophia groaned. "But I always take the snack to the mill."

"And I always have to come searching for you an hour later."

Sophia eyed the baskets on the table like she was tempted to grab them and run. "I will return right away."

"Not today, Sophia." Henriette shot Amalie a stern look, her eyebrows raised. "Amalie needs some fresh air."

Amalie hated to admit it, but the woman was right. Her entire trip she'd looked forward to resuming her work in a kitchen, but with the weight of her disappointment and the weariness of her travels and then her late night reading, she was struggling to stay alert.

She'd like to be excused to rest, but she would never admit her weariness to Henriette. Maybe the fresh air would revive her.

Sophia protested one last time as Amalie pulled on her sunbonnet, but Henriette didn't relent. Instead, she turned to Amalie. "Don't dally at the mill, Amalie."

"There's no reason for me to dally."

At eight thirty, it was already warm outside, though not nearly as hot as the kitchen. Clouds were building overhead to create a gray haze that Amalie hoped would protect the workers from the intensity of the afternoon sun.

As she strolled past the brewery and general store, she marveled at all the work the men had done since they purchased this land eight years ago. Not only had they transformed the fields and trees of the river valley into a town, they'd created a community.

Several visitors passed her on the wooden sidewalk, displaying hooped dresses like the ones she'd seen on the giant doll in Lisbon, except these women were adorned with ribbons and bows, and parasols to keep the sun off their pale complexions. The bright colors of the silk and chemise seemed frivolous and worldly, compared to the dark, simple wardrobe worn by the Inspirationist women. And these visitors looked at her the same way the women had done in Lisbon, like she was an oddity in her calico dress and draping sunbonnet. They didn't seem to realize that here in Amana, they were the oddly clothed ones.

Sophia told her that visitors came often to do business at the mills. Others came out of curiosity to see what type of people lived in a communal society. It seemed like the shopkeeper in Lisbon was right—even though they'd come all the way to Iowa to get away from the world, the world couldn't leave them alone. It was almost as if the very fact they were seeking seclusion intrigued outsiders, making it seemingly irresistible for them to impose on her community.

Visitors didn't understand the bond of their society or the durability of their faith. They didn't understand that the plain clothes the Inspirationists wore only strengthened this bond. None of the men or women were above or below the other in rank or in wealth. They wore the same style of dress, ate the same food, worshiped the same way, slept in the same type of room. And in their sameness, they loved and cared for one another, not because of what they did or how they looked, but because each member was valued as a child of God.

Amalie passed by the butcher shop and the saddle shop and then she heard the steady rhythm of hammer against iron in the blacksmith shop. Ripened fruit and freshly cut grass sweetened the air, even in the village, and she drank in the aroma. Everything about the village celebrated the beauty of life, a celebration of God's goodness.

Just weeks ago, Friedrich had been walking down this street, smelling the fruit and the grass. Even though he wasn't here with her today, she felt the shadow of his presence in the village. He'd helped build these shops and plant the crops of rye and wheat in the fields behind them. He'd walked down this street many times before her, drinking in the sights and the blessed sounds of peace and prosperity given to them by their heavenly Father.

At the eastern edge of town the pleasant scents of fruit and bread deteriorated into more rancid smells from the barnyard. Above her, the bleating of sheep rained down from the smaller village of East Amana. The green hills were speckled with the animals, and she saw the giant barn above that housed them.

One day, after she'd recovered from her weeks of travel, she would walk to the other villages in the Kolonie and visit her school friends as well as friends of her parents and the Vinzenz family.

Or maybe she would wait until Friedrich returned and they could go together to announce their engagement. The thought of being with him, of their reunion, propelled her to walk even faster toward the mill.

At the corner of the main street was a yard with clotheslines strung on poles, a rounded brick building behind them. One of the sisters stepped out of the washhouse, her face steamed red as she shook out a towel and clipped it on one of the lines.

When the woman saw Amalie, she gave a quick nod and ducked back into the washhouse.

Amalie sighed. Pity from the tourists didn't bother her, but there was no reason for her sisters to feel sorry for her. It was this pity from the brothers and sisters in her society that disturbed her the most. The quick, nervous glances from men and women who didn't know what to say to her. The unspoken questions about Friedrich's desertion and the reasons he left.

They weren't privy to the words in his letter nor to the longings in his heart. They might think he was running away from her, but she knew the truth. There was nothing for her to be ashamed of.

As she turned the corner, steam hissed from the engine that powered the woolen mill and puffed into the sky.

In his letter, Friedrich didn't say how long he would be in the army. General Morgan said the war would be finished soon, the Confederates victorious. Maybe Matthias would know how long Friedrich would be gone.

Outside the woolen mill's front door were three men dressed in dark, double-breasted suits. One of them held open a newspaper, and they stood focused over something inside. Normally she wouldn't have cared about the news outside their colony. Normally she would have ignored the men and their paper, scooting around them to get in the door.

But this morning her eyes wandered to the bold letters on the first column. The headline stopped her.

Federal Troops Battling Rebellion in Tennessee

She stopped walking and stared at the words. Which Federal troops were battling in Tennessee?

One of the men looked up and noticed her. He lifted his top hat and stepped aside to give her access to the door, but even then, she didn't move. If only she could read a few words of the paper, just to find out what had happened in Tennessee.

"If you please—" she began, and the other men looked up.

"Would you like us to move?" one of them asked slowly, like she might not understand him.

"*Nein.*" She pointed at the front page. "Could you tell me what is happening in Tennessee?"

The man with the tall hat turned back to the front page and skimmed the headline before he looked at her again. "The Union is trying to force Bragg and his men out of Chattanooga."

"Are there troops from Iowa in this battle?"

He clicked his tongue as he read through the article. "Says there are troops from Indiana, Iowa, and Ohio."

"Are there any from Iowa County?" Her voice shook slightly with her question.

"It doesn't say."

"Martin Smith's son volunteered to fight in the cavalry," one of the men said to his colleagues. "They signed him up for three years."

"They're signing all of them up for three years now."

She stepped back, feeling faint again. Surely Friedrich hadn't signed up for three years. How could they wait for three more years to marry?

The men continued talking to each other, as if she and her calico dress had faded into the backdrop of buildings and fields.

She wanted to tell them that she was going to marry one of the Union soldiers when he returned home. That her Friedrich was willing to leave his home and his community for a call he believed came from God.

Of course, the visitors didn't need to know this about her—or about Friedrich—but for some odd reason, she wanted them and other people to know. It wasn't just those on the outside who were serving in this war. Friedrich was serving too.

The men didn't seem to notice as she remained by the door, listening to them.

"This war was supposed to end at Bull Run."

"No one, not even Honest Abe, can predict how long a war will last."

"The Rebs are getting closer," the man with the top hat said with a sigh. "There's talk of the Confederacy fighting in Iowa one day."

"The war will never come to Iowa."

"I wouldn't be so certain," he replied. "They've already fought in Indiana and Ohio."

Her stomach felt queasy. What would happen if the Rebs came here, men like General Morgan? Would they burn the beautiful buildings that the Amana men erected? It made her hope, in her own selfishness perhaps, that the Union troops stopped them long before they came to Iowa.

The door opened, and Brother Schaube greeted the men with a round of handshakes. She stepped aside as he waved them into the woolen mill. Before the door swung shut, Matthias walked outside, hauling a carved tool chest in his arms. Their eyes met, but he didn't acknowledge her as he moved forward.

She eyed the door, thinking for a moment about Henriette's instructions to be swift, but Matthias needed to eat as well. And she needed to ask him a few questions.

"Where are you going?" she asked as she followed him away from the mill.

He didn't glance at her again, not even to give her the courtesy of a good morning. "To your kitchen."

She expected to feel a rush of enthusiasm that Matthias was beginning to work on it, but any gladness had disappeared with the news of the war. Her kitchen didn't matter much right now.

"Do you know who those men were by the door?" she asked,

trailing behind him. He kept a remarkable pace, even carrying the large tool chest.

"They're business owners from Cedar Rapids. They come each month to place orders for their shops."

"They were reading a newspaper." She struggled to keep up with the stride of his long legs, especially with her arms anchored by the food baskets. "There is fighting in Tennessee."

"We are far from Tennessee," he muttered.

"We are far, but Friedrich might be there."

This time he stopped walking and focused hard eyes on her. "How could you possibly know that?"

"I—I don't know. But he could be."

"Don't borrow trouble, Amalie," he clipped. Like she enjoyed trouble.

She didn't know what she'd done to make him despise her so, except to agree to marry Friedrich. He didn't think she was good enough for Friedrich, but it wasn't his decision to make. They needed to lay down the bitterness from the past and focus on the one person they both cared deeply about.

"They said the army was enlisting the men for three years."

"The war will be finished long before three years."

She set down her baskets on the path, considering his words. If the Union conquered the Rebels in Tennessee, then maybe Friedrich would be home soon. In weeks even.

"Have you received any letters from Friedrich?"

He hesitated. "Not since he left."

"I only want to know if he is safe."

"As long as he is fighting this war, he will not be safe."

She looked down at her baskets. Even if Matthias was right, she didn't want to hear his words. Friedrich was a clockmaker, not a warrior. If he were one of the men in the Tennessee battle, he wouldn't know how to fight. Not with a gun or whatever it was they used to try to kill each other with.

"You will tell me if you hear from him?" she asked.

"Of course."

Amalie nodded, but he had already turned, leaving without his morning snack.

She picked up her baskets and moved back toward the mill. Matthias would do good work on her kitchen, that she was certain, and he would tell her if he heard from Friedrich. Other than that, she would ignore him. Like he said, there was no reason for her to borrow trouble, and Matthias Roemig was trouble.

Though earth be rent asunder, thou'rt mine eternally;
Not fire nor sword nor thunder shall sever me from Thee.
Paul Gerhardt

Chapter Thirteen

The steady drumbeat compelled the soldiers forward, through the small cove. They'd crossed the Tennessee River into Georgia, and the beauty was spectacular, with knobby tree branches arched above their regiment, leaves dripping onto their path. Columbine spiked out of the rocky crevices, the red blooms bowing to the troops as they marched.

The clefts of Pigeon Mountain surrounded him, but Friedrich couldn't enjoy the beauty. They were supposed to be chasing the Rebels, but the soldiers knew if the Confederates trapped them in this gorge, with its steep cliffs on both sides, escape would be almost impossible.

Major General Rosecrans had commanded the Federals to chase the Confederates out of Chattanooga, drive them down into Georgia. The days were hot in the south, climbing past ninety degrees and soaking their skin in sweat, but the nights were so cold that sleep eluded most of them. They hiked at least twenty miles today, over the rough terrain on the mountain with their packs.

Friedrich's division had joined four others to march south, but they'd yet to see a Confederate soldier along their journey, crossing through Tennessee without even a skirmish. And he'd yet to look into someone's eyes and pull the trigger.

He couldn't see them, but the rebels were out there in the trees someplace, ready to fight for the Tennessee border.

Friedrich held his gun a little closer to him. He wanted to fight for what was right, but he still didn't know exactly what that meant for him. Even though his sergeant hadn't said it, Friedrich knew he would send the newest recruits into the battle before the seasoned veterans. Whoever made it out alive would have proven himself to be a decent fighter and move up in the ranks. The green fighters—and the frightened men—would be filtered out on the battlefield.

As he marched, Friedrich pressed his finger to his chest and felt the crispness of paper tucked under his coat. He didn't believe the lock of Amalie's hair would bring him good luck, not like the charms some of the men believed in, but having her hair close to his heart made him feel like she was close as well.

He hoped, wherever she was, that Amalie was praying for him.

The shotgun clutched in his hands, Friedrich tried to pretend he was hunting for deer as they marched along. Shooting a gun wasn't a problem for him, but his mind still struggled about whether he could shoot another man. He didn't know how he could win the battle in his mind at the same time he fought one with his hands.

"Halt!" the sergeant commanded, and then the man lifted his field glasses and looked up the hills.

Before them, Friedrich could see a pile of felled logs blocking their way. The men around him groaned. They would have to climb up the rocky cliffs or turn back to the summit of the mountain.

The drumbeat continued, but above the pounding, he heard a yell. At first he thought one of the men was joking, Earl Smith or another one of them who liked to mimic the Rebel's battle cry, but the cry came again.

The drums stopped and a ball whizzed over his head. He ducked down, his heart racing.

Jonah knelt beside him, his gun ready. "You can do this, Vinzenz."

"I don't know—"

"We have to fight for those who cannot."

The sergeant yelled for them to charge, and Friedrich rushed toward the cliffs with the company of soldiers. Straight into the line of his brothers. His enemy.

He shook his head as he ran, like he could shake off his doubts as well. It was too late to think about his actions now. If he were wrong, he prayed God would forgive him. If he were right, he prayed God would allow him to forgive himself.

He didn't know who fired the first shot, but in an instant, the air popped like kernels of sizzling corn over a fire. Shots echoed all around him, the smells of sulfur and gunpowder stifled the air. He forged ahead with his fellow soldiers, but he didn't pull his trigger. His fingers seemed to be seared to his shotgun. Instead of firing it, he held it at his side.

Next to him, Earl Smith buckled on the ground with a howl of pain. Friedrich stopped running. He looked back down the hill, into a valley of smoke, and then looked above him, at the soldiers rushing toward him, their guns propped over their shoulders.

He could see the holes in the uniforms of the Rebels now. The dirt on their faces and their matted hair. With the exception of the faded gray color on their clothing, the enemy looked just like the soldiers who fought beside him.

Earl cried out again, and Friedrich looked down to see blood soaking the man's leg. Was this how Colonel O'Neill went down, on a battlefield like this? He had lost his leg, but he hadn't lost his life.

The wall of fallen logs was a good forty feet behind him. Fifty even. He didn't know how he could make it to the safe place, behind the wall, but he couldn't let this man die in the blood wash of the battle.

"Close it up, men!" the sergeant yelled through the chaos. "Close it up."

Friedrich pushed the gun back over his shoulder and leaned down to the wounded man. The others would have to do the shooting this afternoon. He would do the rescuing.

He reached down, hooking his hands under Earl's arms. The man screamed out in pain as he dragged him back down the hill. They were almost to the wall of logs when a blast knocked Friedrich off his feet. Where there had been grass, there were bodies now. Fragments exploded in the place Friedrich had been standing seconds ago.

Another soldier cried out below him, holding his hand over his eye. Friedrich wanted to run to him as well, hide him behind the wall, but it wasn't possible for him to rescue everyone.

He pulled Smith behind the logs and then ripped off a piece of his own trousers to wrap around the man's wound. Friedrich leaned Earl back against the wall and propped Earl's gun in his hands. If Earl could ward off the enemy from here, his life might be spared.

As he started to go back into the fight, Earl reached for his arm, stopping him.

"Thank you, Vinzenz."

Friedrich gave him a nod and rushed back to help the other men wounded from the shrapnel. He didn't care what the sergeant or anyone else said. He would start by helping the man who'd hurt his eye.

As he ran to the soldier, he tripped over a body and fell, landing on the chest of a dead man. It was another one of the men who'd ridiculed him back at Camp Pope, but instead of showing mockery, his empty eyes stared up at the sky.

Friedrich vomited the little he'd had for breakfast. This wasn't war. It was hell.

He picked himself off the ground, searching through the smoke for the wounded. The man who had hurt his eye was still alive, sitting up among the dead. Why didn't he lie down, pretend that he was dead as well?

The moment Friedrich spotted the injured soldier, he watched a Confederate discover him too. The Reb raced toward the man, the blade of his bayonet pointed in front of him. In seconds, he would finish what the cannonball started.

Friedrich swung his gun over his shoulder. He didn't stop to think about the repercussions. The Rebel was going to kill the wounded man, and he had to stop him.

The gun kicked back against his shoulder when he shot, and the Rebel fell onto another body. Friedrich felt no sense of glory in his conquest. He had killed one man to rescue another. One life lost, another one saved.

Friedrich raced to the wounded Union soldier and helped the man to his feet, steadying him.

Another Union soldier shoved Friedrich's shoulder with the butt of his gun. "The ambulance will come back for him."

But Friedrich didn't stop.

Few if any of the wounded would be alive if they waited for the wagons to come.

What pleases God, O pious soul, accept with joy,
Though thunders roll and tempest low'r on every side.
Paul Gerhardt

Chapter Fourteen
....

Amalie's fingers trembled with the weight of the envelope in her hands. The paper was smeared with dirt and a reddish blot that she dared not think of as blood. Even with the dark stains, the handwriting was clear. Friedrich had written to her.

She clutched the envelope to her chest for a moment before she looked down at it again. The postmark read Iowa City, and she sighed with relief. Friedrich wasn't in Tennessee.

"Who is it from?" Sophia asked over her shoulder.

"Friedrich."

"Can I read it?"

She pulled it back to her chest again. "Of course not."

The Homestead postmaster tipped his hat as he stepped out of the kitchen, on his way for his weekly mail delivery to all the villages. He could suspect, but he would never know how important it was for her to have a letter from Friedrich.

Friedrich's location was all she'd been able to think about during the past week, since she had heard about the battle in Tennessee. Not even her work in the kitchen had been able to distract her from her thoughts. She'd tried to read more of the book about the slaves, but she couldn't stop thinking about the man she loved, far away on a battlefield.

She wanted to sink down on the kitchen floor and savor every word he'd written, but she didn't want Sophia to watch her. Nor did she want her or Henriette or the two other assistants in the kitchen to see her cry.

"Supper is in ten minutes," Henriette said as she glanced around the busy kitchen. Then she pointed at the door. "But go read it first."

She didn't have to repeat her instruction. Amalie fled outside, to the orchard below the windmill. There in the solitude of the trees, she collapsed on the bench and ripped open Friedrich's letter. A single piece of paper fell into her lap, and she lifted it to read about his weeks in Camp Pope and how much he missed her and Amana. His words were light, but the joviality in them sounded forced. Part of her wished she knew more about what he was thinking, even though she was afraid his thoughts might scare her.

He said he loved her, but in this letter, he didn't mention their marriage, nor did he ask her to wait for him like he did in his first letter.

Had he changed his mind?

He said they were getting ready to transfer away from the camp, but he didn't say where he was going next. Either he didn't know or he didn't want her to be afraid.

She read his words two more times and then refolded the letter. It was probably written in haste, along his journey. He didn't have time to think about their future, only about his present. Their present. She would focus on what he said, not on what he omitted. It was most important that he was alive.

It had been so long since she had seen him; she didn't even remember much of what he looked like anymore. The feelings in her heart might ebb and flow, her excitement about marriage waning with the years she'd waited, but she would remain firm in her commitment to him.

The bells rang out at 11:30, and she prayed again for his safety before she tucked the letter into her pocket and hurried back to her work.

"So what did he say?" Sophia asked as she scooped barley soup into a large bowl.

"He said he is well."

Sophia sighed. "And what else?"

"Nothing is more important, Sophia."

Henriette called to them. "Amalie, you are serving today."

Amalie took one of the bowls with potato dumplings and rushed into the dining room as the people streamed in through the door, single file.

Once the food was distributed, Amalie stood at the side of the room. Everyone bowed their heads before they sat, and she joined them in silent prayer, thankful for Friedrich's letter. She thanked God but she also asked, as she did every time she prayed, that God would continue to protect him. She couldn't bear to pray that God's will would be done, especially if God's will was to call Friedrich home. She only wanted God to send him home to marry her.

Brother Schaube finished with a short prayer for all of them, and when everyone was seated, the meal began.

In minutes the soup disappeared, and Sophia joined Amalie in the kitchen to refill the bowls and platters.

"He's not here again," Sophia said as she held out her bowl for Henriette to fill.

"Who?"

"Matthias Roemig. He's missed the midday meal all week."

"Perhaps he is ill."

Sophia shook her head.

When Amalie walked back into the dining room, she scanned the heads of the men and realized Sophia was right. Matthias had been working so hard on her kitchen house, he'd hardly even stopped to eat. Every time she walked past the new structure and saw him and Niklas putting up the frame, she was grateful for Matthias's tenacity, but she didn't want his dedication to be responsible for his getting ill.

After she set her bowl down on a table, she fingered the envelope in her pocket. She didn't want to see Matthias, nor did he want to visit with her, but maybe she needed to be the one to speak with him about the kitchen house. And it was only right that she tell him about Friedrich's letter. He would want to know that Friedrich was safe.

Dishes were passed quickly, utensils clinked against the ceramic plates, and then Brother Schaube stood and closed their time with prayer. Everyone had a half hour to rest before they went back to work, but she guessed Matthias wouldn't be taking his break.

After a quick meal in the kitchen, Sophia slipped outside with the other kitchen workers. Instead of going back to her room or taking a walk, Amalie ladled soup into a tin and added two slices of buttered bread and a bottle of beer into a willow basket. She appreciated Matthias's determination to complete her kitchen house, more than he would ever know, but he needed to eat.

Henriette eyed her basket as if Amalie was about to feed an outlaw instead of a brother. "Where are you going with that food?"

"I'm taking it to Brother Matthias."

"The man's got two good legs, Amalie. He can come eat in the dining room like everyone else."

Amalie clutched the handles and held the basket to her side. "He's been working almost every daylight hour on my—on our new kitchen." She corrected herself lest Henriette begin to think she was planning to compete with her. "It is only right that I take food to him if he won't stop work to come get it himself."

"Matthias has suddenly become quite dedicated to his work."

Amalie thought back to the days in Ebenezer, watching Matthias build furniture alongside the elder Vinzenz in the carpentry shop. "He's always been dedicated to his work."

Henriette leaned forward as if she was about to confide in Amalie. "The man never missed a meal before you arrived in Amana."

Amalie stepped back. She knew Matthias didn't like her, but was she really so awful that he couldn't even stand to see her during mealtime? She must have done something to offend him deeply, but she didn't know what it was.

"He wasn't working on the kitchen house before I came."

Henriette shook her head. "I don't think the kitchen has anything to do with it."

"So you're saying it's me—"

"I'm only making an observation."

Amalie groaned as she walked out the door.

Why couldn't Henriette keep her observations to herself? Amalie was already weighed down with enough of a burden. She didn't need to add the guilt of Matthias skipping his meals to avoid her.

Physical nourishment was second only to spiritual nourishment among the Inspirationists. Men and women alike worked very hard and they all needed the nutrition to help them maintain their pace. Now, because of her, Matthias wasn't getting enough food. She wasn't going to let him starve because of his unwillingness to either confront her or forgive her.

Matthias was working alone on the building's frame when she arrived, two nails sticking out of his lips and one between his fingers as he nailed a board. When he glanced up at her, she watched his eyes soften at first and then narrow.

Henriette was right. Matthias was avoiding her.

She stepped forward and set the basket beside him. "I thought you might be hungry."

"Danke schön," he mumbled, a nail gripped between his lips, but he didn't move toward the basket.

"You are working quickly."

"I'm building it for the Vinzenz family." He slid the nail from his lips and began pounding it into the wood. "They must have someplace to eat when they arrive."

"Of course," she replied. She already knew he wasn't building it because of her. "I received a letter today from Friedrich."

He stopped pounding. "What did he say?"

"That Iowa City has been hot this summer."

"He's in Iowa City?"

"He was there for a month."

Matthias dropped his hammer to his side as the excitement glimmered in his eyes. "Then I will go to him."

She was warmed again by the loyalty in Matthias's heart. She wished they could both go to Camp Pope and retrieve Friedrich. "He's already gone away."

The light dimmed. "Where did he go?"

"He didn't tell me."

Matthias pounded in another nail and then turned back to her. "Is he well?"

She nodded. "He said he was continuing to pray for God's guidance."

She leaned down and took a bottle of beer out of the basket; the glass was still cold from the ice chest. She hadn't walked down here for him to ignore the refreshment.

He took the drink from her and leaned back against the post. "It's strange, isn't it, how we can all pray to the same God but hear Him guide us in different ways?"

"Maybe He tells us different things because He has different tasks for us to do."

He took a long swig of the beer. "Or maybe some of us aren't listening to what He requires."

"I don't believe God hides information to frustrate us, Matthias. I believe He wants us to continually search for the truth."

"So you believe Friedrich is supposed to fight?"

She shook her head. "I cannot answer for him."

He ate a piece of the bread and hard salami. Then he set the bottle back into the basket and handed it to her. Turning, he began to pound another nail into the wood, dismissing her without even a thank-you or good-bye.

"Matthias—"

"Hmm?"

"What did Friedrich say before he left?"

"He said a lot of things."

"I mean—"

Matthias turned toward her. "I don't understand you, Amalie."

She twisted the handle on the basket. She didn't know exactly what she meant either. She only wanted to experience a bit of what Friedrich was like before he left. "I wondered if he said anything about what it would be like when he returned."

"He wasn't thinking about returning. He was thinking about leaving."

She nodded. "I only wondered—"

"What?"

She shook her head. She wanted a taste of being near Friedrich, but while he and Matthias might be the best of friends, Matthias still considered her to be the enemy. "Nothing."

"If you have something that needs to be said, Amalie, you better say it."

"Did I do something to offend you?"

When he turned toward her, his eyes narrowed. "That's a ridiculous question."

"It's just…it's like you've been angry with me since I arrived, like I was the one who convinced Friedrich to leave."

He shook his head. "Friedrich convinced himself."

"Once we were friends, Matthias. Remember those days?"

"That was a long time ago."

A very long time ago. "I just want to make sure everything is good between us."

"There is no *us*, Sister Amalie."

She turned and rushed back outside the kitchen house.

* * * * *

The hammer missed the nail, slamming his thumb into the wood. Matthias shook his thumb in the air, welcoming the distraction of the pain, but when the throbbing subsided, his thoughts returned in earnest, tormenting him even more than the pain from his hammer.

How dare Amalie come around here, asking him questions about Friedrich? He wasn't privy to Friedrich's thoughts about her nor did he want to be. At one time, many years ago, the three of them might have been friends, but he was no longer part of Amalie's life nor would he ever be except to regard her as Friedrich's wife. Nothing more.

Lifting his hammer, he pounded the nail into the wood. If only he could pound his thoughts away along with it.

Why couldn't Friedrich have written to him as well? Then he could just tell Amalie that he already knew where Friedrich was. He didn't need her to act the messenger. He was grateful for the news that Friedrich was well and he thanked God for it, but he wanted Amalie to leave him alone.

1863

If he knew Friedrich had been in Iowa City for the past month, he would have gone and tried to convince him to leave. Perhaps that was why Friedrich hadn't written him. He didn't want Matthias to come.

He moved the board and set down his hammer. The elders had received a letter from Ebenezer yesterday; the Vinzenz family along with two other families were supposed to leave the second week in September, and it would take them about ten days to travel by steamship and train to Amana. The kitchen house should be done by the time they arrived, perhaps even sooner. Then Amalie could move to her own kitchen and he could resume his normal life eating at Henriette's kitchen. The food might not be as good as Amalie's but at least he wouldn't have to see her every day.

Now if he could figure out a way to avoid prayer services as well.

Niklas stepped up onto the kitchen house floor. "Is Sister Amalie pleased with the progress?"

"She didn't say." He nodded. "She just brought something for me to eat."

"Amalie is a good woman."

He pounded another nail into the wood, trying to ignore the man's praise of her.

"You should have seen her on the trail. I've never seen a woman work harder."

"She certainly knows how to work."

"It was more than that, Matthias. She helped everyone she could."

He didn't want to hear how kind-hearted Amalie was. In his heart, she had to be conniving, vicious even, in order for him to survive.

"Karoline was injured on the trail, and Amalie took charge, nursing her until she reached a doctor."

"Amalie can't stop being in charge."

Niklas moved toward him. "What do you have against Amalie?"

"I don't have anything against her. She just hides behind her work when things go wrong."

One of Niklas's eyebrows slid up. "Sounds like someone else I know."

He hammered another nail. "If you're referring to me, I'm not hiding behind my work."

"Why don't you stop for a break to at least go to the dining room?" Niklas asked.

"I'll stop and eat when the Vinzenz family arrives."

Niklas picked up his hammer and met Matthias's eye again. "Once you marry Hilga?"

Matthias felt like every muscle in his body froze. He should have quick answers to the questions about marriage. After all, everyone in the colony assumed he and Hilga would marry this fall. But he didn't have an answer for himself or for anyone else. He hoped that when he saw Hilga, he would know what to do.

"My business is my business, Niklas."

The younger man nodded and turned away.

Matthias wanted to bang his head against the post beside him. How could he possibly marry Hilga when he couldn't stop thinking about Amalie? And how could he make himself stop thinking about his best friend's future wife?

"At least Friedrich will be getting married," Niklas said.

Matthias eyed the hammer in his hand and was tempted to pound his thumb again.

If death my portion be,
Then death is gain to me.
Sigismund Weingartner

Chapter Fifteen
....

Wind whipped over the river as Friedrich knelt to lap water into his mouth. The dozen or so men alongside him panted like a pack of dogs at the end of a hunt, except they were the ones being hunted.

Once he quenched his thirst, Friedrich leaned back against the muddy bank and folded his arms over his chest to try to stop his arms from shaking. Back in the fields of Amana, he'd imagined himself a heroic soldier with a pressed uniform and gallant horse, fighting for honor and justice, but now his new uniform was torn and stained, and he couldn't stop trembling.

The heroism he so desired had been shattered by the horrors of war and his company's flight across the hills and trees last night when the entire regiment retreated en masse—if you could call it a retreat. The company from Iowa had scattered like grain in the face of the Rebels, taking cover in the brush and branches.

Before they'd come south, their captain proclaimed this fight was a sure win for the Union. He'd been terribly mistaken. Friedrich and the others tossed off their bedrolls as they ran away yesterday, and they slept hidden in the darkness and drizzle, the cold temperatures chilling their bones.

When the sun broke this morning, they continued their run north, hoping to find Rosecrans's camp at the base of Lookout Mountain so they could reunite with the Army of the Cumberland.

Leaning over again, Friedrich rinsed his face and hands in the river water, and then he took a lump of hardtack from his haversack and dipped the hard bread into the water to try and soften it before he climbed back under the shade of an oak tree. Even as the water and food refreshed him, images of war flooded his mind.

The black cloud of gunpowder over the valley. The carnage. Troops dodging the shells and cannonballs as they fled for their lives. He'd never smelled anything like it either—the potent mixture of sulfur and death that still permeated his nose.

And it was only a skirmish with the enemy. The major battles were still to come.

He closed his eyes and tried to pretend he was back in the peaceful Amana Colonies, far away from the border of Georgia and Tennessee, but he couldn't seem to rid himself of the blackness that pressed against his soul. The doubts.

He wanted to do what was right—fight for the freedom of the slaves—but nothing seemed right on the battlefield. In the haze of noise and gunshots and gunpowder, he'd lost sight of Jonah Henson and he'd lost sight of Earl Smith and the man who'd hurt his eye. He prayed the ambulance wagon had found the injured men and taken them to camp.

In the eyes of the Union, he knew he was doing right, but one day, he would have to stand before God and answer to Him alone. He prayed he had made the right decision.

The wind started to turn warm as he swiped his fingers through his wet hair and rested his head against the knobby trunk. His brethren back in Amana would never recognize him with his scruffy beard and overgrown hair and hands that had killed another with a single shot of his gun.

Back in the cove, the life of one Union soldier had been rescued, but the other soldier had slipped into eternity. He would never forget the horror in the Confederate soldier's eyes when the bullet blazed through his chest. His piercing scream. In an instant, the man had left his body behind.

What else had the man left behind?

A wife? Friedrich banged his head back against the bark.

Or children.

What if the dead man did have children? How would they survive without him? With a pull of his trigger, Friedrich had stolen their father away from them.

At that moment, it didn't matter that the Confederate soldier was prepared to take another life. His stomach rolled as he begged God for forgiveness for killing the man.

What did his *Opa* do when he fought against Napoleon? Did he stay focused on the battle or did his mind wander as well?

Friedrich took his Gospel of John, a gift from his father who'd received it from his father. Otto Vinzenz. He turned to the eleventh chapter to read Jesus's words.

I am the resurrection, and the life: he that believeth in me, though he were dead, yet shall he live: and whosoever liveth and believeth in me shall never die.

He prayed quietly that the man in the gray uniform believed in Christ. Perhaps one day they would be reunited in heaven and he would beg the man's forgiveness in person.

And then he prayed for the men he'd helped up to the wall.

Looking around the motley group of troops on the riverbank, he didn't know if they could fight again. Their lips were stained black from the powder cartridges they ripped apart with their teeth, and their stomachs were craving something more filling than hardtack.

Their captain was dead, their company scattered across the mountain in Georgia. None of them knew how to make contact with the rest of their regiment.

In Amana, each day was filled with order and protocol. Rules and consequences. Right and wrong. The army had ordered his days like the Kolonie, with strict times for meals and marching and bed, but yesterday's fight had been messy in so many ways. They'd been told how to fight, but no one had told them what to do if they lost a skirmish.

Closing his eyes, Friedrich rested, and his mind wandered back to Amana. To Amalie.

He needed to tell her again how much he loved her. That one day he would return to her.

Sitting beside a nearby tree, a young soldier named Benjamin took a traveler's inkwell from his bag. Friedrich watched him enviously as he opened the red leather cover and began to carefully pen a letter on a scrap of paper.

There were still two treasured pieces of stationery in Friedrich's bag along with an envelope. He took out the two sheets of stationery and moved toward the man, holding out one of them. "Could I trade you a piece of paper for use of your ink?"

Benjamin glanced up at him. "It's almost dry."

He might be telling the truth or perhaps he wanted to save the ink. Friedrich lowered the paper. "I have nothing else to offer you."

"Are you writing your mother or your girl?" Benjamin asked.

"My girl," he said, though he felt funny using the world. Amalie wouldn't like to be called anyone's girl. He corrected himself. "The woman I'm planning to marry."

The soldier's eyes narrowed. "You still think you're getting married?"

"Of course."

The soldier took the outstretched piece of paper and slowly handed him the well of ink and his quill pen.

Friedrich thanked him and then set the remaining piece of paper on his book. He didn't want to scare Amalie by talking about their battle, but he wanted to tell her a small bit of what was in his heart.

He turned the paper diagonal and at the left corner he began to write Amalie, telling her about their long train ride to Nashville and then their march south. He wrote about how much he missed the beauty of Amana and the food and most of all, how much he missed her.

Then he turned the paper and continued writing diagonally from the right side, the sentences crossing over each other. The blended writing wasn't easy to read, but it was good enough. With this trick, he could pour out much more of himself onto the paper. Much more for them to share.

Halfway through the second side, he told her that the skirmish had frightened him yesterday, but he was safe. He didn't tell her about the man he killed. He wanted to be honest with her, but Amalie hadn't made the choice to come to war. She shouldn't have to carry this burden with him.

He turned his back to the fellow soldiers around him. He couldn't write about death in his letter. One night, while they were resting in each other's arms as husband and wife, he might tell Amalie about the men who'd fallen around him. And maybe he would even tell her that he took another man's life. Together they could decide if he'd made the right decision. If she would forgive him, perhaps he could begin to forgive himself.

Folding the letter, he slid it into his envelope. As soon as he received his wages, he would buy a stamp and mail it.

He rubbed his hand over her name and address. Even though he didn't know when he could mail his words, it comforted him to know that one day she would read them.

He heard heavy footsteps in the trees, and he leapt to his feet along with the other men. Slipping the envelope inside his haversack, he pushed the bag over his shoulder and reached for the gun behind him. Ducking behind a tree, he waited to see who was marching toward them.

There were too few of them left to fight the enemy, and those who'd fled with him were all weary. But if they had to run again, they would run. He only hoped they wouldn't be running farther into enemy territory.

The face of the Confederate soldier flashed into his mind one more time. He didn't know what the future held for him, but he didn't think he could kill someone again—not even to save the life of another soldier. Or to save his own life.

Perhaps he could wound his enemy without killing again.

Leaves rustled in front of them, like the front winds of a tornado about to plow through a crop. He tore open a cartridge and poured gunpowder down the barrel. After he rammed the bullet down the muzzle, he pointed the gun in front of him, his finger trembling on the trigger from the adrenaline that coursed through his veins.

He'd aim for the soldiers' legs. He'd aim to stop them from fighting, not to end lives.

In the branches, he saw the lines of a face and he pointed his gun toward the man, his finger trembling against the trigger. In the next instant, he saw the familiar blue hat on the man's head and dropped his gun with relief.

"Don't shoot," he shouted to the men behind him. "They're Yankees."

Fragments of Iowa's 28th Infantry marched toward them and a small group of other men he didn't recognize. Any joy at being reunited with their men, though, was swallowed by the sadness of losing so many of their comrades.

Friedrich set down his gun as the battle-worn men sank to their knees by the river and gulped the water. Friedrich watched them, unsure what to do. Were the other men unsure as well?

Two of the soldiers carried a stretcher made of canvas and branches. When they laid it down to rush to the river's edge, Friedrich saw a man lying on it.

"Thirsty," the man rasped with a shaky voice.

Friedrich took the canteen out of his sack, full of cold creek water, and handed it to the injured man to drink.

As Friedrich drew closer, he recognized the injured man as the soldier who'd been shot in the eye yesterday. Half of his head was wrapped in cloth, stained with blood, and Friedrich could see the veins weave through the pale skin of his face, but the relief that surged through him was immeasurable. He didn't know what happened to Jonah, but at least this man had been rescued from the massacre.

The injured soldier gulped down the water from the canteen, and when he handed it back to Friedrich, he cringed in pain. Friedrich waited until the pain seemed to subside.

"Can I get you anything else?" he asked, reaching for the haversack on his chest. "Some hardtack?"

"You can get me the head of the man who saved me." The bitterness seethed out of the injured man. "I'd like to kill him myself."

Friedrich stepped back. He hadn't rescued the man to be thanked, but he thought—

Perhaps that was why the man was sitting up in the midst of all the soldiers instead of playing dead. Maybe he had wanted the Confederates to end his pain. Water splashed from the canteen in his hand, another thought slamming him. Was it more cruel for him to wound the enemy than kill him? Like this man, they might be wounded for life or die a slow death out here in these trees, alone.

He shook his head, trying to clear the confusion. At least, in the midst of his pain, a soldier would have an opportunity to make his peace with God before he left this earth. Unlike the Confederate soldier whose life was blown away like a vapor, no time to reconcile with His Maker.

"What is your name?" Friedrich asked the wounded man, but the man passed out on the stretcher before he answered. Friedrich turned toward the two men who'd carried him this far. The taller one was an officer, a sergeant from another company.

"Where are you taking him?" Friedrich asked when the men returned from the river.

"To the Union hospital in Chattanooga," the officer said, looking at the trees around them. "If we can ever find our way out of these woods."

Friedrich stepped forward. "Let me carry him with you."

The sergeant glanced down at Friedrich's torn uniform, as if he could determine the remnants of Friedrich's strength by the state of his attire. "You wouldn't make it all the way to Chattanooga."

"I can make it," he protested. He might not look as strong as some of the soldiers, but long days of working in the fields had strengthened him. He'd gotten the man out of the battlefield; he needed to help take him to the hospital as well.

The officer picked up one end of the stretcher and motioned with his head for Friedrich to take the other. "You best keep up the pace."

Friedrich's legs ached from running and his mind swirled from exhaustion and all that had happened back on the Georgia hills. But, God help him, he would carry this man back to Chattanooga, no matter how far away it was.

* * * * *

Sweat clung to Amalie's forehead as she tried to sleep. Her windows open, she could hear the cows bellowing in the fields and the cicadas serenading her from the grass. She wondered if Friedrich could hear cicadas tonight wherever he slept, or if the sweet sounds of nature were overpowered by the thunder of war.

She sat up in bed and lit her lantern. The flame might make the night watchman pause for a moment, but he would move on. She certainly couldn't lie here in the darkness for hours, doing nothing. She might lose her mind, thinking about what could be happening to Friedrich on the battlefield. How much longer would she have to wonder at how he was? Or where he was?

She couldn't imagine being apart from him for another three years, especially when she spent every night worried about whether he was still alive or if he had gone home to heaven.

Even though it was September now, it was still hot in Iowa. Rain would be a welcome relief from the heat tonight, along with some sort of breeze. Anything to help her cool off and sleep. In the dark hours, sleep was the only thing she could do to escape the reality of what could happen to Friedrich.

What if he left her alone for the rest of her life? No matter what he said, fighting this war was more important to him than marrying her. In her heart, she tried to understand why he needed to go and to respect him for his decision, but it was so very hard.

Opening the drawer of her nightstand, she slipped out the little walnut box that he'd given to her and brushed her fingers over the smooth wood, thinking about the hours he must have spent carving it. Friedrich gave the box to her the morning he asked if she would marry him. The morning he had left for Amana.

They were alone for a few stolen moments as the others prepared to leave. She had wanted to go with them as his wife, but Friedrich was a year away from turning twenty-four. The elders would require a year of separation anyway before they married. Better to separate now, Friedrich had said, when they weren't old enough to marry, than wait until they were.

At the time, she'd expected that she would leave a year later for Amana, but her father convinced the other elders that she needed to stay and cook for the community in Ebenezer. She didn't know why he wanted her there—she rarely saw her parents outside of the quiet meals and meetings. But her father's influence prevailed, and so she stayed and helped cook in the kitchen.

But she never forgot Friedrich. And no matter what Matthias accused her of, she had never been unfaithful. She had only been teasing Mr. Faust on their walk into town, like he had teased her. She wished she could tease Matthias like she had been able to do when they were children, but he would no longer think she was funny.

Friedrich's box represented so much to her. His love, that took the time to carve a work of beauty just for her. His determination to wait for her. She never expected to wait for three years before she saw him again in Amana, nor did she know how long she would have to wait now, but she would be faithful.

She set the box on the pillow beside her so she could see it when she awoke.

She took *Uncle Tom's Cabin* out of her nightstand. Turning to the page she'd marked, the chapter where Tom was being sold to a new master, she slid the book closer to the flame so she could read the words and began to immerse herself in the story.

Understanding was what she sought as she combed through the pages, understanding as to why Friedrich had felt so compelled to leave her and their community, and why he and other men risked their lives to free slaves instead of letting them work to free themselves.

An hour later her clock chimed and she looked up. It was midnight, and she had to be up again in less than five hours. She didn't want to stop reading but her eyes began to droop. Maybe she could actually sleep.

Turning off the flame, she rolled onto her back.

Were there really slaves out there like Tom? Slaves who were selfless in their care for humanity? Slaves who knew God?

The Spirit stirred inside her as she reflected on the story. Sometimes God required His people to wait and sometimes He required His people to act. Friedrich had been called on to act on behalf of those like the character of Tom who couldn't free themselves.

Her heart swelled with her love for him, and as she closed her eyes, she prayed that God would use Friedrich to break the chains of oppression, both the physical ones that bound the slaves and the mental ones that bound their minds and the minds of their owners.

This time she didn't pray that God would bring Friedrich back safely for her sake. She prayed that God would do His perfect will—in both Friedrich's life and hers.

Oh, make in me a heart not free
But filled with wistful need for Thee.
Johann Adam Gruber

Chapter Sixteen

....

A row of shanties was hidden under knots of overgrown vines and pop-lar leaves, ramshackle huts not fit to be called homes. Each roof was thatched with weathered fronds, and there were cracks in the brown clay chinked between the logs. Dark faces peeked out of the windows at Friedrich and Sergeant Mitchell as they slowly walked the stretcher up the dilapidated trail of logs and vines. Friedrich could see the terror in the eyes of the former slaves, eyes that had probably seen the war firsthand.

The sergeant had sent most of the soldiers ahead of them to find camp, but four Union soldiers accompanied them still, standing now in the small field across from the slave dwellings. Many of the plantation trees were lying toppled onto each other beyond the field, like someone had tried to play a giant game of pick-up sticks. Except the soldiers who had chopped them down hadn't left anyone behind to pick up the pieces.

Scattered slats of white-painted wood dotted the grass and fields, fragments of the white fence that circled the property at one time. The barn on the other side of the trees was empty, and a charred founda-tion marked where the grand house once stood, a black eye on the bruised land.

Friedrich shuddered to think that Union men probably burned the structure and ravished the land. He understood why they might have roasted any livestock left in the barn—hunger was a powerful motivator no matter how strong the man—but he didn't understand why they had to cut down so many beautiful trees and destroy the home and fence that the homeowners had worked so hard to build.

Or that the slaves had worked to build for their masters.

He scanned the devastation again with new eyes. Maybe it was fitting for the property to be destroyed. Perhaps it would give these men and women a fresh start at their new life without the monuments of their past to remind them of all they'd endured.

Still, he wished the soldiers had left the main house on the hill untouched and several animals in the barn. Then the freed slaves could move up to the bigger house and have food to eat until this war was over.

He didn't understand why either army, North or South, did what they did. He didn't understand why so many of the Yankees were arrogant about winning this war in spite of all their losses. Even with the destruction of their country and the tens of thousands of casualties, they were still intent on winning this war by power instead of peace.

And he didn't understand why the Confederates continued to insist this war was about state rights instead of slavery, since the only right they were set on protecting was the one that allowed them to own slaves. Friedrich glanced over the ruined land again, over the stumps and broken pieces of fence and circles of stones where the soldiers had burned campfires.

If they kept fighting like this, one side losing a battle and then the other losing the subsequent one, there would be few men left in either the North or the South by war's end. And the slaves would have either run away or starved to death.

The clouds darkened above them. They'd spent a second night out in the woods as they slowly trekked north, but with the rain clouds compounding this morning, Friedrich was grateful to be so close to shelter, no matter how poorly thatched the roof. Sergeant Mitchell stopped walking in front of him, and together they knelt down to place the stretcher on the grass. The wounded soldier didn't awaken.

Sergeant Mitchell stepped toward one of the doors and the eyes rushed away from the window. He called toward the closed door. "We're not here to harm you."

Friedrich glanced over again at the Union soldiers that accompanied him and the sergeant, their uniforms tattered and many of them streaked with dirt and blood. How could the slaves not be afraid? He couldn't even imagine what they had seen from these buildings. Or experienced. They were free now in body, but it might be a long time before they were able to loosen their spirits from the chains.

A Negro boy stepped out into the sunlight, and the child watched them closely, more curious than afraid. He wore only trousers, as tattered as the soldiers' behind them, and his brown hair was matted against his head. Friedrich stayed on his knees, and the boy wandered slowly toward him. When the child reached him, he lifted his dark hand to touch the yellow stripes on Friedrich's cap. Friedrich took off the cap and placed it on the boy's hair.

"Eli!" someone shouted from inside the house. The boy grinned and raced back into the log house.

"You'll never get that back," Sergeant Mitchell said.

"Oh, he'll bring it back," Friedrich said. "Once he shows his mama."

Sure enough, the boy raced back outside moments later to return the hat, leaving the door into the shack open. As Friedrich replaced the cap on his head, the sergeant mumbled something about lice. Friedrich shook his head, smiling. Lice was the least of their worries.

Lightning flashed across the sky, and Friedrich glanced at the doorway of the shack. Rain began to sprinkle down as he and Sergeant Mitchell lifted the stretcher, rushing the man into the house.

It took a moment for Friedrich's eyes to adjust to the dim light inside the room. An elderly woman sat on a chair in the dark corner while Eli and a little girl played by her feet on the dirt floor. A fire smoldered at the other end of the room, stifling the room with its heat. A young woman dressed in rags stirred something in a ceramic pot, and Friedrich's stomach growled at the smell.

Rain beat against the roof and raced across the floor in small streams. It dripped through the cracks in the walls as well, as if it were perspiring from the stress of the storm.

Friedrich's mind wandered back again to the beautiful homes in Amana, each room neatly swept and cleaned. The bountiful gardens and valleys and all the beauty. There was nothing on this Georgia plantation except loneliness and despair.

"Haven't you heard about the Emancipation Proclamation?" Sergeant Mitchell asked the woman cooking over the fire.

A wooden spoon in one hand, the other on her hip, she turned to him. "The what?"

"The President—" Sergeant Mitchell began. "Lincoln has declared that all the slaves in the South are free."

"Free?" The elderly woman clapped her hands. "The good Lord be praised."

The younger woman stared at both of them, her hair pulled back in a handkerchief. "The other soldiers say we be free."

Friedrich looked across the bare surroundings. "Then why are you still here?"

She shrugged. "Where we s'pose to go?"

Friedrich glanced at the sergeant, hoping he would provide an answer. Friedrich had been wondering the same thing himself.

"We will come back for you, ma'am, when this war is over," Sergeant Mitchell said. "To take you north so you can find work."

She shook her head, turning back to the pot. "Something's gonna happen to you 'fore this madness end."

"If we can't come back for you, we'll send someone," the sergeant insisted.

Eli stood up beside Friedrich, his hands stuck in his pockets. "I'm gonna take 'em north."

"Are you now?" Friedrich said, bending down again toward him. "How old are you, Eli?"

He shrugged. " 'Bout five, I s'pose."

"You have to be seven to guide someone up north."

"I be seven soon." He flashed a look toward the woman by the fire. "Won't I, Mama?"

When she didn't respond, Friedrich put his hand on Eli's shoulder. "Until you turn seven, you better wait here. The war will be over soon, and then you can travel wherever you want without a guide."

The woman muttered something as she turned toward the fire, seeming to confide in her pot instead of in them. She didn't trust him or the sergeant, and why should she? They didn't know when they would make it back to the camp or if they would make it back alive.

In the middle of the crowded floor, the man on the stretcher moaned and then coughed, tossing his head from side to side. Friedrich knelt beside him, wishing he could lessen his pain. As he drifted into consciousness, the man cursed the very God who'd made him. Friedrich cringed at his words. He didn't know what he would do if he were ever in so much pain, but he prayed he wouldn't curse God. He wanted to bless the name of his heavenly Father, even in his death. He didn't have the courage to praise God in the face of death by his own strength though. The Spirit would have to help him be strong.

The elderly woman reached for Friedrich's hand as if she felt the turmoil going on inside him. "God bless you, my son."

"I wish I could take you all with me today," he said as she stood up, and she squeezed his hand even tighter.

She reached forward, her eyes staring into space, and at that moment he realized she was blind. She held her hand out and patted his chest. "You take us all right here in your heart," she said. "You keep fightin' for us."

He cleared his throat, wishing he had the right words to say. "I'll keep fighting for you."

"And we grateful, son. Eternally grateful." She smiled. "My years ain't long on this here earth, but I can see the glimmer on those pearly white gates in the distance and they sure is pretty."

"Yes, ma'am." He wished he could get a glimpse into her blindness and see those pearly gates as well. He could only imagine what a sight it must be to see the gates of heaven. To see their Savior.

The wounded man shouted out again as he sat up, his arms flailing as he called for a woman named Liza. Then, with a final scream, he fell back onto the floor.

Eli and the little girls stopped playing. The woman stopped stirring. The elderly woman dropped her hand back into her lap, praying softly under her breath—she could probably feel the shadow of death in this room.

Friedrich hung his head, not knowing what to do or say. After he'd risked his life to rescue this man, killing another to save him and then carrying him through the forest to get him to a hospital, he had slipped away.

Friedrich stumbled back against the rough logs. God's will had been done today, no matter how hard it was to accept. There was nothing else he could do. Except—

Leaning forward, Friedrick patted the man's shirt until he found the small silver disc pinned inside his chest pocket. The man's name was Jonathan Everett.

There was nothing Friedrich could do to bring Jonathan back, but the soldiers could bury him on the estate and then they would find the camp so they could deliver the disc to their commander. If not, Liza would spend her life wondering if Jonathan was coming back to her.

The elderly woman leaned forward in her rocker. "Is he a friend of yours?"

"Not a friend, but he was still my brother."

She sighed. "A lot of people are dyin' on account of us slaves."

"You were never a slave in God's eyes." Friedrich reached down and took her hand again. "Nor in mine."

Her vacant eyes filled with tears again, and he could feel her tiny hand trembling in his. "This man paid a high price for my freedom. His life, it gone from him, and it don't sound like he a-seein' them pearly gates ahead."

Friedrich didn't know what to say. He didn't know what was in the man's heart or if he knew their Savior. His curses must have boiled up from anger, burning those in its wake. But how could he curse God before he died? How could he be so angry at the God who created him?

"You keep them eyes on Jesus," the woman said. "You keep focused on Him instead o' the pain in this world."

He nodded though she couldn't see him. He had to keep his eyes on the Savior or he wouldn't be able to make it through the war.

* * * * *

"He's going to starve himself half to death," Sophia said as she cleaned the few scraps off a plate and then scrubbed it in soapy water at the sink by the window.

"Matthias will do what he wants to do," Amalie said. It was almost like the man enjoyed the secrets that enveloped him.

"He has to eat sometime."

Amalie dipped the plate into the clean water and then dried it with a towel. She didn't want to talk with Sophia about Matthias or his lack of appetite. She already felt guilty that her arrival seemed to push him away from the kitchen house and the food he needed to sustain him and his hard work.

She still couldn't understand why he hated her so. A decade ago they'd been the best of friends—she and Friedrich and Matthias. Unmarried men and women were not supposed to mingle together in the Kolonie, but back when they were children, they'd traveled together from Germany to the States by steamer. Matthias tried to distract her and Friedrich from their nausea by playing games and making up stories about the sea and the giant waves. In Ebenezer they'd played together every day after school, like siblings.

But then the boys turned fourteen and went to work at the mill in Ebenezer. Matthias began learning carpentry from Friedrich's father, and Friedrich was assigned to apprentice with the clockmaker. They'd become men while she was still a girl.

Once they all reached adulthood, they could no longer take her fishing with them or sledding in the snow. They no longer played for hours after school or concocted silly pranks to test on their schoolmaster.

Sophia didn't seem to care about Amalie's lack of interest in the discussion. She prattled on like a schoolgirl herself. "I suppose he lost his appetite when Friedrich left for that"—she lowered her voice— "for that war. He and Matthias were always together, at prayer and at meals and even working together when they could. We all miss him, but Matthias probably misses him most of all."

Amalie's heart cramped. "I think I might miss him a little more than Matthias."

Sophia reached over, patting Amalie's sleeve with her soapy hand. "Of course you do. I didn't mean any offense. I'm just wondering why Matthias won't eat."

Sophia reached for another dish. "Henriette told me all about how Friedrich's family took in Matthias while they were still in Germany. She said Matthias's mother was a witch or something and that she didn't particularly care who reared him as long as she didn't have to do it herself."

"Neither you nor Henriette should be repeating those crazy rumors."

"Crazy?" Sophia asked, sliding her eyebrows up. "I think it's mysterious. Romantic."

"I doubt Matthias agrees."

"So he was abandoned as a baby?"

"I—I don't know," Amalie stammered.

She should know the answer, she'd certainly spent enough time with Matthias when they were young, but she'd never asked because Matthias had never wanted to talk about his family.

Matthias had lived with the Vinzenzes for as long as she could remember. When they traveled to America, their new community became family. Most of them never discussed the relatives they left behind.

"Matthias just turned twenty-six," Sophia said.

"You aren't old enough to marry him."

"Who said I was talking about marriage?" the young woman asked, like she was shocked by Amalie's question.

While men had to wait until they were twenty-four to marry, the minimum age for a woman to marry was twenty. But they could become engaged before this age, as Amalie had been when Friedrich asked for her hand. And there were probably many women like Sophia who hoped Matthias might ask for them as well before they turned twenty.

"I wasn't talking about marriage, but just suppose," Sophia continued. "Do you think Matthias would wait a year to marry me?"

She shook her head. "He's already planning to wed this fall."

Sophia dropped the plate in her hand, and the ceramic shattered in pieces across the floor. Before either of them could speak, Henriette ran in from the dining room with her broom in hand. She waved the handle toward the floor.

"What are you doing?"

Sophia eyed Amalie like it was her fault, but Amalie didn't answer the question for Sophia. Instead she took another plate out of the tepid water and dried it.

Sophia held up a hand, lathered with soap. "It slipped out of my fingers."

"There's a reason God gave you two hands, Sophia."

Sophia put both hands behind her.

With an irritated glance at Amalie, Henriette swept up the broken plate and dumped the pieces outside in the trash barrel. As she marched back toward the dining room, she swiveled to face them again. "Do you think you two can avoid breaking anything else while I finish sweeping under the benches?"

Sophia muttered that she'd be more careful, but Amalie didn't respond. She wasn't responsible for breaking a dish. Sophia and her ridiculous expectations were responsible.

Brother Schaube had said the kitchen house would be finished soon, and she could hardly wait until she could begin doing dishes in her own sink and cook on her own stove. She would motivate her assistants, but she would never berate them. As long as she had women like Karoline working with her, there would be no reason to ever reprimand them. But if she had an assistant like Sophia…

She didn't know what she would do.

When they were finished cleaning the dishes, she would take Matthias a snack. He might not like her presence, but he never returned the food she brought him.

Beside her, Sophia scrubbed a plate so hard that Amalie thought she might break it as well. "Be careful," Amalie said as she reached for it. She slipped the dish into the rinse water.

"Who is he going to marry?" Sophia's whisper sounded more like a hiss.

"I thought everyone knew."

"We all knew you were engaged," Sophia said. "Friedrich couldn't stop himself from talking about you, but Matthias—Matthias has never mentioned leaving behind someone in Ebenezer."

Amalie sighed. That's what happened when you maintained communities in two different places. Rumors blazed across the miles while the truth was often blocked at the state lines.

"He's intending to marry Friedrich's sister."

"Hilga?" Sophia asked as she put the last dish into the water. "She's a year older than me."

Amalie nodded. "Marrying age."

"Why didn't he tell us he was engaged?"

"Did you ever ask him?"

"Of—of course not. It's not a question one asks."

"It might have been a good question, though, before you decided you wanted to marry him."

And must thou suffer here and there
Cling but firmer to His care.
Paul Gerhardt

Chapter Seventeen
....

"Matthias?" Amalie called from the open doorway of the kitchen house.

His heart lurched at the sound of her voice and then he sighed as he moved away from the board he'd been sawing.

He'd done everything he could to convince Amalie to leave him alone, yet she persisted in bringing him food when he missed a meal. Not that he didn't appreciate the food—he did—but he didn't want her to be the one bringing him meals. He'd tried to make it clear to her without being cruel. Perhaps he hadn't been clear enough.

When Amalie stepped inside the frame of the house, she slipped her sunbonnet off her head, over her shoulders. Her light-brown hair fell in light wisps under her cap, escaping from the bun at the nape of her neck. It was as if she didn't even know how beautiful she was.

He cleared his throat. "Amalie—"

"You missed breakfast again this morning."

"I woke up late."

"Then you missed lunch as well."

"It's none of your business when I eat or if I eat."

She set her basket on the sawhorse. "I'm not here to bother you, Matthias. Just to make sure you get some food."

He shook his head. "I'm not hungry."

"Well, that's good because all I have is ham and bread today any-way." She unwrapped the food. His stomach rumbled. "Maybe Niklas would want it for a snack."

"I'll eat it," Niklas called from behind him.

When two of the workers laughed at Niklas, Matthias reached into the basket and snatched up the food. Amalie tried—and failed miser-ably—to hide her grin.

"I'll take it to Niklas," he said.

Her smile fell. "You need to eat," she whispered to him.

He didn't want to hear the concern in her voice, didn't want her to care.

He pushed her toward the door so the other men couldn't hear them talk. It was enough for him to see her in the eleven prayer meet-ings they had every week and at breakfast and supper when he must eat. He didn't want her visiting him at the kitchen house too.

Amalie reached for her basket, draping the handle over her arm, and together they stepped outside, away from the building and ears of the other workers.

"What's wrong?" she asked.

"You can't come here anymore, Amalie."

"Why not?"

"You're—you're distracting my men from their work."

Red streaked up her face as she glanced back toward the door. She hesitated for a moment before she began speaking again. "I'll stop com-ing if you'll stop working long enough to eat at the dining room."

"I'm not your responsibility, Amalie."

"Heaven forbid if you were," she said. "I can just drop the basket off at the door. I won't disturb you or your men."

Irritation flamed within him. He had done everything he could to discourage her, but she wouldn't be deterred.

"I don't want you around here." His words came out as a growl, but he didn't care.

"Someone needs to feed you."

"I don't want it to be you!"

Her lips pinched together, but she didn't say anything.

His heart seemed to tear within him. He wished Amalie were bringing the meals because she wanted to see him, but even that thought was wrong, terribly wrong. What would Friedrich think if he knew he'd even entertained that thought?

Dear God, Amalie had to leave him alone. More than anything, he strove to be an honorable man, loyal to his community and his friends. His loyalty to Friedrich was waning, though, stripped away a little more every time Amalie showed up with her basket of food. He was a traitor, flirting in his mind with Amalie while his friend fought battles for their country.

Why wouldn't she just stop? Stop bringing him food, stop smiling at him, stop being so persistent and irritatingly kind.

He leaned forward. "I keep asking you to not deliver my food, but you ignore my request."

"Because you need to eat."

He shook his head. "No, Amalie. You are doing this because you want me to finish your kitchen house."

"I'm doing it for Friedrich." She glanced down at the hem of her dress and then looked back at him. "He'd never forgive me if I didn't care for you while he's gone."

"You think you're taking care of me for Friedrich's sake?" Heat crawled up his face. "Do you even realize how selfish you are?"

Her lip quivered, and he knew she was about to explode. "Selfish?"

"You are pretending to help me, but you are really doing it so you can get out of Henriette Koch's kitchen. The faster I work, the faster you will be working in here."

"I'm not—" she replied, but the confidence was gone from her voice.

"And you are feeding me to get accolades from your fiancé."

Her eyes narrowed, and he could see the anger in them. *Good.*

"Not only because of that," she said.

"Then tell me why."

"You're my brother, Matthias, same as the rest of these men. We are supposed to take care of each other."

"There you are." Brother Schaube rushed around the corner, waving a piece of paper in his hands. "I've been looking for both of you."

Amalie crossed her arms, the basket draped at her side.

Matthias glanced at the paper but couldn't read it. "Did something happen to Friedrich?"

He shook his head. "It's from Ebenezer. The Vinzenz family and fifteen others have started their journey."

"They're coming—" Amalie whispered.

Matthias didn't say anything.

"Will you be ready in a week?" Brother Schaube asked.

Matthias glanced back at the building. The faster he was finished with this building, the better. "It might be two weeks."

Brother Schaube nodded. "We will make do until it is complete."

As Brother Schaube turned away, Matthias turned back to the door. "Amalie—"

The elder turned around abruptly, his smile gone.

"Sister Amalie," Matthias said.

She glared at him. "What?"

He waited until Brother Schaube was out of sight, and then he leaned down to her.

"Don't come back until your kitchen is done."

Turning, he stomped back inside. If that didn't make her leave him alone, he didn't know what would.

* * * * *

Lee and Gordon's Mill was located on the West Chickamauga Creek—named the River of Death by the Cherokees. Friedrich and Sergeant Mitchell and the other four soldiers had dodged Confederate brigades and skirmish lines up and down the creek until they found where the Federals had set up camp. And Friedrich found Jonah Henson.

Friedrich embraced his friend. "I thought we'd lost you back on Pigeon Mountain."

"And I thought we had lost you," Jonah said. "I saw you helping Earl and the others."

"Have you seen Earl?"

Jonah nodded and directed him toward a tent that had been set up along the edge of the property. They combed through a row of cots until they found him,. Thank God, someone had gotten Earl away from the fight.

The man's eyes brightened when he recognized Friedrich, the mocking gone from his lips.

"Darn bullet got me in the leg," Earl said, holding up his cast. "But the doc said they don't have to saw it off."

Friedrich sat down on the edge of the cot, grateful the man was still alive and they hadn't had to amputate his leg. Maybe it was better to wound a man than kill him.

"They are sending me back to Iowa tomorrow," Earl continued.

"Your family will be glad to have you home."

"I wish I could have stayed longer."

Friedrich gave Earl a long sip of water from his canteen.

"Why did you save my life?" the man asked.

"God gave me the strength to do it."

Earl shook his head. "I don't deserve God's mercy."

"None of us deserve His mercy," Friedrich said. "And yet He bestows it on us willingly."

Earl leaned his head back against his pillow. "I will forever be grateful."

Sergeant Mitchell marched into the tent. "Get some rest, Private Vinzenz."

"I want to spend time with my friend."

"You'll have to spend time with him after the war," the sergeant said. "We're marching out of here early tomorrow. The Confederates are running south, scared as kittens, and we're gonna chase them out of Georgia this time around."

Friedrich slowly stood to his feet. The Rebel cry was still vivid in his mind. He didn't think the Confederates were scared, not like kittens anyway. More like cougars backed against a wall.

But if they were sent to battle in the morning, he had no choice. And if they won this one, with the much larger brigade of men, they would be continuing south to take back the southern states for the Union.

"I wish I could take your place and fight," Earl said.

Friedrich nodded and then turned to walk away. He wished he could go home.

Chapter Eighteen

· · · · · · · · · · · · · · · · · · · ·

The breeze rushed through the open windows in the great room where the Community of True Inspiration met each night for *Nachtgebet*, their evening prayers and worship. Matthias wiped the sweat off his brow with his sleeve as the cool air refreshed his tired body. He opened his hymnal and began to sing with the others, but his mind wasn't on the lyrics. Instead his gaze wandered to the other side of the aisle where Amalie sat, singing the familiar hymn with her eyes closed.

When she opened her eyes, Matthias looked back toward the front of the room. He didn't even realize the song had ended until one of the elders led out in prayer. He bowed his head.

Most nights he controlled his eyes through sheer effort, not turning even once to look at the row across from him, but he couldn't seem to help himself tonight. He overcame physical challenges every day, but lately it seemed that mental discipline was proving much more troublesome. In his weakness, he kept slipping to a place he didn't want to go.

When the short service ended, he stepped through the men's doorway. Darkness had begun to fall across the village, and everyone, including Amalie, should be on their way to their rooms to rest for the night.

In Henriette's kitchen he found a tin of coffee and a plate with sliced ham and cheese. After Amalie brought him his noon meal, he'd skipped supper—he didn't have it within him to face her again today—but at least he could eat now.

He started with the food and then took a long sip of the coffee. Every night the women left coffee on the kitchen table for the night watchman, but this was the first time he remembered them leaving a snack as well. He took another sip of coffee and told himself that it was Henriette or Sophia who thought he might need the food.

No matter how tired he was, it was his turn to spend the next four hours walking through the village to make sure a fire didn't break out while the community slept. John Keller would take his place as a watchman around one so he could have a few hours of sleep before the morning work began again. Until John came, he had to keep himself alert.

Several lanterns glowed in the rooms above the street as he strolled down the center of Amana. Most of the village was asleep by nine. During the week, bedtime and worship were the only times that the people in Amana were idle with their hands so they could reflect on the day and offer rest to their bodies.

The night's quiet was usually a welcome relief from the busy din of the Amana workdays, but tonight, instead of reflecting on the blessings God had given him and the work he wanted to accomplish tomorrow, Matthias couldn't stop thinking about his conversation with Amalie. Four hours to contemplate his words to her.

He tried to stop thinking about her, her thoughtfulness at taking care of him, and her kindness to feed him. But he couldn't stop himself.

An involuntary smile crept up his face, and he stopped walking, trying to purge the wicked thoughts from his mind. He would do everything he could to finish the kitchen house in less than two weeks so he could move on to another project, another village even. If they moved him to, say, South Amana, he might never have to see Amalie again.

He shivered in the darkness. He couldn't move to another village, not with the Vinzenz family arriving soon. He wanted to respect the elders and the parents who adopted him into their family, but for the first time in his life, he felt trapped.

What would it be like to leave the Society like Friedrich had done? Run away from the woman he should marry? Run away from the woman he couldn't have?

The lantern swung in his hands as he resumed his walk toward the woolen mill. He might try to run away from his troubles, but no matter where he went, he would carry them with him.

As he paced up and down the street, he searched the small windows at the top of each building for an orange glow. They'd had only one fire in Amana since they began building almost eight years ago. In the washhouse. The night watchman had rung the bell and people poured out of their homes to extinguish the flames before they spread.

He circled the mill and turned to pace back beside the barn and orchards and then under the dark windows of the residences and shops.

Bigger cities like Buffalo were ridden with crime, but he didn't walk the streets tonight because of crime in Amana. They didn't have a single police officer patrolling their streets—they'd never had need of law enforcement and he prayed they never would. All the residents strove to live their lives by the Word of God and the testimonies of their Werkzeuge. Any sin was addressed by the Bruderrath, any discipline administered by them as well.

Usually the discipline meant members were banned from meetings for a season or they were moved back in their seating during services. This form of discipline, along with their personal accountability before God, was enough for members to respect the rules of their authority and to strive to live at peace with their fellow man. They had no need of guns in their community except to hunt and no need of prison cells.

Without much of a threat of fire and no crime, the job of a night watchman was a dull but necessary duty. Matthias's thoughts were his only companion, and tonight they weren't good company.

Fireflies playing in the apple orchards, the lights blinking in random discord. Or was it harmony? Sometimes it was hard to tell the difference between the two.

His own heart was in discord right now. Hilga and her parents were coming and he didn't know what to say to them. Three years ago, when he left Ebenezer, Hilga didn't seem to love him like a woman should love her husband. Even though he'd tried to muster stronger feelings for her, there was nothing inside him except a brotherly love. He'd do just about anything for her, but he didn't want to marry her.

He could pray diligently that God would fill his heart with feelings for Hilga, but it didn't seem fair to marry, not until he could devote himself fully to her.

A long time ago he'd confided to Friedrich that he hadn't developed feelings for Hilga. Friedrich thought Matthias felt like this because of his past abandonment. And he thought Matthias would develop love and trust over a lifetime with Hilga.

Maybe Matthias would always wrestle with his past, but the real reason he didn't love Hilga was trapped inside of him, like a prisoner in his heart. He didn't dare tell Friedrich that he was incapable of loving Hilga because he was deeply in love with another woman. Friedrich would insist that he tell him who had captured his attention, and he could never do that.

Passing by Amalie's kitchen house, Matthias wished he could

resume his work tonight instead of walking aimlessly up and down these streets. Niklas was right; he was just as bad as Amalie about losing himself and his problems in his work. But hard work was much easier than confronting these feelings, especially when there was nothing positive to come out of the confrontation.

As he turned at the western edge of town, something screeched in the darkness, and he jumped. They didn't have criminals in Amana, but Brother Fehr's collection of peacocks had stopped Matthias's heart several times. He couldn't see them tonight, but he could hear them rustle behind their fence. Part of him wanted to screech back at the spoiled birds, but he left the peacocks behind, hiding in the dark, as he walked back through the village.

All the windows were dark in Amana, except one.

As he passed the Koch Kitchen House, his eyes locked on the light flickering in a front window. He watched it closely, telling himself that it was his duty to make sure there wasn't a fire.

Perhaps it was good that he was supposed to be outside tonight, walking. It wouldn't be possible for him to sleep right now, not with all the thoughts raging through his mind, electrifying his skin.

He wasn't thinking about fire though.

He was thinking about Amalie.

* * * * *

Amalie paced across her bedroom, turned, and crossed it again. Did other people in their community think she was selfish as well?

She rubbed her hands in front of her, over and over, until they felt raw. Matthias was wrong. She wasn't being selfish. God required all of them to care for their brothers and sisters in need; He certainly required it of her. She couldn't judge other people, but she had to respond when God asked something of her.

While Matthias might not want to be obligated to anyone, he needed to eat. Even so, it was wrong of her to disregard his demand that she leave him to his work.

Why did he have to be so exasperating? Yes, she wanted him to finish the kitchen house quickly so she could work on her own, but it was more than that. She wanted to help him as a friend. A sister in Christ. Someone who'd cared very much for him in their younger years.

Well, she wouldn't distract him or his men any longer from their work. If Friedrich asked her why she hadn't helped Matthias, she would tell him the truth. His friend was an idiot.

When she reached the wall, she swiveled again.

When had Matthias become so cruel? It was like he'd lost his heart somewhere between here and New York. Back in Ebenezer, he had always been kind to her. A good friend and brother. After Friedrich asked to marry her, she'd looked forward to having Matthias as a brother, of sorts. She had once thought they would all be grand friends after they married, almost like the days of their childhood. She and Friedrich. Matthias and Hilga. But Matthias made it quite clear that he didn't want her benevolence or her friendship.

Well, that was fine with her. She certainly didn't need his friendship and she had things she could do during the minutes of her afternoon break other than bring him food.

Climbing into her bed, Amalie leaned back against the pillows. Even though it was well after nine, she couldn't sleep.

She retrieved a needle and thread from her nightstand to monogram her pillowcases with her name and newly assigned number so she could send them to the laundry on Monday.

As she stitched, her mind wandered back to the evening meeting.

She had stolen a glance over at Matthias as they prayed, his pious head bowed. Perhaps he was praying for forgiveness. If he wasn't, he should be. She couldn't understand the state of his heart, so pious during the prayers, while being so cruel to his sister. How could he be so rude to someone who was only trying to help him?

She hoped that if someone saw Friedrich in need on the battlefield, they would help him. Give him food if he needed it or a place to rest. And she hoped Friedrich would be humble enough to accept their offer.

She dropped her needlework into her lap.

Perhaps that was the problem with Matthias. Perhaps he was too proud to allow her to bring him food, like he would be indebted to her for her service. And he was too stubborn to allow her to continue. Someone, other than she, needed to talk to him about humbling himself. She had heard enough ill words from him already, but maybe he would listen to one of the elders or even Friedrich when he returned.

There was nothing wrong with allowing someone to help you.

Our souls they could not capture.
For as a bird from nets released, we have escaped in rapture.
Martin Luther

Chapter Nineteen

....

The foe is before us in battle array,
But let us not waver or turn from the way.
The Lord is our strength and the Union's our song,
With courage and faith we are marching along.

Blue-clad soldiers surrounded Friedrich as they marched down a hill and into a valley, singing their song of war. But instead of singing about their battle, Friedrich sang under his breath, "O we ain't gonna thresh no more, no more. We ain't a gonna thresh no more."

He was homesick for Amana, aching for his work in the fields and the bounty of delicious food in the kitchen house. Even more, his arms ached for Amalie, and he wished he could spend one day holding her close to him, breathing in the scent of her hair. He never should have left Iowa before he said good-bye to her. Never should have left Amana at all.

The rumble of thunder echoed across the rolling hills and distant mountains, but there were no clouds in the sky. Instead of lightning and showers, the incoming storm would be one of bayonets and rifles and clubbed muskets.

The blast from another cannon echoed through their regiment, and then the hills surrounding them were silent. Friedrich expected the loud noises of battle, but he hadn't anticipated the quiet. The eerie silence pierced the air, even more than the cannonading.

The singing continued around him, some of the voices strained, but Jonah's voice sounded upbeat in spite of his fatigue. They'd started marching before sunlight, and the singing kept them marching in sync, in spite of their exhaustion, through the woods and fields.

Our wives and our children we leave in your care,
We feel you will help them with sorrow to bear.
'Tis hard thus to part, but we hope 'twon't be long,
We'll keep up our heart as we're marching along.

The intensity that breathed through Friedrich's fellow comrades was palpable. Though none of them would admit it, even the most boisterous among them were frightened. Like Friedrich, it was the first real battle for many of them. Some of the soldiers might have kept their hearts strong, but his felt as weak as a willow.

It was good to know that his parents and Matthias and others would care for Amalie if something happened to him, but he wanted to be the one caring for her, for the rest of his life.

"We ain't gonna thresh no more," he sang again.

Wind blew through the forest on the valley floor, around the soldiers. A break from the summer heat. Last night he and the others without blankets had been bitterly cold again, trying to get some sleep under the stars, but today men were collapsing with heat exhaustion. He hadn't had a decent meal since they left camp two days ago, but as he sang, he could almost feel the scythe in his hand, hacking through the grass in the fields. And he could pretend he was back in Amana.

In spite of the Union losses more than three weeks ago, they were marching around Pigeon Mountain again. General Rosecrans was intent on driving the Confederates out of Georgia like he had in Tennessee. The last skirmish had crippled their regiment, but not the brigade. And according to their new sergeant, the enemy had been hurt even more. He hadn't seen the fall of the enemy, but perhaps it was because he was running the other way.

Even in their weakened state, their company would keep going through Georgia, driving the retreating Confederates southward until there was no one left to fight. They would take the South in this last battle and end the war.

A loud cry rippled down the hill in front of them, a thousand voices screaming in frightful glee. The yell sent goose bumps down his back and arms. There was no turning back for the 28th Iowa Infantry. The Confederates were coming.

The sergeant shouted above the roar. "You ready, soldiers?"

He wasn't ready, but it was too late to change his mind. Jonah nodded at him, and Friedrich stood taller as the Rebel soldiers swarmed like bees at the base of the hill, their guns poised in front of them. He didn't know where they'd come from, but it didn't matter. They were still screaming, running up the slope with a hatred of mind and soul.

At least it sounded like hatred. How many of them were as terrified as he was?

The scars seared on Joseph's arm flashed through his mind, the humiliation on the man's face. He was fighting for Joseph and for children like little Eli who had their entire lives in front of them enjoy to freedom. He couldn't turn back now. He had to fight.

He straightened his back and joined the trailing voices of soldiers who finished the song.

The flag of our country is floating on high.
We'll stand by that flag till we conquer or die.

The Rebels streamed down the hills on every side of the valley now like a thunderous waterfall that threatened to drown them all. Jonah and dozens of soldiers shot back at the enemy on every side of Friedrich, but Friedrich didn't know which way to shoot. He didn't want to hit one of his fellow soldiers, nor did he want to hit a Rebel.

God help me, he whispered. The country he loved was about to annihilate itself, killing off thousands and thousands of its sons in one bloody battle.

The Union soldiers clumped together as they marched across the valley, facing their enemy as one, but the layers of the outer soldiers began to fall until Friedrich and Jonah were both on the front line. In front of him, Rebels continued to stream down the hill.

He stepped over the bodies of his comrades, but he couldn't think about their death in this moment. Later he would have time to think over all that had happened here, but now he had to protect the men around him. A Rebel charged toward him, and he aimed his gun at the man's legs. The soldier went down with a cry.

Friedrich's eyes watered as he ripped open another cartridge with his teeth and stuffed it down the barrel of his gun. He hated this—the yelling and the killing and the destruction of so many. Death was all around him, the love of God seemingly far away.

Choking in the smoke and gunpowder, he moved forward.

Someone grasped his elbow, and he looked down into the face of a boy. Sixteen maybe. His eyes were wide with fright, his leg drenched with red.

"Help." The boy coughed as he clung to his knee. "Please."

Then he collapsed onto the chest of another soldier, a Rebel who had departed this world. Friedrich glanced at the forest around him, at the madness of the fighting, and all the men falling down.

When he looked back at his feet, he didn't see the boy's gray uniform. The soldier was supposed to be his enemy, but looking into his face, all Friedrich saw was a brother.

Bending over, Friedrich picked up the boy and carried him up the hill toward the rear of the Union brigade, away from the fighting. A life was a life, and if this boy was willing to fight for his, then so would Friedrich.

Friedrich collapsed behind a cropping of rocks, laying the boy beside him. Friedrich wanted to fight for freedom, for Joseph and the others, but in this moment, with bullets whizzing by him and cannonballs exploding on the ground, the Spirit urged him to protect his injured brother. He wouldn't leave the boy until the battle was over, not until an ambulance took him to a hospital.

"What's your name?" Friedrich yelled above the clamor.

"Taylor," the boy shouted back, his words ending in a cough that seemed to paralyze him. "Taylor Barnes."

Taylor wasn't much younger than his sister or Inspirationist boys like Niklas Keller. He wondered if the boy had been conscripted into this fight, like Friedrich, or if he'd volunteered. Either way, he should grow up with his family, wherever he was from. He had to live.

Friedrich turned his shotgun, pointing it toward anyone who dared to attempt to hurt this boy. This time he wouldn't run away from the fight like he had before. He would follow Sergeant Mitchell's lead and take a wounded man with him to safety when the fighting was done.

Taylor squeezed his leg again, balled up in pain. As Friedrich bent to comfort him, a shot of pain seared his back. The fire lasted only a moment, and then he saw a dim light through the dark cloud of gunpowder.

Taylor shook his arm, crying out, but his voice sounded like it was tunneled. Then he heard Jonah Henson's voice, calling his name.

But it was too late to answer him.

The hazy light over Friedrich grew brighter, overcoming the darkness, and the heat seemed to disappear along with the despair. Peace enveloped him and cradled him like a child as he slipped away in the beauty and the warmth of Christ's everlasting light.

My Savior, be Thou near to me
When death is at my door.
Bernard of Clairvaux, Paul Gerhardt

Chapter Twenty
....

Steam hissed out of the passenger train's engine, its brakes squealing as it slowed to a halt. Homestead's platform was packed with women in calico dresses and men with plain shirts and straw hats. When the train stopped, Matthias could see the people inside the car, noses pressed against the windows as they saw their new home for the first time.

He should be elated this morning at the thought of finally seeing Hilga, but his stomach felt bitter instead. He wanted to welcome the Vinzenz family, the entire family, but the thought of seeing their daughter terrified him.

He was a wretch. From the time he was a child, the Vinzenz family had been nothing but kind to him. Today, instead of being exhilarated at the possibility of seeing them again, he dreaded it.

Some of the people around him waved. Others clapped quietly and a few people were even crying. Every time they welcomed their Ebenezer sisters and brothers to Iowa, it meant they were one step closer to becoming a whole community again. In a year's time, they would no longer be a divided society.

As they waited for the men and women to emerge, Matthias scanned the crowded platform and saw Amalie standing beside Niklas

Keller. As he eyed the two of them, the familiar feelings of jealousy tugged inside him, the same way he had felt when she and Friedrich used to slip off together in Ebenezer.

He refocused his gaze on the train, trying to refocus his frustration as well.

Was he going to spend the rest of his life tormented by Amalie? Or allowing himself to be tormented by her? He had fled temptation when he volunteered to be one of the first carpenters to move to Iowa, and for three years he had been safe from his feelings, only reminded of his weakness when Friedrich wanted to talk about the woman he was going to marry or about the fun they'd had as children in Ebenezer with Amalie at their side.

He shook his head, forcing himself not to steal another glance at them. No matter his feelings, he must focus on the arrival of the Vinzenz family today. Amalie was allowed to talk to Niklas Keller if she wanted. Niklas was two years away from twenty-four anyway. Amalie was too old for him.

The train door opened in front of him, and the first person to step down the stairs was Louise Vinzenz. The woman who'd been like a mother to him for twenty-one years.

"Mama," he called out as he rushed to her.

Louise was a large woman with an even larger heart. She wrapped her arms around him, squeezing him tight, and his shoulder dampened with her tears.

When she stepped back from him, still holding his shoulders with her hands, tears swam in her dark-blue eyes. "Has he really gone to war?"

"I'm—I'm so sorry."

She gave him a long look, like she was searching within him. The crowds seemed to quiet around him as they blended into a blur. "This is not your fault, Matthias."

He shook his head, wanting to make her understand how sorry he was. "I tried to talk him out of it."

"There was nothing you could say to stop him." She wiped the tears that wet her sagging cheeks. "It is that stubborn streak that runs through the entire Vinzenz line of men. It parked itself in Friedrich and won't let him go."

More people followed her off the train, grasping hands and shoulders clustered around them. Louise glanced around the people, searching. "Where is Amalie?"

Before Matthias could direct her toward Amalie, she was standing beside him.

"I'm right here, Sister Louise."

Louise wrapped Amalie in her arms. "I wish you'd stop calling me sister and start calling me Mama like Matthias does. In no time at all, I will be your mother."

Amalie stepped away from her and tried to smile. "How is my mother?"

"She's fine, dear," Louise said as she patted Amalie's shoulders. "She misses you, of course."

Matthias saw the glimpse of hurt in Amalie's eyes. Salome Wiese had never spent much time with her daughter when Matthias and Amalie were children. Sister Salome was always too busy working as a midwife to care for her only child. He wondered how it was with Amalie's parents today, but it was none of his business.

"Oh, there she is."

He broke his gaze from Amalie's face as Louise reached for Hilga's hand and helped her daughter down to the platform. He could feel the stares of people around him, waiting to see how he greeted her.

Amalie was beside him, Hilga in front of him. And all he wanted to do was run away.

Instead of running, he nodded at Hilga. She looked as pretty as he remembered her to be, even in her plain dress. Her honey-colored hair was tucked under her black cap, the ribbon tied under her chin. Her blue eyes met his briefly before her gaze fluttered to the ground.

He wanted to feel something, even the slightest twinge of his heart, but there was nothing except warmth at receiving her and her family.

He cleared his throat. "*Willkommen.*"

She still didn't meet his eye. "Thank you," she whispered.

He should say something else to her, inquire about her trip, but asking about her trip seemed so formal. He should be telling her how much he missed her, that he loved her. But he couldn't lie, not to himself or to her.

Niklas Keller joined them, and Louise hugged him and then the person beside him. "Oh, it is so good to see all of you."

Members of their society poured out of the train now, hugging their loved ones and hauling luggage. No one seemed to be looking at him or Hilga any longer. It would be the perfect time to whisper something to her, but there were still no words for him to say.

She deserved so much more than him. A man who was speechless, not because he was confused but because he was completely enthralled with her.

Even as Amalie and Niklas scooted around him to talk to Hilga, he seemed frozen in place. In his failure to muster up some enthusiasm at welcoming Hilga, he'd made all of them uncomfortable.

He was an idiot.

The last person off the train was Carl Vinzenz. His hat was tipped low on his forehead, and in his eyes was a mix of happiness and sorrow.

He clasped Matthias's hand. "At least one of my sons is here to greet me."

"Friedrich wanted to be here."

Carl looked back and forth between Matthias and the crowd surrounding his daughter. He seemed oblivious to how uncomfortable Matthias felt and to the silent gulf between him and Hilga. "We need to find you two a private place so you can reacquaint yourselves."

"Oh, no—" he stuttered. "Hilga has so many friends to see."

"How far is it to Amana?"

Matthias nodded toward the woods behind the platform. "Three miles."

"Hilga." Her father edged through the wall of people to retrieve his daughter.

Matthias eyed the forest behind the station. Everything within him wanted to run, all the way back to Amana, to the safety of his work on the kitchen house, but if he ran, he would still have to face Carl and Hilga on the other side. No matter how difficult this was, he would stay and do what was required of him.

Seconds later, Carl returned with his only daughter and a smile plastered so thick across his face that it looked like it might crack into pieces. Hilga wasn't smiling.

"I'm tired, Papa."

"A walk will be good for you," Carl insisted. "A long, leisurely walk."

Matthias stared at the man who had been like a father to him. Some of the betrothed men and women stole moments together before they wed, but no man and woman in their society were supposed to be alone before they married. What was he supposed to do when an elder instructed him to walk alone with his daughter, through the forest?

Run.

Hilga stood straighter beside him. "We need a chaperone."

"Well, of course you do," Carl stammered.

A sigh of relief slipped through Matthias's lips, but neither of them seemed to hear it.

"Amalie," Carl said, directing her toward them. "And Niklas."

Matthias stuck his hands into his pockets, his stomach sinking inside him. It wasn't possible for this day to get any worse. He hated feeling trapped like this, like others were making all the calls for him while he sat on the sidelines and awaited their beck and call.

Carl put his hand on Niklas's back and turned toward Amalie. "Could you two walk back to Amana with Matthias and Hilga?"

With Amalie and Niklas a few yards behind them, Matthias led Hilga toward the forest. The sun streaked light onto their pathway as they walked quietly under the canopy of walnut and cedar trees. Four wagonloads of Inspirationists rolled past them, on their way to Amana. The people waved as the wheels hammered the ruts in the road.

Then the silence folded over them as they walked toward the bridge. He could hear Niklas and Amalie whispering behind him, and it only made matters worse. Maybe Friedrich was right. Maybe the abandonment he'd endured as a child made it impossible for him to communicate with women as an adult. Maybe he had feelings for Amalie because he could never actually be with her. It was easy to love someone who didn't know you loved them and whom you never had to tell how you felt.

The river raced under the bridge as they stepped onto it, and Hilga paused to breathe in the fresh air. Behind them Amalie and Niklas stopped walking, and Matthias wished they would join him and Hilga. At least the torment of their nervous silence would end.

Matthias picked up a twig from the bridge and tossed it into the water. The current swept it down the river for a moment, and then an eddy trapped it. The twig swirled around in the whirlpool, not going anywhere except in circles. When he glanced over at Hilga, her eyes were on the twig as well.

He broke the silence first. "Was it a good journey?"

She nodded in response.

"Was it long?"

"The steamer trip was long."

He paused. "Do you miss New York?"

"I suppose."

And that was it. She didn't ask him any questions nor did she embellish her answers.

As silence poured over them again, he shivered. If they couldn't even have a simple, polite conversation, how could they have a happy marriage? He didn't need the blaze that seemed to spark whenever he spoke with Amalie—he'd rather not have it, in fact. But it would be nice if he and Hilga could maintain a conversation.

He threw another twig in and watched it wash down the Iowa River with the current.

"Your parents want us to marry," he said, and then he turned to search her face. "But do you want to marry me?"

She looked away from him. "Oh, Matthias—"

"Because we used to be able to talk in Ebenezer but now conversation seems to escape us."

Her lower lip trembled. "I will do whatever the Lord requires of me."

The heaviness of her words washed over him. Would the Lord require this of them? A marriage that neither of them desired?

"Your parents think this marriage is what the Lord wants."

"*Ja*, they do."

"But what do you think?"

She glanced behind them, at Amalie and Niklas talking along the pathway. "I—I don't know."

"We must pray, Amalie."

Her voice fell to a whisper. "My name is Hilga."

He turned from her so abruptly that something twisted in his neck. But he couldn't let her see his burning face. Or sense the burning in his heart.

"We will pray," he said before he turned to walk again.

God help him in his prayers.

* * * * *

Poor Niklas, Amalie thought. He waited in agony beside her even as he tried to carry on a pleasant sort of conversation. Or maybe the talking was to distract him from the beautiful girl on the bridge in front of them.

He chattered on about the upcoming harvest and the fact that her kitchen house was almost complete and he kept talking about the beauty in the forest. Amalie tried to appreciate his interest in the wilderness around them, but she would rather be in the kitchen house, over a stove, than hiking this muddy path through the woods.

In spite of his attempt at conversation, Niklas's eyes kept wandering back to the slender figure in front of them and the sight of the handsome man hovering over her on the bridge, intent on her every word.

Surely Matthias would treat Hilga better than he did the other sisters in their society. For Niklas's sake, he had to be good to her.

When they started walking again, Niklas groaned as if he was in pain.

"Why don't you talk to Carl and Louise?" Amalie asked as they stepped off the bridge onto the dirt pathway.

"What would I say?"

"That you love their daughter. That you want to marry her."

"I won't be old enough to marry for two more years."

"Then you should talk to Hilga," she countered. "And ask her to wait."

Niklas pointed to Matthias's back. "But she loves him."

"How do you know that?"

He shook his head, resigned to a life without Hilga. Amalie wanted to shake him. Like so many others, she'd been watching Hilga at the train station, and the woman clearly wasn't as excited to see Matthias as she should have been. Even as they walked through the forest, reunited after three years, they didn't appear to be talking.

Amalie loved Carl and Louise Vinzenz, but they were clearly blind in this instance. In wanting Matthias to be their son, they were sacrificing their daughter's happiness.

"Hilga knows how you feel, Niklas, and I believe she feels the same for you."

He glanced over, questioning her. "She has never said anything to me."

"I've seen how Hilga looked at you in Ebenezer, how her face would light into a smile whenever you were near. It seems to me that she loves you just as much as you love her."

His voice climbed. "Do you think?"

"It's clear to everyone except perhaps you and her parents."

He shook his head slowly. "I've loved her for a long time."

She smiled. "I understand."

"But she is supposed to marry someone else."

"You have to fight for her, Niklas."

"But what—what would Matthias say?"

"Exactly what he thinks."

Niklas paused. "*Ja*, he would."

"You aren't afraid of Matthias, are you?"

He paused. "I'm more afraid that Hilga will laugh at me."

"You will spend your lifetime wondering, Niklas, if you don't ask her how she feels."

"If she says no—I will see her for the rest of my life, walking around with Matthias and their children. I don't know if I can bear it, knowing that she knows how I feel."

"It's possible that you might be the one walking beside her instead."

She looked at Matthias and Hilga walking silently in front of them, and her own mind wandered. In no time Friedrich would return to her. He would get off the train, and the two of them would stroll under the trees together, back to the village.

There would be much for them to talk about, so many words and thoughts that they hadn't been able to communicate in letters while she was still in Ebenezer. She could almost hear him, entertaining her with stories about the war and the reasons that he had to leave her. Then he would tell her how much he missed her, and she would tell him she missed him as well.

Matthias and Hilga weren't like that. They walked through the forest like they were strangers. Or maybe they were just nervous after being apart for so long. Maybe that was why Matthias had been so irritable lately—he'd been nervous to see the woman he would marry.

She and Friedrich might turn out like that if they weren't careful. Lovers through their letters but strangers in person.

She and Niklas followed Matthias and Hilga out into the fields at the edge of the forest and then into the village where Carl and Louise and many others were waiting. The celebration continued as half of them crowded into Henriette's kitchen. They would be eating in shifts until Amalie's dining room was complete.

As Niklas left for the dining room, Amalie brushed her hands across her apron and walked toward the kitchen door. It was time for her to return to the kitchen, to help Henriette and Sophia and the other assistants who'd been assigned to help with the dinner rush.

Reaching for the door, she turned and saw a flash of blue over her shoulder. Brass buttons gleaming in the sunlight. Her heart leapt, her fingers frozen around the doorknob.

Friedrich?

She squinted at the soldier, trying to see his face under the brim of his hat. Clutched at his side was a cane, supporting his left side as he moved through the village.

Had Friedrich been hurt in the war?

This man seemed shorter than Friedrich, more husky than the man she remembered.

But it had been three years since she'd seen Friedrich. Perhaps she'd forgotten how tall he was.

It felt like she was in a trance, as she released the door handle and moved to the man. Drawing closer, she saw his mustache, a grayish tint that matched his hair. And she saw the solemn expression frozen onto his face. It wasn't her Friedrich, but why—

Dear God.

Why was this soldier in Amana?

Ah God, my days are dark indeed,
How oft this aching heart must bleed.
Martin Moeller

Chapter Twenty-One

....

Amalie's body trembled as she stepped farther away from the safety of the kitchen house. There were thousands of soldiers in Iowa, seeing one shouldn't alarm her so. She tried to approach the man, to welcome him to the village, but she didn't want him here. If he brought news with him, she didn't want to hear what he had to say.

Matthias appeared unexpectedly beside her, and she welcomed his presence. While she couldn't seem to find the words to say, he didn't hesitate. "Are you here to take more of our men away?"

The soldier shook his head. "No."

She waited, wishing the man would change his mind and say he had come to Amana to deliver more conscription letters or that he was here to tell them about a new law.

"Then what do you want?" Matthias's words sounded hollow. Scared.

"My name is Colonel O'Neill," he said. "I'm looking for a woman named Miss Wiese."

Amalie stepped forward with a shaky smile. "I'm Amalie Wiese."

He didn't return her smile.

She struggled to take a deep breath, fighting to control her voice. "Do you know Friedrich Vinzenz?"

The man's head dropped. "Friedrich was a good soldier."

She swayed to the side, and Matthias secured her arm before he spoke with the colonel.

"What do you mean, he *was* a good soldier?"

"Friedrich—he was killed during the Battle of Chickamauga."

The world seemed to spin around her.

"Killed—" The word tasted bitter in her mouth. She could say it, but she couldn't comprehend it. The brick houses around her blurred, and the kitchen house seemed to disappear as she collapsed onto the dirt street. If only God would take her away as well, take her to Friedrich.

"Amalie."

She heard Matthias whisper, but she didn't see him. His arms scooped her off the dirt, and she buried her head on his shoulder.

"Where is he?" she heard Matthias ask.

"The Federals lost the battle, so they will have to wait to retrieve those men who were killed."

"But how do you know he is dead?" Matthias demanded.

Hope surged within her. Maybe Friedrich was still alive. He could be wounded or captured or something else. If they didn't have his body, they couldn't know for certain he was gone.

"I received a telegram this morning." The man's voice was filled with regret. "One of his fellow soldiers saw Private Vinzenz fall. He said Friedrich would want me to tell Miss Wiese."

"How—how did he die?" she whispered.

The colonel shook his head. "I don't have any more information."

Matthias thanked the man for delivering the news, and Amalie wanted to scream at them both. The man wasn't to be thanked.

"I'm sorry," Colonel O'Neill said, and she moaned at his words.

"I'll take care of her," Matthias told him.

She lifted her head and tried to push away from him. She wanted to run and hide. Cry. Scream. Anything but be near Matthias right now.

"Let me go," she hissed as he carried her away from Colonel O'Neill. Friedrich Vinzenz was gone.

* * * * *

Matthias carefully lay Amalie down on the sofa and closed the room's curtains to ward off the sunlight and the curiosity of all those who loved her. She mumbled something he didn't understand, so immersed in her own pain that she didn't seem to realize where she was or whom she was with.

He slid down into a chair, his head in his hands. Everything within him ached. He wanted to pretend the colonel was wrong, that it wasn't possible for Friedrich to be gone. But in his heart he knew the man was telling the truth.

The village doctor raced into the room, his black bag anchored to his side. He opened his bag and lifted Amalie's head, spooning something into her mouth, and she collapsed back onto the cushions. Drifting away again.

When the doctor glanced his way, he lifted the spoon as if to offer Matthias some of his medication. Matthias shook his head. He would have to be strong for Hilga and her parents first. Then maybe the doctor could give him something to try and block out the pain.

He raked his fingers through his hair and then leapt to his feet. Amalie was asleep, and he couldn't stop to let his mind work through the ramifications of losing his friend. Not until he found Carl and Louise and Hilga.

The Vinzenz family was in the kitchen house, eating their noon meal. When Carl looked up at Matthias, he dropped his fork onto his plate, and the clatter echoed through the room.

"What's wrong, Matthias?" Carl demanded.

He motioned for Carl to come outside and both Louise and Hilga followed them. He struggled in his mind, trying to form the right words, but there was no right way to tell them that their son was dead.

She loves you, Matthias, but she can't come back.

Louise's words echoed in his mind. The words she'd told him twenty-one years ago when his mother left. How had she done it then, tell a boy that his mother was gone for good?

And how could he tell them today that the son they loved was gone as well?

The three of them stared at him, waiting for him to speak. Louise's eyes were wrought with panic, her fingers fastened around Carl's arm. Matthias wanted to tell them there was nothing to worry about, that Friedrich had only left them for a season. But right now, eternity seemed far away.

They followed him into the parlor next to the kitchen house, and Louise gasped when she saw Amalie, asleep on the sofa. Louise teetered on her feet, and Carl helped her into a chair as the doctor reached back into his bag.

Tears streamed down Hilga's face even before she heard the news, but he couldn't wrap his arms around her to comfort her.

The doctor helped Hilga into the remaining chair, and as they all mourned together, Matthias shared the colonel's words.

"My son...," Louise muttered. "I want to see my son."

When Matthias finished speaking, Carl lifted his voice in prayer. He begged God for guidance. For strength. Friedrich was already basking in the light and peace of God, but they needed God's Spirit there with them today. Desperately needed Him and the hope they had in the cross. The power of the cross.

"I want my son," Louise repeated, looking at Matthias as if he were hiding Friedrich from her.

Carl knelt beside her, tears streaming down his face as he took his wife's hands. "He isn't coming back, *Liebling*."

Matthias knew Carl loved his wife, but he had never heard him call her darling before.

"I want my son," Louise said again.

Matthias turned and slipped out of the room. He might like to pretend that he was the son of Carl and Louise, that they loved him as much as they loved Friedrich. He didn't doubt their love, but he wasn't Friedrich nor could he ever replace him.

Out of the village he walked, back through the fields and trees to allow them time to grieve as a family.

Instead of turning on the trail back toward Homestead, he walked to the Indian Dam. The place where he and Friedrich spent hours and hours fishing.

He hadn't been to their fishing hole since Friedrich left. As the weeks passed, he didn't want to go without his friend, so he kept waiting until he and Friedrich would fish together again. But now Friedrich would never return to fish with him or work with him or eat their meals together. Their time together on this earth was gone.

He picked up a rock and ripples sliced the surface when he tossed it in. The book of Revelation talked about a river of life pouring out of the throne of God, clear as crystal. Did the river have fish in it? Perhaps Friedrich was fishing somewhere right now, basking in the glory and wonder of Christ.

All this time they'd been waiting for Friedrich to come back to them. Now Friedrich was waiting for them to come to him.

Looking up into the heavens, he wondered if Friedrich could somehow look down upon them all, see how many people were grieving over his death. If Friedrich could say last words to them from the next life, what would he say?

Friedrich's unopened letter was tucked away in Matthias's room, and when he was ready, he would open his friend's final words to him.

Collapsing onto a flat rock, his dropped his head into his hands. Out in the wilderness, far away from the brothers and sisters in his community, he grieved for his friend.

Life's hourglass flows swiftly on and soon my course on earth is run,
And what is past is gone forever! Eternity is now my goal.

F. A. Lampe

Chapter Twenty-Two

....

Hidden amongst the branches and fallen leaves in the forest were flocks of wildflowers. Orchids. Wild petunias. Amalie plucked the stems of the flowers and formed a purple and yellow bouquet. There was a large garden with both autumn flowers and vegetables at the edge of Amana, beside the cemetery, but it didn't seem right to place garden flowers on Friedrich's grave.

His heart was passionate and beautiful, and unlike her, he loved the forest. His grave should be covered with flowers just as wild and colorful as his life.

As she walked out of the woods, she saw the Vinzenz family and Matthias standing in the prairie grass, among the dozen white headboards that marked the graves of the brothers and sisters who'd gone before them into eternity. The wooden headboards on each grave were identical, no grave more or less important than the others. God loved Friedrich the same as every other man and woman in this cemetery, but she didn't love them all the same. This grave would be closest to her heart.

There would be no hymns today or a member of the Bruderrath reading Scripture. When a member of their society died, hundreds of people gathered at the cemetery to commemorate their life, but when

Friedrich left for the war, he also left their society. Only his family and Amalie were permitted to remember him.

She hoped the elders would let Matthias's marker remain among the other headboards so that many years from now, no one would know that Friedrich had left their community. Nor would they know his body was lost in Tennessee instead of buried in Amana. The grave would remain as a memory of Friedrich's life for the next generations of their community.

Matthias dug a small trench for the headboard and secured it in the hard ground. When he was finished, Amalie placed her bouquet beside the marker.

Matthias offered her his arm as she stood to her feet, and he escorted her toward Louise. Amalie had spent the past two days fluctuating between grieving alone in her room and hoping that perhaps Colonel O'Neill was wrong, that Friedrich had been wounded or taken prisoner instead of being killed. But Matthias and the elders and even the Vinzenz family had resigned themselves to the loss of Friedrich's life on this earth.

Louise cried out in the silence, and Amalie felt like she should join her in her tears to honor Friedrich and his legacy, but she felt numb inside, as if her body had ceased to feel anything except pain.

Beside her, Carl read from the book of Revelation.

And God shall wipe away all tears from their eyes; and there shall be no more death, neither sorrow, nor crying, neither shall there be any more pain: for the former things are passed away.

Friedrich was free of pain—and she was grateful for it—even if she had to bear the weight of the pain for both of them. There were no tears for God to wipe from her eyes, but she prayed that in time, God would heal her heart. She didn't know how she could go on day after day with this pain constricting inside her, paralyzing her.

Carl finished his reading, resting the Bible at his side, and they all bowed their heads to pray silently. Inspirationists didn't mourn their dead, at least not in their dress or by wailing like those of the world did. Friedrich had been freed from the burdens of this life, and she was certain he was now enjoying eternity with their blessed Savior.

But even as she tried fervently to rejoice, Amalie couldn't muster any joy. Friedrich's body and his spirit had been released from pain and suffering, but those he left behind would continue to suffer for a long time.

* * * * *

Matthias's hands ached to work after the small funeral, to stay busy, but his mind couldn't seem to focus on even the simplest of tasks. Instead of joining Niklas at the unfinished kitchen house, he escaped to the quietness of his room.

Friedrich's letter was on top of his desk, waiting for Matthias to open. He'd tried to read it multiple times over the past two days, but he couldn't bring himself to even touch it. He didn't know why, but something about opening the letter meant that he had resigned himself to the truth that Friedrich was really gone.

He sat down by the desk and turned the envelope in his hands several times. Then he took a deep breath as he slid his fingers under the glue.

You are the most loyal of friends and brothers, he began to read and then he dropped the letter into his lap, his hands shaking.

He knew it would be hard to read Friedrich's last words to him, but he had no idea how hard.

The letter in his lap, he glanced out the window, at the vibrancy of the summer sky and people hurrying in straight lines along walkways. Life in Amana continued on without Friedrich, at the same steady pace it had when he was here and after he'd left for the war. But everything had changed for Matthias.

> *I don't think I ever told you, Matthias, but long before you arrived in our home, I had prayed for a brother. I was too young to realize exactly what was happening in the weeks after your mother left, but I remember begging Papa and Mama for you to stay. I needn't have begged. They had already made up their minds to take you in as their son.*

Matthias closed his eyes for a moment. He remembered that day so well, back in 1842, when he was five years old. His mother with her soft brown eyes and her dark hair tucked back in a handkerchief, leading him down to the castles and estates in the province of Hesse-Darmstadt. They traveled for three days, and as they walked, she told him grand stories about the pietist people residing there known as the Community of True Inspiration, people she said would care for anyone in need.

At the gates of one of the estates, his mother kissed the top of his head and asked him to wait there for her while she found him something to eat. As his stomach cramped with hunger—strange how he could always remember that feeling of hunger—he'd wondered about the tears in her eyes. He'd thought maybe she was crying because she was hungry as well.

Minutes passed and then turned into hours as the daylight faded to darkness. His mother never came back.

Louise Vinzenz found him, taking him to her family's rooms for food and rest. Friedrich made a bed for him on the floor and told him grand stories about the persecution of their people and the fact that they might be voyaging over to the Americas soon.

No one in Amana seemed to care about his heritage, or if they did, they never discussed it with him. He was an Inspirationist. The Vinzenzes were his family. And Friedrich had helped him become a member of this Society.

> *I can't say good-bye to you in person this morning. If I try, I won't ever leave, and I believe this is what God requires of me—to fight for those who cannot fight for themselves. And so I go today to face the evils of the world, the unknown, and I pray that I am used by His hands, in whatever way He asks.*
>
> *Even as I struggle against my own will and desires, I want to be used as His vessel.*
>
> *I will strive to be just while I have mercy. To pray for love even as I fight. And to remember to pray for you and Amalie and our family.*
>
> *You know I have loved Amalie for most of my lifetime. Please take care of her for me while I am gone.*
>
> *Your Brother Always,*
>
> *Friedrich Vinzenz*

The words complete, Friedrich's letter fluttered to the floor. Matthias left it on the ground as his gaze wandered back out the window.

Why had God required this of Friedrich? It was too much, to say good-bye to his friend, to face the rest of his life without him.

Take care of Amalie for me.

The words rang back to him.

Did Friedrich know what he was asking? Had he guessed at Matthias's affections? His friend had spent a lifetime loving Amalie, while

Matthias had spent his life trying to hide his love from her. From all of them.

A wave of guilt passed over him. There was no way he would dare tell Amalie what Friedrich had said nor would he ever tell her. He could never pursue her after the death of his best friend.

Friedrich hadn't mentioned caring for his family, but Matthias would help care for all of them.

Someone else would have to care for Amalie.

Who has not stood the battle's strain
The crown of life shall ne'er obtain.
Johannes Scheffler

Chapter Twenty-Three

· ·

The leaves above the pathway were tinged red and orange. The birds no longer sang out, intoxicated by summer's bounty and joy of new life. Autumn was upon them, and a chill replaced the heat that settled in the valley over the summer months.

Amalie didn't feel the cold, but her body was tired as she trudged down the path toward Middle Amana. Her soul felt even heavier. Sleep had fled from her during the past two weeks, daunted, it seemed, by the depths of her grief. Even when she forced her eyes to close and her breathing to slow, she couldn't seem to escape.

The doctor's medication helped her to finally rest, but when she woke in the morning, her senses subdued, the shock of her loss would flood over her again. It was like reliving the moment Colonel O'Neill told her Friedrich was gone, over and over again.

Her kitchen house was almost complete, but the elders insisted that she rest for several days before she began working in it. The thought of overseeing her kitchen didn't chase away her sorrow, or even mollify it.

Amalie's thoughts swung like a pendulum in her mind. Part of her wanted to stay in bed for days while another part of her wanted to escape back into her work. She kept wondering what happened to

Friedrich in his last hours, wondering how he died, wondering if he knew how much they would miss him in Amana.

Last night, when she couldn't sleep, she finished reading *Uncle Tom's Cabin*. She knew the story was fiction, that Tom wasn't any more real than Christian in *Pilgrim's Progress*. Yet Tom and Eliza and the other characters in this novel came alive to her because of what they stood for. Tom had given up his life to protect other slaves, as Friedrich had done. In very different ways, they were standing up for God's justice and incredible love.

The storekeeper was right, this was a book about Christ. She could see Him in these characters, just as she could see His face in the many members of His community, and she could see the many parts of God. His grace and His peace and His justice. But what she couldn't understand, what she battled and fought within herself, was why God would ask Friedrich to fight the war...and then take the life of His servant away?

Just like God had done with Tom in Harriett Stowe's novel.

In the story, God had allowed Simon Legree to kill Tom so the other slaves would turn to Him, so Cassy and young Emmeline would live, so Legree himself would have an opportunity to reconcile with God. But Amalie might never know if God had a purpose for taking Friedrich, or if he was a mere casualty in this cruel war that man had wrought on himself.

Smoke billowed up from Middle Amana. Like Amana, wood, brick, and stone buildings clustered together to form a small village. There was no mill in Middle Amana, nor did she see any shops, but she found the kitchen house, following her nose to the place that smelled like onions and smoked meat.

When she stepped into the kitchen, Karoline squealed and jumped up from her chair to hug her. Then she quickly pulled her closer to the stove. "Where's your shawl, Amalie?"

She looked down, realizing for the first time that she probably should have put something over her dress to insulate the thin material. "I guess I forgot it."

"You'll freeze out there, wandering around like that."

Karoline pushed Amalie toward a stool and handed her a steaming cup of black coffee though Amalie didn't relish the scent like she once did. She didn't seem to feel much these days, not even the heat from the coffee or the cold in the air.

The long table was filled with dumplings, and Karoline worked across the table from Amalie, simmering the dumplings in a skillet on the stove. "How is the Vinzenz family?"

"I—I don't know."

"Why don't you know?"

"I haven't seen them in a few days." She'd avoided them and so many others, the pain being too great for all of them.

"I suppose you haven't seen Matthias either."

She shook her head.

"You should all be hurting together, Amalie. Not alone."

She twisted the cup in her hands. "I don't know what to say to them."

"They probably don't know what to say either," Karoline replied. "But I don't think you need to say anything at all. Just be together."

She couldn't imagine that Matthias wanted to see her, any more than he had before Friedrich died, but perhaps she should visit with Carl and Louise and with Hilga.

"You are like a daughter to Carl and Louise, Amalie," Karoline said. "And I think you will always be a daughter to them, even when it's time for you to marry another man."

Amalie's chin jerked up. "I'm not going to get married."

Karoline sat back down on her chair. "Someday, Amalie, not now."

"There is no one else for me. Not even ten years from now."

Karoline reached for Amalie's hands and squeezed them. "Some women are called to stay unmarried, my friend, but God has not put that call on you."

Amalie's stomach felt sick. They could talk about anything else, but not that. She could never imagine herself courting or marrying anyone but Friedrich.

"I don't want to talk about marriage."

Karoline let go of her hands, and an ornery smile crept up on her face. "There's always Christoph Faust."

"Karoline!"

"You could travel with him for the rest of your life, across the country and back again. And you could cook for him day and night, and for whoever he was taking west."

A giggle escaped Amalie's lips, and she clutched her hand over her mouth before she laughed again. She should feel guilty for laughing just weeks after she'd found out about Friedrich's death, but the laughter felt good. She hadn't laughed in a long time.

"You could fill one of those chuck wagons with your stove and all your supplies. Every night, you could cook under the stars and sleep under them too." Karoline giggled now. "You and Christoph would be a happy little couple, out there under the moon."

Amalie picked up a lump of dough from the table and threw it at Karoline. Her friend dodged it and it landed on the stove.

"I can see you now, Amalie." She twirled around and then curtsied. "Queen of the wagon train."

"You're not helping," Amalie said, but it wasn't true. Her heart felt lighter than it had in a long time.

"A half-dozen little Fausts would be galloping around your ankles, for miles on the trail."

"I'm not marrying Mr. Faust!"

Karoline's eyes twinkled. "You never know what could happen."

"Maybe you should marry him."

"He will remember me as the woman who got injured on his watch." Karoline's eyes sparkled when she laughed again. "I don't think he will ever forgive me."

"And he will remember me as the woman who almost drowned trying to cross the river."

"You are blessed with tenacity, Amalie."

"And you are blessed with a heart of joy."

Karoline scooted around the table and hugged her. For the next hour, Amalie helped Karoline roll the dumplings to fry, and after the noon meal, Karoline made her borrow a woolen shawl for her walk back to Amana.

Amalie's shoulders and chest were bundled tight in the heavy wool, but her steps were quicker on her journey home. There was a future ahead of her, one that most certainly didn't involve Christoph Faust, but a future nonetheless. It was good to have a friend in Karoline, someone who knew she needed to laugh and someone who could talk about the life in front of her instead of only her present sorrow.

As she walked into her home, past the good room,, she stopped. Matthias was sitting there in a chair, next to another soldier, but this man was much younger than Colonel O'Neill. His arm hung in a sling, and his uniform was not pressed and clean like the colonel's. This soldier looked like he had just walked away from the war.

"Amalie." Matthias rose to his feet. "This man needs to speak with you."

She stared at the man, not noticing when Matthias moved across the room toward her. He pulled her to the side of the doorway.

"Who is he?" she whispered.

"His name is Jonah. Jonah Henson." He paused. "He knew Friedrich."

She peeked around the corner and eyed the man on the sofa again as if she could tell if he was telling the truth. She didn't know what motive he could possibly have to lie to her.

"Does he know what happened to Friedrich?"

Matthias nodded.

"Tell me—"

"He needs to tell you himself."

Amalie lingered in the arch of the doorway, wishing she were back in Middle Amana with Karoline where the grief from Friedrich's death seemed so far away. Then she stole into the good room, taking the chair on the other side of the sofa. Her fingers fidgeted on her lap. She thought she wanted to know what happened to Friedrich, but at this moment, her certainty was gone. She didn't know what to say to this man, nor did she know if she could bear to listen to the truth.

The soldier took off his cap, exposing red hair that needed to be trimmed, and he drummed his cap with his good hand as if he wasn't sure exactly what to say to her either.

"I'm sorry for your loss," he said in broken German. He stole a glance up at her and then looked back down at his toes. "I was with Friedrich at Chickamauga, and I thought—I thought you might want to know how he died."

She met his eye and then looked over at Matthias. He nodded at her.

Jonah held out an envelope to her, and she saw Friedrich's familiar writing was scrawled across it, addressed to her. She was grateful for the chair underneath her or she might have collapsed again.

She reached for the letter and clutched it to her heart. "How did you get this?"

Jonah handed over a small leather bag with strings. "It was in his haversack."

Opening the bag, she took out a silver tag with Friedrich's name on it and some crackers.

Amalie looked back up at him. "Did you see him fall?"

The soldier's long nod spoke of solemnity. Reverence.

"How—" She hesitated. "How did he die?"

"He was killed rescuing someone else." She could hear the bitterness in the man's voice, mixed with admiration. "A wounded Reb."

She fell back against the hard upholstery. Her Friedrich had given his life for the enemy. He was really dead, she knew that now. What other Yankee soldier would rescue a Confederate?

Jonah leaned forward. "He was a hero."

Her heart began to swell. She could almost see Friedrich, ignoring his own safety to save another. He probably didn't even have time to think of the consequences. Someone needed help and he had gone to the man's rescue.

"Did he suffer?" Her voice quaked, her fingers brushing over her hastily scrawled name on the envelope.

"I saw him get hit, but by the time I reached him, he'd already passed on."

"And the Confederate?"

"I don't know." He held up the sling around his shoulder and arm. "I was shot in the battle and they sent me home when it was over."

"Did you know Friedrich before this battle?" Matthias asked.

Jonah seemed relieved to turn from Amalie.

"We trained together at Camp Pope," he replied. "Some of the men scoffed at Friedrich for his strange beliefs, but I can tell you that none of them are laughing anymore. Those of us who didn't get killed in the battle will always remember him for his bravery. And for rescuing another man instead of protecting himself."

Amalie wrapped her arms around herself, rocking gently on

the seat. Instead of destroying his brother, Friedrich had saved him. "Thank you for telling us."

Matthias stood up beside Jonah. "Friedrich always carried his grandfather's copy of the Gospel of John with him."

The soldier shook his head. "It wasn't in his haversack."

Matthias directed him to the door. "Friedrich's parents need to hear your story."

Amalie looked out at the fall leaves adorning the large window. None of the Inspirationists might have agreed with Friedrich's decision to join the infantry, but they could do nothing but admire his courage as he laid down his life not only for his friends, but for his enemy as well.

I can rest in thoughts of Him,
When all courage else grows dim.
C. Titus

Chapter Twenty-Four
....

Jonah accepted the invitation to join Matthias and the Vinzenz family for supper. Carl led the soldier with reverence and perhaps a bit of pride into the dining room. Jonah sat between Carl and Matthias, and his eyes widened at the bounty of food on the table. He seemed to bask in it all—the food and the quietness and the fifty men and women eating together in solemn appreciation for all God had given them.

Jonah ate three bowls filled with chicken and rice soup, several pieces of bread, two servings of cottage cheese, and two slices of rhubarb pie. Matthias guessed the man would have eaten more if Brother Schaube hadn't stood up and ended their meal with prayer.

The diners filed back out into the cool night, walking around Matthias and Jonah as they moved toward evening prayers. Jonah stuck his free hand into his pocket and looked up the street as if he didn't know exactly where to go from here.

"Where are you from?" Matthias asked.

Jonah nodded west. "Marengo."

"Your family must be glad you are back from the war."

"I don't have much of a family anymore," he said with a shrug. "My parents died in a carriage accident when I was fourteen. I have an uncle who farms outside of town, but I don't see him very often."

Matthias understood. Without the kindness of the Vinzenz family and the entire community, he would be on his own as well. "Yet you came back to Marengo."

"I didn't have anyplace else to go."

Matthias hesitated. He understood a bit of what that was like. "Have you been home yet?"

Jonah shook his head. "I wanted to come here first."

Matthias searched the man's face for a moment, and he realized that Jonah Henson had traveled all the way from Tennessee, finally home from the war, and there was no one to greet him or thank him for all he had done.

"It's too late for you to travel tonight," Matthias said.

"The darkness doesn't bother me."

"Perhaps you can leave at first light." Matthias pointed at the sand-stone house next to him. "There's a free room up there where you could spend the night."

Jonah hesitated. "Are you certain?"

"You've done all of us a tremendous service, coming to tell us what happened to Friedrich," he said. "It is only a small way for us to thank you."

Jonah blinked, glancing up again at the dark window above them. "I would like to stay."

Several more people wandered around him and Jonah on the nar-row walk, on their way to Nachtgebet. Everyone in the village attended the prayers, but just for tonight, he didn't think Brother Schaube or the other elders would mind if he stayed away to entertain their guest.

Matthias pointed him to the doorway of the sandstone house. They could wait in its good room until the others were finished.

"What was it like," Matthias asked as they walked, "out on the battlefield?"

"The days, they were terribly long when we weren't fighting, but the battle itself was terrifying." He shifted his arm under his sling. "I didn't know when I would get hit, and when my turn finally came, I almost felt relieved. I no longer had to wonder how it would end."

"You thought you would die?"

Jonah nodded.

"I can't imagine."

Jonah seemed lost in his memories. "It was mighty cold as we tried to make our way back to camp. There weren't enough blankets, even for the wounded men."

Over Jonah's shoulder, Matthias could see the tip of the woolen mill in the distance. He didn't feel God's call on his life to join the fighting, not like Friedrich had, but perhaps there was something else they could do to help.

Two men lifted their hats to him as they rounded a corner.

"Where are they going?" Jonah asked.

"To evening prayers."

Jonah watched them wistfully, and then he turned back to Matthias. "Do you think I could join them?"

Matthias hesitated for a moment and then he guided Jonah toward the residence where they prayed every evening for their community and their country.

* * * * *

Amalie watched Matthias escort the soldier into the bottom floor of the residence where they prayed. None of the elders asked him to leave, and she was grateful for it. She'd never seen an outsider in their prayer meeting before, but after what Jonah had endured, he probably needed prayer even more than the rest of them.

Brother Schaube led out in prayer, and then Matthias prayed. Gratefulness poured out of his heart with his words, and she reveled in the strength of his voice. His petitions. Perhaps Matthias did miss Friedrich as much as she did.

Louise followed Matthias, thanking God for the life of her son and for taking him on to heaven before them. And then she thanked God for bringing Jonah to them.

In Amalie's lap was the letter Friedrich had written to her. She'd read his words before supper and she would read it again before she went to bed. And then she would give it to the Vinzenz family to read as well.

His handwritten lines crossed over each other to conserve paper, blending the words in an odd pattern that made it difficult but not impossible to read. He hadn't known this was his last letter to her. He probably thought it was like the letter he'd sent from Iowa City; he would follow it with another and another.

He said the Confederates had surprised them with an attack, but he wasn't injured. He and his company were enjoying the cool water from a stream as he was writing her, and he was missing Amana's wonderful food. If the war didn't kill him, he tried to joke, then the army food would.

His words were no longer funny.

He finished the letter with words to his parents and he told Matthias that he would return soon to fish with him.

And he said he missed her, even more than the food.

She opened her Psalter-Spiel to hymn sixty-four and began to sing. She missed him too.

Joy and peace, like balmy showers,
In Thy smile come gently down.
Matthias Loy

Chapter Twenty-Five

....

Two brothers carried pots and cookware into the new kitchen house. The stove and icebox were already in place and the cellar was stocked full with colorful canning jars, contributions from the other kitchens in the Kolonie. Sunshine flooded through the wide windows into the dining room, and the walls shone with fresh light-blue paint.

Matthias sat on a bench, surveying his and his team's handiwork, as he always did when a project was complete. In solemn awe he looked around the dining room. Part of his contemplation was pride, he supposed. Part of this moment, though, was in pure wonder at what could be accomplished in eight weeks. With the determination of their men and the abundance of supplies God had provided for them, a new building had been born.

What never ceased to amaze him was that not one person received payment for their work or for the materials needed to erect a building. It was the perfect picture of what it meant to be a community. Without anyone vying for money or credit or power for what they had done, they could do great things. The results were extraordinary, and all glory was given to God.

The door cracked open, and Amalie peeked inside. His heart softened at the sight of her.

He stood up, motioning toward the kitchen. "Come and look."

She stepped back toward the door, as if she was about to run. "When are you leaving?"

"I don't know."

"I'll return later."

His own words rang back to him. He'd told her not to come back to the kitchen, not while he was there, and now she was doing exactly as he once asked.

"This is your kitchen now." He swallowed hard. "I'd like to show it to you."

She crossed her arms. "I thought you didn't want to see me ever again."

"I shouldn't have said those things to you. I—I don't know why I did."

"Really, Matthias?" she questioned. "Because it seemed to me like you knew exactly why you were doing it."

"I was wrong," he said simply. He couldn't explain it to her.

She stepped into the room, glancing at the tables and benches, and the wood-burning stove in the corner that would keep the diners warm during the winters. He couldn't tell if she was in awe as well or if she was dazed.

"Are you all right?" he asked as he guided her from the dining room to the kitchen.

She avoided his question as she ran her hands across the smooth top of one of the tables. "You've done a good job."

"Thank you."

She peeked through the doorway, into the kitchen. He wanted her to be excited about their handiwork and her new stove and the display of all the pots and pans she'd brought from New York. But when she turned back toward him, there was only sorrow in her eyes.

"It's not the same without him, is it?" she asked.

He sat back down on one of the benches. "There's certainly not as much laughter these days."

"I think you might miss him even more than I do."

He searched her eyes, wondering what she meant. "We all miss him."

She leaned back against the wall. "I can hardly remember what life was like with Friedrich."

"He hadn't changed a bit, Amalie. He was just as strong and as passionate as he was when we left Ebenezer."

"I think I miss him, but it's more like I miss the memory of him. I miss knowing that his letters are on their way and the expectation of seeing him again." She wrung her hands together. "There is no future now."

He stopped her. "You still have a future, Amalie."

She shook her head, and he didn't try to dissuade her again. She would have to begin realizing her future without Friedrich on her own.

"He never stopped loving you. Not once."

"Nor I him."

"I will help you remember him," he said quietly. "Neither of us will forget."

She sat down on a bench, across from him. Her eyes were on the window behind him, lost in her thoughts. He wanted to reach out and hold her like he did when they first learned the news of Friedrich, but even the act of comforting her, even if he wanted it to be innocent, would mean so much more to him. He saw now the kindness in her heart, the love she harbored for Friedrich. And he had to control the turmoil inside him—for his sake and for hers.

"What do you miss most?" she asked.

"His silly singing, especially when he sang so loudly they could hear him up in East Amana. And I miss our Sunday afternoons fishing on the river and walking with him every night to evening prayers."

She met his eyes. "You were the best of friends, Matthias."

He shook his head. "A good friend would have stopped him from going to war."

"Louise told me you tried to change his mind."

"I didn't try hard enough."

She spread her hands over the smooth tabletop. "I remember that time, back in Ebenezer, when you tried to talk Friedrich out of skating on the pond. You did everything you could, but he still wouldn't listen to you."

"And neither would you."

She shrugged. "I wanted to skate with him."

He remembered the sound of the ice cracking across the water, the horror that filled him when Amalie fell through the ice. His heart had almost failed as he rushed to her. The water was shallow, so only the bottom of her dress and her skates were wet, but he'd still rushed her back to a residence to warm her by the fire. Amalie and Friedrich had laughed about the accident, but he never thought it was funny.

"No one got hurt then," he said.

"If anyone could have deterred him, it would have been you, but no one could change Friedrich's mind when he was determined to go." She paused. "Do you remember how sick he was on the ship over here?"

"We were all sick."

"Yes, but he was sick more than the others. Even as a child, you spent hours sitting with him in his cabin while the rest of us played on the deck."

AMANA
1863
IA

"He was like a brother to me."

"He was your brother, Matthias."

She pushed something across the table at him, a blue book with silver pictures.

"What is this?" he asked.

"A shopkeeper in Lisbon gave it to me," she said. "It helped me… helped me to understand slavery. And why Friedrich had to go."

He slid the book back toward her. "What does this author know about slavery?"

She raised her eyebrows at his tone. "If you would read the book, you might understand the horrors of slavery as well."

"I already know about the horrors of slavery."

"But we can't really understand it—"

Irritation flared up inside him. She didn't know how much he understood.

"Does it explain why Friedrich had to die?" he asked, and she hesitated at the bitterness in his words. She could never understand his anger nor could he tell her. "I'm sorry, Amalie. I know he gave up his life protecting another man."

"No, it's all right to be angry," she said. "To question."

"There are no answers to our questions." He shook his head. "God works in ways we will never understand."

"Someday," she said. "Someday I think we will have answers."

"We will miss him together, Amalie," he said, and then scolded himself at his words. He shouldn't do anything with her.

"Thank you." She began to stand. "I need to get busy organizing the kitchen."

"Amalie," he said, stopping her. "There's something else I wanted to speak with you about."

"What is it?'

"Jonah Henson said that it was bitter cold in Tennessee this time of year. Many of the soldiers are getting sick from exposure."

She blinked, and he wondered if she had the same spark of an idea that he had. "Don't they have blankets?" she asked.

He shook his head.

"The Council of Elders meets next Wednesday," he said. "If you think it's a good idea, I want to ask them to let me collect blankets and other supplies for the soldiers and for their prisoners. We could help the Union and the war effort without sending any more of our men to fight."

Life sparked in the dullness of her eyes. "It's a good idea, Matthias."

"I would want to do it to honor Friedrich's life."

This time she shook her head. "We should do it to honor the men who are still fighting for freedom."

"You are certain?"

"Friedrich would not want to put himself above the others."

"No, he would not."

He had been thinking more of her and the Vinzenz family than Friedrich, but Amalie was right. None of them would want to esteem themselves higher than either the Federals or their prisoners.

"Let's collect blankets for the soldiers, and anything else they might need."

He stood up by the table. "I will speak with the elders."

She stepped toward the kitchen and then turned back to him. "Hilga is a blessed woman to have you, Matthias."

His chest tightened with her words. If only he could be certain he would be able to be as loyal to Hilga as Amalie had been to Friedrich.

* * * * *

Amalie slid a knife out of its sheath and removed the cores from the ten heads of white cabbage she'd collected from their fall garden this morning. She fed the cabbage through a hand-cranked shredder and added the thin slices to a large pot with fried bacon. She would let the cabbage simmer until it was tender enough to make coleslaw.

White curtains framed the sunlight streaming through her new windows. Matthias and the other carpenters had built tall shelves, cupboards, and a six-foot-long sink, and then they added plenty of hooks above the long tables to hang baskets and her kettles. The craftsmanship was impeccable, and in spite of their differences, she would always be grateful to Matthias for his detailed work.

Her hands worked quietly and quickly as she loaded wood into the box under the stove to build a fire. It felt good to be back in a kitchen. Her kitchen.

And whatsoever ye do, do it heartily, as to the Lord, and not unto men.

The Lord had given her this job and she would work with all her heart to please Him.

As the fire blazed below the stove, she lifted a kettle of water and set it on the left burner. Then she placed the pot with cabbage and bacon on the burner behind it. She would boil beef for the first meal tonight along with the coleslaw and make spiced apples when Karoline returned from the orchard.

The door opened beside her, and she looked up, expecting to greet Karoline, but Louise walked into the kitchen instead.

The older woman moved toward the sink and washed her hands in a bowl. "I am here to help you."

"You need to rest, Louise."

Louise didn't seem to hear her words. Instead she reached for a knife and began cutting the arm roast into chunks. "It will be like the days of old, when I used to feed our whole family at home instead of going to communal kitchen, except I'll get to feed both my daughters and my son."

"I'm not your daughter, Louise," Amalie said, as if she had to remind the woman that she and Friedrich never married. She would spend the rest of her life as a Wiese, not a Vinzenz.

"Oh yes, you are." Louise set down the knife and reached out to give her a hug. "You are still one of my daughters, just like Matthias is my son."

Amalie welcomed the hug, though she didn't know how to respond to the woman's love for her. Even though she'd spent most of her life living in the room next to her mother and father, she'd never known what it was like to have a mother who cared about her well-being.

Her mother did the typical things a mother should do. When Amalie was a child, her mother escorted her to meals and school and to prayers, but even as she took her to different places, she rarely spoke with her. She couldn't imagine her mother volunteering to help her work in the kitchen, or saying how grateful she was that Amalie was her daughter.

It wasn't that her mother didn't care about her, but she was ever busy in her role as the doctor's assistant and town midwife, and she thrived in her busyness. Someone was always knocking on her door, asking for her help, and it seemed like she was always available to help everyone except the child she had birthed herself. The busyness fulfilled her in some way, but Amalie missed having a family.

Louise eyed the bowls of rutabagas lined up on the shelf. "Would you like me to mash them for dinner?"

"That would be wonderful."

"We will work," Louise said as she lowered a bowl to the table. "And we will talk."

Amalie added the pieces of roast to the warm water before she stirred the cabbage. She wasn't sure what she would talk about with Louise, not without talking about their memories of Friedrich. It had been hard enough discussing what she remembered with Matthias. She didn't know if she had the strength to talk to Friedrich's mother about him as well.

Louise stepped outside the back door and filled a kettle with water from the pump. When she returned, she placed the kettle on the stove.

"This is a dream for you, isn't it? To have your very own kitchen."

"It is."

"I'm happy for you, Amalie, that you've been blessed with this kitchen. And that Matthias built it for you."

"He didn't build it for me."

"Oh yes, he did."

Amalie shook her head as she sprinkled salt into the boiling beef. "He did it for you and Brother Carl and for his future wife."

Louise retrieved the potato masher from the cupboard and placed it on the table. "You think Matthias is going to marry Hilga?"

Amalie hesitated, the saltshaker suspended in her hand. She avoided gossip, and she didn't know Louise to be a gossip either. Was this what mothers and daughters did, as part of friendly conversation, or was Louise fishing for some type of information?

Amalie set the saltshaker beside the masher and turned to spoon the softened cabbage into a bowl. Then she sprinkled oil and vinegar over it. "I cannot comment about the state of his heart."

"Neither can I, but a mother knows her children, and Matthias's heart is conflicted."

As she added dried parsley to the coleslaw, Amalie thought back to her conversation with Sophia weeks ago. Had Matthias changed his mind about Hilga? Perhaps his heart had changed to love another woman. Sophia would be pleased by the news....and so would Niklas.

She turned away from Louise, setting the oil and vinegar back on a shelf. She should be happy for Matthias and the others, but her emotions warred inside her.

She didn't even understand the state of her own heart.

Let Thy grace, like morning dew falling soft on barren places,
Comfort, quicken, and renew our dry souls and dying graces.
Christian Knorr von Rossenroth

Chapter Twenty-Six
....

The Bruderrath met every month in one of the seven villages, and this morning the board of thirteen elders gathered in a small room off the stone meetinghouse in Amana. Fifteen minutes before they were scheduled to begin, Matthias walked into the meetinghouse beside Jonah Henson.

Jonah sat on a wooden bench in the lobby, but Matthias paced the floor. He wouldn't allow himself to predict what the council would decide, but he wanted to collect these goods, for himself and for Friedrich and on behalf of the sacrifice Jonah and so many other men were making for their country. Friedrich had given up his life for their country, and part of Matthias wished he could go fight. But another part of him knew his motives would be all wrong.

"Welcome, Brother Matthias," Brother Schaube said as he opened the door. "Jonah."

Jonah stood up and shook the man's hand while Matthias went into the room. Society members were rarely allowed to petition the Bruderrath; outsiders were never allowed to speak to the board. Still,

Jonah wanted to wait for Matthias outside, prepared to answer any questions the elders might have about the soldiers in Tennessee.

Brother Schaube directed Matthias to a wooden chair that faced the men. The thirteen trustees sat in an L-shape, six against one wall and seven against the other. They were all dressed alike in their dark coats and trousers, and every man was clean-shaven, but there was no similarity in regard to age. The men were elected from the church elders, and their ages ranged from men in their thirties to those in their eighties. A combination of wisdom from experience and a desire to embrace new technology and ideas. Matthias fidgeted in his chair as they stared back at him. He hoped all the men would embrace his idea.

"You have a request," Brother Schaube began.

Matthias scooted forward on the seat. "In Matthew, our Savior curses those who knew someone was hungry and didn't offer him something to eat or knew someone who needed clothes and did nothing to clothe him."

Brother Schaube's eyes filled with concern. "Do you know someone in need?"

He nodded slowly before he spoke again. "The Federal soldiers in Tennessee need both food and clothing."

"What do you know of the soldiers?" Brother Schaube asked.

"Jonah said that when they were fighting in Tennessee, it was already bitter cold at night. Some of the men no longer have shoes to wear and others lost their bedding on the battlefield. I thought—" Matthias took a long breath before he continued. "I thought we could collect woolen blankets and clothes and socks for these men and then send the extra supplies down to Chattanooga to help the soldiers."

Brother Schaube leaned forward. "How many soldiers are down there?"

"I don't know the exact number, but Jonah said there were thousands."

Brother Schaube paused as he considered the request. "The need is great, but we have no way to deliver supplies to these soldiers."

"I would like to go to Marengo to speak with Colonel O'Neill," Matthias said. "I'm certain he would help us get clothes and blankets to the soldiers."

The elder studied him. "Why do you want to involve yourself with this war, Matthias?"

"I want to help those in need, not involve myself in a war of any kind."

Another one of the elders rubbed his hands together, his gaze intent. "We are all concerned that you want to do more than help the soldiers. We are concerned that you want to fight."

Matthias squirmed under the man's gaze. If he was honest, he had thought about what it would be like to join the army, but his motive wasn't selfless like Friedrich's had been. He didn't want to rescue anyone; he wanted revenge. In his anger, he wanted to kill the men who had murdered his friend on the battlefield. A brother who was rescuing one of their wounded soldiers.

God hadn't spoken to him to go, as He had to Friedrich, and Matthias feared within himself what he would do if he were to fight in a battle. He didn't think he could rescue the enemy as Friedrich had. But even if he never went to war, he could pray for peace and he could help the men who were compelled to go fight.

He glanced into the eyes of all thirteen men who waited silently for his answer. "I want this war to end, but it is not for me to fight against the Confederacy." He took a deep breath. "Our community can help those who are fighting, though. We can demonstrate God's love and desire for peace to those soldiers from Iowa and other parts of our Union."

The elders paused for a moment before the head elder spoke again. "God is pleased with your heart, Matthias. We will pray about this opportunity as a council and then notify you when we reach a decision."

Matthias nodded and then met Jonah on the other side of the door. They could only pray that God would inspire the elders to allow them to proceed with collecting the supplies.

Matthias relayed the discussion to Jonah as he escorted the man to the western edge of town. Two of Brother Fehr's peacocks squawked behind the fence beside them, one of them fanning his iridescent feathers as he and Jonah drew close. Jonah stood mesmerized as the regal bird defended his territory.

"I hate to leave," Jonah said as he watched the bird.

"Will you start back to work soon?"

Jonah shook his head. "I clerked at a dry goods store before I went to war. The owner said he wants to hire me again, but he doesn't have enough business right now and probably won't until the war ends."

They continued their walk through the trees and plants in the specimen garden, toward the cemetery.

"What made you want to join the army?" Matthias asked.

"I never wanted to join," Jonah said as he buttoned his coat. "A recruiting agent came to the store and asked me to take the place of a man who'd been conscripted. I needed the money to pay off a debt."

Matthias's throat constricted. He glanced at the sling across Jonah's shoulder and his mind went back to the line of men waiting by the enlistment office in Marengo. Had Jonah been the one to fight in Matthias's place, or had the man sent as his substitute been killed in the battle like Friedrich?

"You didn't want to fight?" Matthias's voice cracked.

"I wanted to do what was right."

Matthias nodded. The answers weren't easy. Jesus told them to render unto Caesar what was Caesar's, and their Caesar had commanded him to fight. Yet they were also supposed to obey God over man, and Jesus blessed the peacemakers. And He told His followers to turn the other cheek.

Perhaps God did speak differently to those who served Him, asking each of them to serve in a way that exemplified God's heart. Some He commanded to seek peace while others were supposed to fight for the poor. And others were supposed to care for the needy—offering even a simple cup of water in Jesus's name.

He couldn't take water to Chattanooga but he could offer warmth to the soldier in Jesus's name.

Matthias shook Jonah's hand.

"You are welcome to come visit Amana anytime you'd like."

"I appreciate it."

"Stop in the Middle Amana kitchen on your way home," Matthias said as Jonah started down the road to Marengo. "They'll be happy to serve you a meal."

Jonah nodded. "Thank you."

Matthias turned and looked back toward the village. He and Niklas were building a new hotel to host the influx of businessmen and tourists visiting their community. He should join Niklas this morning, but his gaze wandered to the trees that surrounded the cemetery. Even though Friedrich wasn't there, it was a quiet place away from the clamor of town. A place to think about all that had happened.

As he stepped through the shelter of the trees, he stopped. Amalie was there, kneeling in front of Friedrich's grave. He should retreat, leaving her to her privacy, but he couldn't seem to break away his gaze. Mesmerized, he watched her place the flowers in her hands in front of the cross, and then she bowed her head.

Watching her, he felt sick to his stomach. Never once should he have thought that Amalie could be his. He had entertained the idea, even when he knew it was wrong. Even when he knew she was promised to Friedrich.

How could he have done this to his best friend? To this woman who had been faithful to Friedrich? He had longed for what he couldn't have, and if he didn't release it, it would destroy him.

He backed away from the trees.

Amalie had loved Friedrich with her entire being, and she would always love him, no matter how long he was gone. Matthias had nothing to offer her, to care for her, nor would he ever have.

Shaking his head, he turned around. Friedrich had been wrong to even ask.

* * * * *

"You can't go to Chattanooga," Colonel O'Neill told Matthias. "The entire town is surrounded by Confederate soldiers."

Matthias scooted forward on the wooden chair in the man's office. "Private Henson said the soldiers need blankets and clothing."

"They need blankets. They need food." The colonel slammed his fist on his desk. "And they need to win this blasted war."

Matthias steadied his voice. He had thought the challenge would be for the Bruderrath to approve his collection of supplies, but they'd voted unanimously for him to pursue this. He never thought the colonel would disapprove. "We can't do anything about winning the war, but we can get them the supplies they need for comfort and strength."

"You don't understand." The colonel shook his head. "Chattanooga is under siege. The U.S. military can't even get supplies in or out of the town. How do you expect you and your unarmed inspirational people to get the stuff to them?"

Matthias wanted to shake the man and tell him that *he* didn't understand. If God wanted them to deliver the supplies, it didn't matter if they faced the entire Confederate Army. None of them lived or fought or served with their own strength. Everything was given to them by God.

Matthias leaned forward. "If He chooses, God can make blind eyes see, Colonel, and He can make seeing eyes blind. It was God who empowered a boy named David to defeat the entire Philistine army with his sling, and if He chooses, He can impart this same strength and courage to us."

The man laughed roughly. "You really do think you're inspired."

"You may not think that God speaks today, but we still believe it. And we believe He is directing us to collect and deliver these supplies."

"I need men like you to fight."

Matthias shook his head. "I am not supposed to fight."

"Then you are a waste of my time," the colonel said. "A waste of a man."

Matthias stood up. "We would welcome your help to deliver these supplies, but if you choose not to assist us, we will still do what God has called us to do."

"You are a fool, Rocmig."

Matthias stomped out the door, saddened that the man didn't recognize his own foolishness. What the world thought was foolish, though, God often redeemed for His good.

Chapter Twenty-Seven

....

Matthias pulled back on the reins and the workhorses stopped in front of the meetinghouse in High Amana. Men and women loaded the back of the wagon with their offerings of blankets, woolen shirts, knitted socks, leather shoes, and jackets.

With the wagon full, Matthias pulled forward and Jonah drove the next wagon in front of the meetinghouse. Their brothers and sisters quickly filled that wagon as well, and Matthias was overwhelmed by their generosity. The donations from the other six villages already packed the Amana meetinghouse, and the men in Amana would carry the boxed supplies over to Homestead tonight for their journey by rail in the morning.

With every bundle passed into the back of the wagon, another soldier would be warm for the winter, or at least warmer than he would be without the blankets or coats.

Matthias thanked the people of High Amana on behalf of the Bruderrath and then carefully drove the team down the steep hill to return on the path to Amana. Not only had the women worked on knitting socks and the crew at the woolen mill worked late into the night to produce more blankets, but people had given sacrificially of their personal clothing and belongings.

Clouds filled the sky and Matthias buttoned his coat as he steered the team home. The temperature dropped a few degrees more every day, and the nights were even colder, dipping into the low thirties. Snow would fill the river valley soon. He couldn't imagine how cold the soldiers must be at night.

He hadn't been back to visit Colonel O'Neill, but the elders received the national newspapers. The reporters predicted that the siege around Chattanooga would end any day, but until then, supplies continued to be cut off from the Federal soldiers who occupied the town as well as the few citizens who remained.

He drummed his fingers on the seat to keep them warm. The only way to ensure the safe delivery of these goods was for him to go with them. Brother Schaube had arranged the details of their shipment all the way to Nashville and then he insisted on hiring a guide to accompany Matthias. While Matthias initially balked at the idea of going with someone, it was apparent to him that the only reason he didn't want a guide was founded in his pride.

He thought he could get the supplies into Chattanooga alone, with God's help, but the elders believed that he needed someone familiar with the ways of the world to escort him. In the end, he agreed. He might know the intricacies of workings in their Kolonie, but he knew nothing of how things worked on the outside.

Not only did they have mounds of donated blankets and coats and shoes to deliver to the soldiers, but the women in the community had packed boxes full of canned fruit and salted pork and hard candy along with bags of coffee beans.

He hadn't counted the supplies, but they had at least a thousand blankets, maybe more, and hundreds of coats and pairs of shoes. Nor could he guess how many socks the women had knitted. On his night watch, he'd seen the candles burning in the windows and knew that many of them were knitting for the soldiers.

He wished Jonah would accompany him, but with the exception of his short stint in the infantry, Jonah hadn't spent much time outside Marengo. These days, the man rented a horse and rode to Amana almost every weekend, eating at Amalie's kitchen house and encouraging Matthias and the others in their collections. Often he spent the night in one of the guest rooms as well. It wouldn't be long before his arm was completely healed, but he didn't seem to be in much of a hurry to find a new position in Marengo or anyplace else.

Matthias had wondered before how any man could stand in a store or sit behind a desk for an entire day and be content in his work. He feared he would go crazy if he couldn't be out in the fresh air, working with his hands. Jonah didn't seem like the kind of man who could be content indoors either, but he supposed a man had to make a living in whatever way he saw fit.

He leaned against the hard back of the wagon seat as he rode through the village of Middle Amana. His guide was supposed to arrive sometime tonight, but it made him nervous, waiting for him at the last possible minute. He had no choice but to resign his concerns and wait, something he would probably have to do multiple times on his journey ahead. But he would be ready to leave at first light.

* * * * *

Inside the main room of Amana's meetinghouse, Amalie folded a blanket and placed it on top of the neat pile. She'd lost count a long time ago of how many blankets she had folded and stacked, ready to transport to Chattanooga. Matthias and Jonah had collected enough supplies to feed and clothe hundreds of soldiers along with blankets for each one of them as well.

Tonight teams of Amana women divided the clothing into piles and others packed them into crates while the men transported the packed crates to the train station in Homestead. The wood stove burned in the corner of the room, but with all their work, and the dozens of women inside, they probably didn't need the heat from the stove.

Matthias and Jonah left after their midday meal for High Amana, and she'd expected them to be back by supper, but an hour had passed since they'd eaten and the men had yet to return. Brother Schaube had postponed prayers this evening, until Matthias and Jonah could join them.

"Here's another one," Karoline called before she tossed her a navy blanket. Amalie folded it and set it on the pile.

As the weeks and then months passed, the shock had worn off a bit that Friedrich was gone. Nothing had changed for her—she was still working in the kitchen every day, going to prayers every night. The only change was the loss of her hope for the future, for Friedrich's return and their subsequent marriage. Her life stretched ahead of her, full of peace but also of monotony. The sameness of it frightened her, but this week had been different. They'd worked every night, trying to get everything ready for the shipment.

"Do you think we'll be done soon?" Sophia whined beside her.

Rosa Schaube handed Amalie another blanket and she began to fold it.

"We must be done soon," Rosa said. "The men are delivering the supplies to Homestead tonight."

Sophia collapsed onto a mound of socks. "I don't think I can fold another blanket."

"Then start folding socks," Rosa retorted.

Sophia picked a sock off the pile, sighing as she matched it with another.

When Rosa moved away from them, Sophia scooted close to Amalie. "I wish I could go with them to Tennessee."

"No, you don't."

Sophia didn't seem to hear her. "Just think of all the soldiers down there, thrilled to see a woman. It wouldn't even matter that I wasn't wearing some fancy dress."

Amalie's stomach clenched at the thought of being among all those worldly men. "Why would you want that, Sophia?"

"I just think it would be fun."

Amalie turned the blanket over and made another fold. She didn't think it would be fun at all.

"There are plenty of good men here in Amana."

"But very few of them are good enough for me."

The door opened, and Matthias stepped inside. His hat and over-coat were dusted with snow, and his arms carried a large bundle.

"Except one perhaps—" Sophia moved toward the door.

At that moment, Amalie hated the girl. Really hated her and she didn't know why.

Was it because she liked to flirt with Matthias?

It shouldn't matter to her if Sophia flirted with Matthias or even if she married him, but Matthias deserved a woman who was devoted to him and to her faith, not someone who needed the attention of multiple men.

"Let me take that," Sophia said, taking the bundle out of his hands.

"Thank you," he replied, but he wasn't looking at Sophia. His eyes scanned the room until they rested on Amalie. When his gaze met hers, she looked down at the floor, hoping for another blanket to fold, but there were none left. She stepped toward Rosa and began digging through the pile of supplies left to divide. Anything to divert her from Matthias's gaze.

She found a blanket in the mound and folded it. From the corner of her eye, she watched Sophia speaking to Matthias, with not even an attempt at subtlety. Apparently the woman didn't care if all of Amana observed her fawning over him.

She sighed and realized she was almost envious of Sophia's boldness. Sophia didn't let others deter her when she wanted something. And right now she wanted Matthias's attention. Amalie was bold, but her boldness usually involved her work, never her relationships.

Was there someone in her life she was willing to risk everything for, even being singled out in their community?

Not even with Friedrich had she been willing to do that.

When Sophia returned to her side, her voice plunged even lower. "I sure would like to go with Matthias on that trip, just so we could be alone."

"Don't let the elders hear you."

Sophia winked at her and then she twirled around before she landed on the stack of blankets. "Think of how fun that would be."

Amalie didn't dare.

"Isn't he the most handsome man?"

"I hadn't noticed."

The door opened again, and Jonah stepped through the door followed by a third man. Christoph Faust.

Amalie's stomach rolled as Mr. Faust found her face in the crowd.

"Who's that?" Sophia whispered, another grin creeping up her face.

Sophia didn't wait for Amalie to reply. Instead, she sauntered slowly back to the entrance.

Disgusted, Amalie threw down the blanket and rushed toward a door at the other end of the room. They would have to finish without her.

All the stars, the moon's soft light,
Praise Him through the silent night.
Joachim Neander

Chapter Twenty-Eight
....

What was wrong with Amalie?

Moments after he met her gaze, she marched out the side door. Had he done something to anger her? Glancing behind him, he saw that Christoph Faust had walked into the room. Perhaps seeing the man had upset her.

Turning, Matthias went back out the door to unload another armful of the donations. He remembered well the day that Amalie arrived in Amana and watching her smile up at the captain of the wagon train. What he thought was righteous anger had flooded his mind, but now he realized that he was only fooling himself. Perhaps he had been a bit angry for Friedrich's sake, but more than anything else, he was jealous.

He carried an armful of coats back into the building. Amalie hadn't welcomed Faust with her look. No, it was more like disdain.

Once again, he had been wrong about her.

Matthias threw the blankets onto a pile and turned back toward the wagon. If only he could run after Amalie and ask her what was wrong.

He couldn't go after her now, not with so many people relying on him, but he wished he could see her before he left in the morning, if only to tell her good-bye.

Niklas and his father brought two more wagons to the front of the meetinghouse. Harvest moonlight beamed down as the men hoisted crates onto the back of the wagons to take to Homestead.

The bell tolled across Amana for evening prayers, and Carl Vinzenz rushed to Matthias's side.

Hilga was behind him with Louise, and Carl nudged his daughter forward. "Would you like to escort Hilga to Nachtgebet?"

He wanted to find Amalie, but he couldn't refuse Carl, not with Hilga next to him.

When Hilga joined Matthias's side, she didn't look happy about going to prayers with him either. They left the meetinghouse and strolled slowly up the pathway, neither of them speaking a word.

He shivered in the night air and put his hands into his pockets. Like Jonah said about fighting in the war, perhaps he should marry Hilga because it was the right thing to do. Even if he didn't love her, he would treat her well for the rest of their lives.

Or maybe it wasn't the right thing—to offer only part of himself to Hilga when his heart belonged to another. And when he was certain that Hilga didn't love him either.

"We are leaving in the morning." He paused, waiting to see if there was anything else she wanted to discuss, but she didn't say anything.

She stopped walking. "You shouldn't go."

He looked over at her. "Why not?"

"Something bad might happen to you." Her voice faded into a whisper. "Like Friedrich."

'I'm not going into the battle."

"But bad things happen close to the battlefields as well. Mistakes."

He glanced over again, touched by her concern. How he wished he loved her with such a passion that he couldn't help but take her in his arms and whisper in her ear. Even with her parents behind them, even with the community surrounding them. He wished his love for her overwhelmed him.

But it didn't. He felt no different for her than for Karoline or Sophia or any of the other younger sisters in their community.

When they arrived at the residence, he nodded at Hilga and she slipped into one of the rows for the women. He sat down on a bench and bowed his head.

He appreciated her concern about his leaving. His safety. But even as he thought of letting Christoph Faust deliver the supplies without him, something nudged at his heart, perhaps the same sensation Friedrich had when he was supposed to go fight this war. Something, the Holy Spirit maybe, was telling him he needed to take the blankets and clothing all the way to Chattanooga.

Amalie walked through the door, her head bowed, and he squeezed his eyes closed, trying to pray quietly with the others. When the prayers finished, Hilga didn't look for him. She walked back toward her residence with Amalie and Karoline, and he was alone.

Carl stepped up beside him, clapping his hand on Matthias's shoulder. "What are you waiting for, son?"

Matthias strode down the path next to the man. Carl was right—he shouldn't wait a moment longer.

"May I speak with you and Louise in private?" he asked.

A smile spread across Carl's face. "Of course."

Instead of going into the good room where someone might hear them speak, Carl directed them to the carpentry shop. He hung a lantern in the corner of the room.

Tools hung from the ceiling and wood scraps littered the benches and floor. Matthias took a deep breath of the musty wood scent. He spent most of his time away from the shop, building walls and floors, but he always relished the simple pleasure of carving a piece of wood into a work of art.

He rubbed his hand over the rough edges of a chair and then turned to Carl and Louise.

"You have both been like a mother and father to me for almost as long as I can remember."

Louise stepped forward, taking his hands in her thick fingers. "You are a son to us, Matthias. No matter what."

He nodded. More than anything, he wanted to be able to tell them he wanted to marry their daughter, that he would care for her the rest of his life.

"I know you want me to marry Hilga," he said.

Carl smiled. "You will make a fine couple."

He squeezed his eyes closed for a moment before he looked at Carl again. "But I cann. marry her."

"What?" Carl exclaimed, pouncing forward. "What are you talking ?"

" oesn't—" he started to explain, but Louise stopped him.

at's a relief," she said with a grin.

Carl turned to his wife as if she were mad.

Louise reached out and took Matthias's hands, looking into his eyes again as if she knew what was inside of him. "Hilga will be ha hear that as well."

think?"

w she will."

He sighed with relief. He didn't want to hurt Hilga or any of them.

"She won't be happy," Carl insisted with a shake of his head. "None of us are happy."

He glared at his wife, but she ignored him.

"You can't marry her, Matthias. Not when you love another," Louise said. "Or when Hilga loves another as well."

"But you're supposed to be—" Carl's voice broke. "I wanted you to be my son."

"Don't be ridiculous, Carl," Louise said. "God gave us Matthias as a son, just like he gave us Friedrich."

"Thank you," Matthias whispered.

"And it's almost like he gave us two daughters as well—Hilga and Amalie. They both need good husbands."

Matthias stepped back, banging into a sawhorse. He tried to scoot around it and knocked a tool off the wall.

Did Louise know what was in his heart? Judging by her hearty laugh, she did.

How long had she known?

Carl's gaze ricocheted between Matthias and Louise as if they were both crazy.

"Hilga has two parents who love her," Louise said, "and I believe there is another man here in Amana who does as well. But Amalie needs someone to care for her."

Matthias looked at her. "Friedrich asked me to take care of Amalie, but I don't know how."

"You and Amalie need to talk," Louise said, pushing him toward the door. "About something other than Friedrich."

* * * * *

Matthias gazed up at the light that flickered above the dining room—Amalie's new room. There were no lights in the windows next to hers where Brother Schaube and his family slept.

"*Guten abend*, Matthias."

Matthias slowly turned away from Amalie's window and saw fellow carpenter Gottlieb, ready for his duty as the night watchman. Even with the bright moon, he held a lantern in his hands.

"Are you going to Homestead tonight?"

Matthias shook his head. "In the morning."

Gottlieb glanced up at Amalie's window and back down. "We will all miss you."

Matthias took a step away from the kitchen house and the thoughts that captured his mind.

"I think I'll take a walk tonight, to calm my mind," he said.

"You better hurry," Gottlieb replied. "We've got snow moving in."

Gottlieb continued his guard duty west of town, and Matthias moved east. Perhaps Louise was right, and he and Amalie needed to talk about something besides Friedrich, but he didn't know how to begin that conversation. He could talk to her about the supplies they were gathering for the soldiers, but that conversation would lead back to Friedrich.

With the bright moonlight, he didn't need a lantern this evening, but he needed his gloves. He reached into the pocket of his coat and his hand slid over the lid of a small box hidden there. He had carved it long ago and kept it in his room, not knowing what to do with it. Now he knew who he wanted to share it with but he wasn't sure how to get it to her.

He took his hands out of his pockets and slid on his gloves.

The mill was silent now, the moon making it look ghostly against the black night. And his mind began to wander again.

What would it be like for Amalie to join him, out here on this quiet night? When everyone except Gottlieb was asleep?

His heart seemed to burn within him. They didn't have to speak about Friedrich, about anything for that matter. He just wanted to be alone with her, in the quiet, before he left for Tennessee.

All the windows were darkened as he hurried back down the street, except Amalie's window. What was she doing so late at night, while the others were asleep? Or perhaps she was still having trouble sleeping, as he was as he lay awake so many nights. There was so much he didn't know about her.

What would he and Amalie talk about if they didn't talk about Friedrich?

A lantern moved toward him, and he slipped behind a tree as Gottlieb passed by. If the elders found out that he and Amalie were alone on his watch, they would both be banned from services for at least a month. And he probably wouldn't be permitted to travel to Tennessee.

But then again, what if something did happen to him while he was gone? He might never be able to tell Amalie how much he cared.

His mind whirled, but he dared not think about the consequences any longer. Instead, he lifted a stone from the ground and threw it as softly as he could toward her glass. The tap echoed back down to him, and he cringed. He would be mortified if Brother or Sister Schaube came to the window to inquire about the noise.

When Amalie didn't come to the window, he threw another rock. It pinged off the glass, louder this time, and he almost hurried back down the street.

But then he heard a creak above him and watched her window lift. Amalie leaned out into the night. Her long hair dangled over her shoulders, the contour of her face seemed to glow in the moonlight. He should turn and run away right now, but he couldn't seem to move.

"Who's there?" she whispered.

He glanced over at the Schaubes' room, but no one had opened their window.

He cleared his throat. "It's me."

"Matthias?" She scooted her head back into the window, but he could still hear her voice. "What are you doing here?"

"I—I want to speak with you."

She hesitated and then whispered again so softly that he had to strain to hear her words. "Can we speak in the morning?"

"Not if we want to be alone."

The window closed, and he waited in the darkness. Perhaps she wouldn't come down—if she didn't, it was clear to him that Louise was wrong. Amalie didn't care for him as he did for her.

Minutes passed slowly, and he almost turned to go to his room, but then she was in the doorway. A candle illuminated her face and the black cap that covered her hair. He'd never seen her looking so beautiful.

Even with the shawl wrapped around her, Amalie shivered in the cool night. His eyes locked on her, he leaned forward and blew out the candle.

"Come," he whispered.

Amalie didn't complain as he led her off the main street, away from Gottlieb's watch and onto a muddy path in the orchard. The chill of winter silence enveloped the spindly trunks and branches around them, but even with the coolness, his skin burned. It had seemed like a good idea to throw that stone at Amalie's window, invite her to join him this night, but now he wasn't so certain. He had never been this close to her since they'd become adults, with no one else nearby.

Instead of sitting on a bench, he looked up at the windmill before them, at the sails turning slowly in the breeze. "Have you been up there yet?"

She shook her head.

"Let me show you."

Amalie followed him up the steps, onto the wide platform below the wind wheel. In the moonlight, far beyond the village, they could see the valley and a silver shimmer in the fields as they stretched to the trees.

"It's beautiful," she whispered.

He leaned forward, his elbows on the railing as he surveyed the growing village. He couldn't look over at her in the moonlight. If he did, he would lose his nerve.

"Christoph Faust is traveling with me in the morning," he said.

"So I guessed."

"I was wrong to accuse you of flirting with him."

"I was wrong to speak with him like I did." She turned to look at him, and in the moonlight, shadows from the windmill's sails flickered across her face

"How are you doing?" he asked.

"I don't know how I am."

He stared back down at the orchard as if the dark trees harbored the answers to his questions. "Hilga and I are no longer going to marry."

She was quiet for a moment. "Why not?"

He didn't want to frighten her, but he no longer wanted to hide the truth either. "It wouldn't be fair to marry Hilga when my heart belongs to someone else."

His words hung in the chasm between them, and for a moment, he wished the gap would swallow him. Even as the words rang back to him, they terrified him.

"No, it wouldn't," she finally whispered.

A breeze gusted through the trees, turning the sails above them, and the windmill swayed with it. Was it possible that Amalie was as confused as he was? She trembled beside him, but her words lightened the burden in his heart. He could only hope that perhaps Louise was right, but he wouldn't push her. They both needed to heal before they thought about the future.

He dug into his pocket. "I have something for you."

She reached out and took the walnut box from his hands. Her fingers smoothed over it. "Where did you get this?"

"I made it," he said. "A long time ago."

"It's—it's lovely," she said as she tried to open the lid. He reached out to stop her, and at the touch of her skin, fire sparked through him again. He withdrew his hand.

"I have the key," he whispered as he held up a small brown satchel. Then he slid it into his pocket. "When I come home from Tennessee, I will open it for you."

She slowly lowered the box. "I'm afraid for you to go."

"I'm a bit afraid myself."

For the slightest of moments, she took his hand in hers and squeezed it. Gottlieb's lantern bobbed in the orchard below them and she let his hand go, quietly waiting until the watchman was gone. "Please be careful."

He thought of telling her about the Confederate soldiers that held the town of Chattanooga under siege, about the warnings Colonel O'Neill had given him. The task ahead was impossible, but God so often dwelt right in the midst of the impossible. He didn't know what awaited him, but he hoped the siege might be lifted by the time he and Faust arrived in Tennessee. If it wasn't, the burden would be too much for Amalie to carry. He wanted her concern, but he didn't want her to be afraid.

"I will come back to you, Amalie."

She shook her head. "You don't know."

He touched the softness of her face, lifting her eyes to him again. When he gazed down at her, he felt like his own heart might stop its beat. "I will do everything I can to return to you."

Chapter Twenty-Nine

From her window, Amalie watched Matthias walk away from her window until the outline of his body disappeared into the darkness. Was it really possible that Matthias Roemig loved her?

In spite of the cold, her body radiated with warmth, and her fingers rolled over the smooth varnish on the lid of Matthias's box. What was he keeping locked inside it? A letter, perhaps, or something of value. As much as she wanted to know what he was giving her, she would guard the box and its lock until he returned.

She struck a match and the tip blazed in her fingers as she opened the drawer to her nightstand and reached inside, searching for Friedrich's box. The box that she had thought he made for her.

She remembered well the morning he had given it to her. They'd taken a walk to the creek in Ebenezer, talking about what awaited them in the west, and he gave her the box so she would never forget him.

And she hadn't. She had been true to him for more than three years, treasuring the box as a small part of Friedrich's love for her. A reminder that he cared for her.

Now she held both boxes, one in each hand. They were carved from the same type of wood, the same design. She'd always assumed that

Friedrich had made the box in his father's shop, but perhaps she was wrong. Perhaps Matthias made both boxes.

She placed the boxes into the nightstand, easing the drawer shut.

What if Matthias had cared for her all of these years? That would explain why he'd acted so unkind toward her when she tried to feed him. He was being loyal to Friedrich and was helping her to be loyal as well.

Matthias Roemig was truly an honorable man.

She sat down on her bed and moved back against the wall. She didn't remember much about what Friedrich looked like, but she knew every inch of Matthias's face. She knew his frown and his handsome smile and the woodsy brown of his eyes. She knew what made him smile and what made him angry, and tonight she had seen a glimpse of his heart, something she hadn't seen since they were children.

But that didn't mean that she should or even could offer any promise to him. Quietly she thanked God that he hadn't asked for one.

As she scooted down onto her pillows, fear plagued her at the thrill that Matthias's touch brought. It was much too soon for her to begin to think about loving another, Matthias or anyone else.

I pray that you will wait for me as well, but if I don't return, my desire is that you will live a life of dedication in the Kolonie. And that you will find love.

The words of Friedrich's first letter haunted her. She would remain dedicated to the community, but he said he desired that she find love as well.

She tossed on her pillow. Even if she wanted to love Matthias, she didn't have anything left in her heart to give.

In the morning, long before the sun began to rise, Amalie opened her nightstand drawer one more time to look at the boxes, to reassure herself that last night hadn't been a dream. Then she dressed quickly and crept down the stairs to the kitchen.

While most of the people in Amana awakened, she hummed as she beat together egg yolks and milk to make apple fritters. And as she worked, she prayed that sunshine would warm their village today and that it would follow Matthias and Mr. Faust all the way to Chattanooga.

Amalie was sifting together flour, baking powder, and cinnamon when Karoline crossed under the archway that separated the kitchen from the residence.

Karoline reached for her apron and tied it around her waist, eyeing her as if she wasn't certain if Amalie was happy or confused. "You're in pleasant spirits this morning."

"I believe the sun is going to shine today."

"That is a good reason to smile."

Amalie leaned over to fold the egg whites into the batter. She didn't need to explain why her heart felt so light today, nor did she even quite know why she felt this way.

"I saw that Christoph Faust has returned to us."

"*Ja*," Amalie replied. "He is supposed to accompany Matthias to Tennessee."

"I will prepare a basket of food for their journey."

Amalie hesitated. She wanted to prepare the basket for Matthias. But then she changed her mind. Perhaps it was better for Karoline to put it together.

Two other girls arrived to help, and the kitchen was soon awhirl with activity. Amalie stirred chunks of apple into the batter and then she fried the fritters in lard. The other women fried bacon and boiled coffee and set plates and silverware on the table. She was sprinkling powdered sugar on the fritters when the diners began to arrive.

Amalie didn't even peek outside as Karoline and one of the other girls began to serve breakfast. She didn't know if she could bear to see Matthias, not after last night. If she blushed at the sight of him, people would wonder and they would talk. She didn't need that kind of scrutiny from him or anyone else. It was much safer for her to stay in the confines of her new kitchen.

Karoline swooped back into the kitchen. "Matthias is out there."

"Is he?"

"Along with Mr. Faust and Jonah Henson. He said they are leaving within the hour."

She scooted another platter of fritters toward her. "Make sure they have enough bread and beer for their journey."

"I will."

"And don't forget to add the Handkäse."

Karoline grinned at her. "Of course."

"And some dried meat." She sounded just like Henriette, but she didn't care.

"Amalie—" Karoline stopped her. "Something is different about you, and I don't think it has anything to do with the sun."

Amalie glanced out the window. Sunlight had indeed replaced the darkness, and snow iced the trees and rooftops outside the window. Everything looked white except the sky.

She turned back to the fritters bubbling in the pot of lard. "The sun always brings good cheer."

"The sun and other things."

Amalie grunted in response.

"You have no reason to feel bad for your joy, Amalie. It is a blessing from God."

When Amalie fished the last fritters out of the pot, the grease splattered on her finger and she raced to pour cold water over it. As she

1863

soaked her finger in a bowl, she glanced out the kitchen door and saw Matthias eating his breakfast beside Jonah. There was strength in his posture. A confidence that she'd always admired.

She was grateful this morning for many things, including that God had given Matthias a new friend in Jonah. Jonah could never replace the childhood bond of friendship he had with Friedrich—just as no man could ever replace the love she'd had for him—but perhaps God had given both Matthias and her a way to help mend their brokenness.

When Matthias stood up, she scurried back to the stove. There was no batter left for her to fry, so she frantically searched the cluttered table to find something to busy her hands and her mind.

"Amalie?" Karoline probed, concern bolstering her voice.

"I'm fine."

Karoline placed her hands on her hips. "Are you sure you don't want to marry Mr. Faust?"

Amalie picked up a spoon and glared at her friend. "I'm certain."

"Because I'm sure the option is still open," Karoline teased her. "You could marry when they return from Tennessee."

Someone stepped into the kitchen behind Amalie, and her heart raced. Turning slowly, she expected to see Matthias, but Christoph Faust stood there instead.

"What's this talk of marriage?" he asked.

She wished she could crawl under the worktable and hide from the questioning in his eyes.

"You'll have to ask Sister Karoline," she finally said.

He didn't look toward Karoline. "I thought you would be married by now."

She hesitated, not daring to tell him that Friedrich was gone. If Matthias hadn't told him, then neither would she. "In time I will marry."

"Perhaps it isn't too late for you to break out of this cage."

The Amana Colonies weren't a cage to her; they were a cocoon.

"I'm not leaving here, Mr. Faust. With you or with anyone else."

Matthias appeared behind Mr. Faust, and on his handsome face was a grin she hadn't seen since he was ten or eleven. And he was smiling at her.

"The train won't wait for us," he told Mr. Faust.

Mr. Faust stuck his hat back on his head and turned toward the door. "Then we must leave."

Matthias was still looking at her, still smiling. Karoline thrust two baskets of food toward Matthias, and then she seemed to disappear, out the door behind Mr. Faust perhaps.

"We will all be praying for you," she said.

Matthias held her gaze, his tone so low that she was the only one who could hear him. "I will not forget it."

Her heart raced along with her voice. "Mr. Faust is a good guide."

"He knows that Friedrich was killed." He held her gaze steady within his. "But he doesn't know Friedrich was planning to marry you."

"Thank you."

He tipped his hat and then he was gone.

* * * * *

Fresh snow covered the road as Matthias and Faust rode through Amana on the wagon. He lifted his hat to Jonah and Karoline and dozens of other people gathered in clusters to wave as they began their journey east. Even though Amalie wasn't on the street, he caught a glimpse of her face inside the kitchen window, watching him leave, and he lifted his hat one last time.

She had promised him nothing with her words, but her eyes had held a hint of promise. He would relive their last moments together over and over during this journey.

Louise, Hilga, and Brother Schaube waited for him at the edge of town. Louise kissed his cheek and whispered to him that Carl wouldn't be mad at him for long. Hilga didn't appear mad at all.

Brother Schaube prayed protection for him and Faust and then handed Matthias a small burlap bag filled with gold pieces and greenbacks to pay for their journey along with their train tickets.

Matthias stowed the money inside his coat. He'd never used money in his life, and wasn't sure exactly how to exchange it, but that was one of the reasons why Faust joined him on his journey. In spite of his rugged appearance, the elders trusted the man to help Matthias make wise decisions.

He urged the horses ahead on the snowy road. In the back of the wagon was the load of blankets and clothing to be delivered to Homestead, and the baskets filled with food were on the bench between them. Crates filled with the remaining supplies awaited them at the Homestead station, ready for the nine o'clock train heading east.

So much had changed since the last time he traveled through this forest, with Hilga at his side and Amalie trailing behind them. Hours before Colonel O'Neill came to the village and shattered their world.

Now his hope was being renewed. Their Savior had mercifully reached down to this world, into Matthias's sinful heart, and was transforming it. Amalie gave him hope for his future on earth, but only God could make him whole.

Faust pulled his hat low over his face and leaned back on the bench. "Is it strange for you to leave?"

"Very," he said slowly. "Friedrich was the one who longed for travel and adventure."

"Surely you wanted to see other places besides Iowa."

He shook his head. "I'm content in the Kolonie."

"Your colony sounds a bit too much like jail to me."

"There is much freedom in a community like ours."

Faust laughed. "You say that because you were born into it."

"No," Matthias replied. A clump of snow fell on Matthias's coat, and he brushed it off. "I was born a gypsy."

Faust stopped laughing, his eyebrows raised as he turned toward Matthias. "A gypsy?"

"I spent most of my childhood sleeping in tents or under the stars."

"It sounds like the perfect life for a boy."

"It wasn't."

Faust paused. "I suppose you had enough traveling as a child then."

Matthias nodded. "Why aren't you already in Tennessee, fighting for the Union?"

Faust leaned back against the bench, his boot on his knee. "I'm a wanderer, not a warrior."

"You never received a conscription letter?"

"I'm not an easy man to find." Faust nudged back the brim of his hat when he glanced over. "Were you conscripted?"

Matthias thought about Jonah and the battle wound he sustained, an injury he never complained about. "The elders hired a warrior to take my place."

The two men rode out of the white trees, toward the Homestead platform, and Matthias saw a man in full military attire standing by the depot. The buttons on his jacket gleamed in the light, and in his left hand he held a cane. Standing just as stolid beside him was a black man.

Matthias tied the horses to a post and walked toward Colonel O'Neill, but instead of speaking to the colonel, he acknowledged the man standing beside him.

1863
IA

"Are you Joseph?" he asked.

When the black man nodded his head, Matthias reached to shake his brother's hand. He understood, if only a bit, the wounds Joseph must have experienced as a child. "It's a pleasure."

Joseph's somber gaze dissolved into a smile. "Pleasure's all mine."

Matthias glanced between the men. "Are you planning to go to Tennessee?"

Colonel O'Neill lifted his cane and limped closer to him. "I'm not going and neither are you."

"What do you mean?"

"Chattanooga is still under siege. The Rebels won't even let Yankees deliver food into the city."

"All the more reason to get these supplies down there."

"There is no way into the town," the colonel insisted. "Confederate troops are guarding the roadways and the river within sixty miles of it."

Matthias glanced over at Faust and read the determination in his eyes. Then he scanned the dozens of crates the Homestead men were putting on the platform, ready to transfer to a boxcar. He couldn't turn back now.

"With the Lord's help," he said, strength filling his voice. "We will get these supplies to the troops."

"You don't understand—" The colonel tried again.

"I have to try," he said.

The colonel bowed his head for a moment as if he was asking for help from the Lord as well, but when he lifted his head, there was a slight smile on his gruff face. "Then you must go."

The platform began to rattle under their feet.

"Take this." Colonel O'Neill held out an envelope and hobbled forward to give it to Matthias. "When you get to Nashville, ask to speak with Major Oldham. He will help you."

"Thank you."

The freight train whistled, and seconds later the brakes squealed as it stopped next to them. The brothers from Homestead began to load the crates into an open boxcar.

"When we met before, I said some things I didn't mean," the colonel said.

"I've said things as of late that I didn't mean either."

"If you can get the supplies through the barricade…" He paused. "They will help sustain our troops."

As Matthias stepped into the boxcar, he watched Joseph place his hand on the colonel's shoulder. "I got to go with 'em, sir."

"Oh, no," Colonel O'Neill said. "There are still slave traders roaming the southern states."

"I know the terrain," Joseph insisted. "I can help 'em get to Chattanooga."

The colonel shook his head, but as the train crept forward, he didn't stop Joseph as he climbed into the boxcar beside Matthias and Faust.

Matthias lifted his hat to the man and then leaned back against a crate as Faust slid the door closed.

He didn't know what lay ahead of them, but he was glad that both Joseph and Faust were with him to help guide his path through this strange world. And he was even more glad that Amalie was praying for him.

From morn till eve my theme shall be thy mercy's wondrous measure;
To sacrifice myself for Thee shall be my aim and pleasure.
Paul Gerhardt

Chapter Thirty
....

Amalie and Karoline draped pine boughs along the tables in the dining room and arranged pink and white cyclamen blooms to sprinkle color into the green foliage.

She didn't know the couple being married very well, but as she and Karoline prepared their wedding luncheon, she tried hard to be happy for them.

These days it seemed like everyone in their village was scrutinizing her every emotion, trying to weigh if her love for Friedrich was true. She didn't know exactly what to say about anything, nor did she know how she should feel.

When a man and woman in their society made a formal declaration to marry, it was after much deliberation. Even with a period of separation, they almost always went forward with their marriage. She didn't know any women who had lost their betrothed before their marriage. Elderly men and women in Amana, and a few of younger people as well, understood the heartache of losing a spouse, but Amalie wasn't a widow. She was a woman who'd lost the man she loved, a man she'd never married.

Karoline stepped away from the table and gave a clap. "It looks beautiful."

Amalie surveyed the greenery and the assortment of nut and feather cakes stacked on a separate table at the side of the room. Hopefully the bride and groom would be pleased with the dining hall.

"One day I will prepare this room for you and your husband," she told her friend.

"No, you won't," Karoline protested. "There's no one in Amana for me to marry."

Amalie pretended not to hear her words. "We'll celebrate in the summer, though, so we can decorate this room with dahlias and phlox and dozens upon dozens of peonies."

Karoline rolled her eyes as she turned back toward the kitchen. "You must be dreaming about your wedding."

Instead of hurrying back with Karoline, Amalie lingered by the cake table. A wedding celebration was a rare holiday for their workers, and for a moment, she wondered what it would be like for Matthias to join them for the afternoon of singing and eating and celebrating the couple's future as man and wife.

But he and Mr. Faust had been gone for a week now. The elders received a telegram from the men soon after they'd left, saying they and their crates had arrived in Nashville. They didn't say how long it would take for them to travel to Chattanooga or when they would return.

Part of her didn't want Matthias to think she cared for him, not any more than a sister in Christ would care for him. But her mind wandered back to Ebenezer, the strength in Matthias's arms as he rescued her from the ice so long ago, and the fire of youth in his eyes. Then she thought about him as a man, in Amana. His determination to finish her kitchen and protect Friedrich's honor.

But now—now Friedrich was gone. And he had been gone from her since she was twenty-one.

What if, one day, she did decide to marry?

She straightened the cakes as she tried to force that thought out of her mind. Matthias might not even come back from Tennessee. She could no longer allow herself to focus another moment on her hopes; she need only pray for his safety.

"They're coming," Karoline called from the kitchen.

Amalie glanced out the window and watched the smiles of the newly married couple as they hurried across the street with dozens of family members and friends trailing behind them.

God in His time would direct her, but for now she would guard the broken pieces of her heart.

* * * * *

Fog shrouded the river and the forest along the shoreline, so thick that Matthias couldn't see the water over the side of their boat. It was the perfect covering for them to sneak across the enemy's line.

They'd carried the supplies by wagon down the Sequatchie Valley since the railway had been destroyed, then over a mountain pass. The three wooden pontoons that Major Oldham promised them were waiting along the Tennessee River, the captain and his crew of freed Negro men having paddled up from Bridgeport, Alabama.

They'd emptied the crates of supplies into the boats and covered the clothing and food with canvas to keep out the rain, but nothing would save the supplies if Rebel soldiers sank the boats.

Four crewmen paddled each boat, and at the captain's signal, they stopped paddling and listened. Behind the curtain of fog, soldiers marched near the shoreline. Matthias could hear the pings of musketry in the distance, and he prayed quietly for protection. None of them knew where the soldiers' loyalties lay, but a Yankee would be just as likely to shoot at an unidentified boat as a Rebel would.

"Stay low," Faust whispered from across the floor.

The man needn't worry. Both Matthias and Joseph lay flat against the hull—Matthias hadn't moved for a good hour. He wished he knew how to swim—in case the soldiers aimed their fire toward the boats—but he figured he could paddle to shore if he had to, preferably on the north side of the river.

When the soldiers' footsteps quieted, the captain's words slurred slightly as he commanded his men to continue paddling. Whiskey seemed to provide the man with the courage he needed to navigate through enemy territory. Matthias only hoped the captain could keep his wits about him while the enemy was so close. The captain said he didn't sympathize with either side of the war, but he was glad to profit from the madness.

The Confederates still surrounded the town, but according to Major Oldham, they were also fighting against the Federals on Lookout Mountain. The fog was a blessed deterrent this early morning, and with God's help, Matthias hoped they could maneuver around those left to guard Chattanooga.

The captain directed the boats around the river's rocky crags. They were about ten miles from the town of Chattanooga now, and if they could keep up this pace, they should be there by nightfall.

Matthias's fingers slipped into his pocket, the warmth long replaced with cold, and he felt the satchel inside that carried the key to the box he'd given Amalie. More than anything, he wanted to do this job well, and then he wanted to return to Amana, to open the box for her.

Shaking his head, he let go of the satchel and lifted himself up on the bench. Joseph quietly joined him, and together they looked out toward the fog. The trees and most of the cliffs were still obstructed from their view, but Matthias could see the ripples of dark water alongside their boat.

Faust pinched tobacco leaves out of a pouch and tucked them inside his cheek. Joseph took a pinch, but Faust didn't ask Matthias if he wanted tobacco. "Are you afraid?" he asked instead.

"A little."

"You know, I think a bit of that gypsy blood still runs through you. Most men would be terrified by now."

Matthias leaned back against the canvas side, the cold air ruffling his hair and coat. Perhaps some good had come out of his childhood. He didn't want to leave Amana, but when he did, he wasn't nearly as afraid as he thought he would be.

"You are a lucky man to have a girl like Amalie waiting for you."

His fingers brushed over his pocket again. "I hope she does wait for me."

Matthias glanced to the bow as the captain shuffled back toward them.

"This is my last favor for the major," the man slurred. He kept calling their trip a favor, but they were paying him handsomely for it.

"How long until we arrive in Chattanooga?" Matthias asked.

The captain's eyes were on the water. "By nightfall, if we're lucky."

A shot rattled through the fog and reverberated across their boat. The captain took a long swig from his flask and wiped his face with his sleeve. "Darn lucky if we get there at all."

Yield to God in true submission, He will free you from on high.
For your sorrow, grief, and strife, He'll bestow the crown of life.

Joachim Pauly

Chapter Thirty-One

....

Amalie hurried outside when she saw Jonah ride into the village.

"Is there any news?" she asked before he dismounted. They'd had no word from Matthias since they'd received the telegram from Nashville.

Jonah shook his head. "The colonel said there is substantial fighting near Chattanooga. They won't let anyone in or out of the town."

"I thought the troops were resting for the winter."

"It's hard to rest when you don't have food or clothing."

"Matthias is in danger, isn't he?"

He lifted his recovering arm, as if she needed the reminder. "No one is safe near the front lines."

As much as Amalie wanted the supplies to reach the soldiers, she hoped Matthias would wait outside Chattanooga until the siege was over.

"The colonel said he would send a messenger as soon as he receives word from Matthias."

Amalie nodded, stepping back to the kitchen. There was nothing else she could do but wait. "Come and eat some pie," she said.

Jonah hitched the horse to a post and followed her into the kitchen. The sling on his arm was gone now, and the despair once etched around his eyes had been transformed into a familiar contentment. It was a slow process of healing for all of them, but she was glad to see the smile on his face.

Last week Brother Schaube offered Jonah work as a carpenter until Matthias returned, and Jonah had accepted the offer immediately. He only went to Marengo these days at the elder's request to inquire about Matthias at the colonel's office, though it seemed to her that Jonah didn't even want to go back to his hometown for news. He stayed above Henriette's kitchen and ate there as well.

Karoline was by the stove when Amalie walked into the kitchen, stirring the chicken noodle soup in a stockpot.

Jonah paused in the doorway. "Good morning, Miss Baumer."

Karoline nodded at him, but she didn't respond.

Amalie eyed her friend curiously and then turned back to Jonah. "Karoline and I would be honored if you would join us for the noonday meal." She glanced over at the stove. "Don't you think, Karoline?"

"Ye—Yes. You should join us."

Did Karoline just stutter?

Faint ribbons of pink fluttered up Karoline's face as Amalie studied her. Then Amalie turned back to Jonah. "Have you tasted Karoline's chicken soup before?"

Jonah shook his head. "No, ma'am."

"It's the best in the Kolonie."

His eyes were still on Karoline. Karoline's eyes were on her soup.

"I'm sure it is," he said.

Amalie handed Jonah a fork along with a piece of warm apple pie.

"I need to pump some water," she said as she patted one of the stools for Jonah. "Why don't you sit and enjoy your pie?"

"Amalie—" Karoline protested, turning her head.

"I won't be gone long."

Amalie grinned at her friend as Jonah took a seat, and then she slipped out the back door.

* * * * *

Matthias and the others ducked down into the open hull as gunfire rattled the boat. Pockets of water splashed around them, and he prayed the shots would continue to pelt the river instead of their pontoon.

The winter sunlight was melting away the fog, and as the minutes passed, thick layers of gray peeled back until Matthias could finally see the shoreline. He'd thought they were in the middle of the river, but a grassy beach lay only yards away. And the tall grass was peppered with at least a dozen soldiers, the butts of their guns aimed at his boat.

He saw the blue tatters of their Federal uniforms. A few of them wore caps, while others had holes in their coats and shirts. Bare toes stuck out from the frayed hem of one soldier's trousers while another man wore only one shoe.

Faust rose above the canvas sides, his hands in the air, but instead of lifting his arms like the others, Joseph reached down and opened one of the boxes beside Matthias. Standing slowly beside Faust, Joseph held up a shoe for the men to see. "These men," he called. "They got shoes and food and blankets for all of you."

Joseph pitched the shoe forward, but before he released it, Faust yelled, "Don't throw that."

It was too late. The shoe sailed through the air and landed on the shore.

Matthias cringed at the man's error—a mortal one for all who had helped them—and he braced himself for the retaliation of fire. But instead of shooting, half the soldiers were focused on Joseph. The rest of them were focused on the shoe.

When the shoe didn't detonate, the soldier in front lowered his weapon and poked at it with his bayonet. Then he waved at the others and a cheer echoed across the rocky beach and the trees.

"How did you know what to do?" Matthias asked Joseph as they paddled toward shore.

The man shrugged. "If you'd of thrown it, they woulda shot you."

Matthias and the others passed around the jackets to the cold soldiers. Men with bare feet tugged on socks and laced on new shoes. Then they devoured the cheese and salted pork. Many of them had lost or burned their blankets weeks ago so the Confederate soldiers couldn't use them, but the Rebels never captured them. Now they had new blankets to keep them warm at night.

The baas soldier directed Matthias away from the others. "Name's Brayden," he said as he chewed on a piece of the salted pork. "We're from Pennsylvania."

Matthias introduced himself.

"I don't know how much longer we could've lasted without food," Brayden whispered, then he glanced down at Matthias's plain clothes. "Why aren't you soldiering?"

"I—" Guilt washed over Matthias for a moment, and then he stood taller. He had done the right thing, following his leaders in their pursuit of peace. "I belong to a group called the Inspirationists. We believe there are peaceful ways to resolve this war."

"I wish you'd tell that to the folks in Washington."

"We tried, several times, but they wouldn't listen to us."

"I'm glad you didn't enlist," Braydon said. "My men and I are grateful for the supplies."

Matthias pointed to the two boats waiting in the river behind his. "We have plenty more for the soldiers in Chattanooga."

Braydon eyed the boats and then smiled. "I've been looking for a way to get us back to town."

Sergeant Braydon commanded six of his soldiers to embark on the first boat and they slipped easily into the spaces that once held boxes. The other soldiers divided up to ride on the other two boats. With their muskets honed on the rocky cliffs and trees, the crew shipped their oars and rowed for another two hours without confrontation, into the town of Chattanooga.

At the river's edge, ragged clusters of men greeted them. Their clothing was no longer recognizable as uniforms, their cheeks sallow from hunger. The soldiers they'd met earlier began to unload the boats before they docked, and Faust and Joseph joined them in handing boxes of food to the waiting men who then sat down on the shore and devoured the contents.

Matthias stepped out of the boat, marveling at all God had done, marveling that He had brought them into the town safely under the cover of the fog. At that moment, Matthias had never been so grateful to be part of the Inspirationist community. Their sacrifices were different than the sacrifices of those who enlisted to serve their country, but they offered what they believed God required of them.

Faust pushed him forward. "Tell them your people gave them this food."

Matthias stuck his hands in his pockets, shaking his head. "We were only the hands, like all of these men passing out the food. It was God who provided it."

Faust gave him an odd look, one that Matthias was beginning to grow used to in the world outside Amana. "Don't you want them to know about your Kolonie?"

"I want them to know that God hasn't forgotten them."

Matthias watched the men on the shore, wrapped in woolen blankets as they ate. For the rest of his life, he would continue to fight—but not with weapons. He would fight to help those in need.

A heart full of pleasure is better than gold,
I would not exchange it for riches untold.

Author Unknown

Chapter Thirty-Two

....

Plunk.

Amalie flew up on her bed and listened. The wind rattled her window this first night of the new year, but nothing else hit the glass. She pulled her quilt up to her neck, but she couldn't rest her head back on her pillows. Not with her heart leaping inside her chest like a candle's flame.

Night after night, she'd dreamt about a stone hitting her window, but nothing except tree limbs had banged against it in well over a month. Winter was upon them now, snow crusting the streets and rooftops, and with the long nights, she dreamed more often. Matthias Roemig had taken over most of these dreams.

All those years that she'd spent with Matthias along with Friedrich. She'd loved Friedrich back then, but she cared for Matthias as well—as a friend and a brother. Something had happened inside her heart during the weeks he'd been away. She couldn't explain it nor did she know if she wanted to, but she desperately wanted Matthias to return to Amana. To stay true to their Savior and to the community...and to her.

She lifted the walnut box he'd made off her nightstand and held it close to her chest, wondering again what he'd locked inside. Carl Vinzenz or Jonah could probably open it for her, but as much as she wanted to see its contents, she wouldn't open it until Matthias returned to her.

Weeks had gone by without any word from Matthias or Mr. Faust. Not even a telegram. Every night, their community prayed together that Matthias was safe, wintering with the troops someplace. Last week Jonah returned from Marengo with the news that the Union had won back Chattanooga, and supplies were beginning to trickle into the town. The whole community rejoiced.

She began to scoot back down into her covers. She didn't dare allow herself to compare her fear of losing Friedrich with her fear that she would lose Matthias, but in the dark hours of the night, when her hands were idle, she was terrified that he would be taken from her as well.

Plunk.

Her heart leapt again at the sound of something hitting her window. It was probably a tree limb, but still, she had to know for certain. Holding her breath, she stole across the bare floor, to the window, and she looked down at the yard below. At the dark form looking back up at her.

Her fingers shaking, she struggled to open the window. Wind blasted her face, her hair swirling around her head. As she pushed her hair back, she squinted into the darkness.

"Who's there?" she called, her voice hushed.

There was a long pause before he spoke. "I'm home, Amalie."

She caught herself against the windowsill, her knees wobbling at the sound of the familiar voice.

"Don't move," she said, louder this time. She didn't care if she woke everyone in the residence. Matthias was home!

Amalie buttoned her dress quickly before wrapping her heavy shawl around her shoulders, a scarf around her hair. Securing Matthias's box inside the folds of her shawl, she rushed down the stairs and out into the night, right into Matthias's open arms.

She could smell the dust on his collar, feel the soft bristles from the beard he'd grown in Tennessee. And she didn't want him to let her go. Time seemed to stop for a moment before he held her out in front of him, searching her face in the dim light. "I couldn't wait until morning to see you."

"I would have been disappointed if you had."

"There's so much to tell you," he said, but the words faded away. For now, silence was enough.

"Come," he said gently, reaching for her hand.

It wasn't until they stepped onto the dirt street that she realized she had forgotten to put on her shoes, but even with the coldness, she didn't care.

A fire roared inside the carpentry shop, shadows from the tools flickering across the wooden walls. The heat warmed her skin, and the presence of Matthias soothed her. This was exactly where she was supposed to be.

He patted a bench and she sat down beside him, tucking her cold feet under her dress. "I missed you, Amalie."

"You were gone too long."

He nodded. "We made it to Chattanooga without harm, but Faust didn't think it was safe to return until after the Federals took back the town."

"Did they need the supplies?"

"Very much."

"Then I'm glad you went," she said. "And I'm glad you returned."

"The war is almost over now."

"Does that mean they will free the rest of the slaves?"

"I pray so." His eyes softened in the firelight. "Did you bring the box?"

She unwrapped the walnut box from her shawl and slid it toward him. "I wanted to know what was inside."

"You could have broken the lock."

She shook her head. "I wanted to wait even more to open it with you."

He took the satchel out of his pocket and removed the key. His gaze on her, he took the box out of her hands and then looked down for the briefest of moments to unlock the box.

"Can I open it?" she whispered.

He lifted the box up to her hands and she slowly opened the lid.

Something sparkled inside, green and red and blue dancing with the firelight. The box didn't harbor a letter or flower petals or locks of hair. It held a piece of jewelry.

Reaching inside, Amalie lifted out a gold chain with gems and trinkets dangling from it. She stared at all the colors, mesmerized. She'd never seen anything so beautiful.

Her fascination turned slowly into fear as she looked back at Matthias, her eyes wide. "Where did you get this?"

"It was my mother's."

Her fingers brushed over the stones and a gold coin and copper pendant. Part of her was frightened by this information while another part of her was intrigued. Sophia had said Matthias's mother had been a witch—did this piece carry some sort of enchantment with it?

But that didn't seem right. Why would Matthias keep a piece like that, even if it had been his mother's?

"My mother was a gypsy," he said softly.

Amalie stared at the stones on the bracelet again. Her father had told her stories about the gypsies in their Fatherland. The Roma. Many of them were enslaved in Europe and the few who weren't slaves were despised and often feared, so much that the German government often took away the children of gypsies to give to families they considered more respectable.

1863
IA

"Was she—was she a slave?"

He nodded. "She ran away from her owner when I was three."

Amalie tried to speak, but the shock seemed to capture her tongue. If Matthias's mother had been a slave, then he would have grown up as a slave as well.

Finally she spoke again. "Do you remember it?"

"A little. It was a hard life, but my mother protected me as much as she could."

He took the bracelet gently from her hands, his voice distant for a moment as if he were traveling back to a place she couldn't possibly understand. "My grandmother made us this bracelet so we would remember."

"Remember what?" she probed.

"The secrets passed down through our family."

The trinkets and gemstones traveled between Matthias's strong fingers, and she had a feeling that he had clung to this piece often, remembering his past.

He held out the blue gem on the bracelet. The edges weren't as smooth as some of the other stones, but the color was as vibrant as the winter sky.

"This is a blue quartz. My mother used to say that the flaws in its beauty represented life's greatest secret."

Amalie leaned forward.

"She said no one can buy joy nor can any man take it away. It is a gift bestowed only from God, and it was a gift she wanted to pass down to me."

"That's a beautiful gift." She rubbed her fingers over the roughness of the quartz and then he showed her the gold coin, tinged orange in the light.

"This piece represented wealth. Even though we had no pillow to lay our head on at night, we were blessed with abundance because we had each other."

"You were very blessed," she repeated in a whisper.

He dangled a piece of leather against his palm. "This was from a whip, once used to beat my grandfather," he said, and she cringed at his words.

"My grandmother cut one of the tassels off the whip and made my mother promise that when she received her freedom, she would cherish it forever."

Tears filled Amalie's eyes. No son should ever have to carry the burden of slavery for his family. And no mother should ever have to tell her child to cherish his freedom.

Not long ago, she had tried to educate Matthias about the evils of slavery. No wonder he had been so irritated with her. He knew much more about it than she could ever imagine.

"You're crying," he whispered, wiping the tears gently off her face with his sleeve.

She nodded. For the first time since childhood, her tears flowed outside the solitude of her room. And Matthias didn't try to stop her.

She pointed at a copper piece that looked like a small butterfly. "What is this one?"

"It represents new life," he said. "The old passes away when God redeems us. No matter our circumstances, we are a new creature in Him."

The fire popped, and he glanced over at it before his gaze fell back on the bracelet.

Amalie pointed at a piece of green-colored glass that glowed in the light. "And this secret?"

He held up the smooth glass. "We look through the window of this life like glass, into the splendor of eternity," he explained with a smile. "The hardships in this world last only but a short time, and if we endure, we will be harbored by our Savior forever."

He skipped over several of the gems and trinkets until he held out one last jewel, this one a bright red. He paused, staring at it for a moment before he lifted his eyes back to her. "My mother added this ruby to the bracelet as our secret. It was her promise to me."

She swallowed at the intensity in his eyes. "What did it mean?"

"That she loved me from the day I came into this world, and no matter what happened, she would never stop loving me." He looked back down at the bracelet. "But she didn't keep her promise. She left me alone at the castle gate, with this bracelet hanging from a chain around my neck."

"She never stopped loving you, Matthias."

He shook his head. "She gave up."

"Or she was afraid. Maybe she thought you would have to return to slavery if she kept you or maybe she didn't want you to have to wander anymore."

A little boy seemed to emerge from within him, the hurting child who had been abandoned by the one person who was supposed to love him forever. "The Vinzenz family would have adopted her into their family, like they did for me."

Amalie stared at the red gem again and marveled at its beauty. Then she reached out and touched the butterfly.

"She sacrificed her heart for you, Matthias. She gave up what she loved most so that you could have a new life, like the butterfly."

With her words, the hurting child swelled back into the strength of a man. "Sacrifice is what love is about," he said.

"Yes, it is."

He held out the bracelet to her. "I'd like you to have this."

Her hands froze in her lap, and she couldn't seem to move them. "Oh, Matthias."

"They're the secrets of my family," he said. "Of my past." His eyes blazed like the fire behind him.

"And I want to share them with you."

She reached out slowly and took the bracelet—his secrets—in her hands. "My heart," she whispered. "It's been shattered."

He brushed a stray wisp of her hair behind her ear, and then his hand slipped back into his pocket. He removed a smooth stone from it, a shiny gray color with tan and red strands that rippled across it. "I found this along the riverbed in Tennessee," he said, holding her in his gaze. "And I want it—I want it to represent my promise to you."

"What promise?"

"I'm a carpenter, Amalie," he said quietly. "I build things, and I help put broken pieces back together again."

She couldn't seem to breathe. "My heart?"

"Only if you'll give me the pieces."

When he held out the stone, she rubbed her fingers over it and then looked back at him. "I'm not the only one with a broken heart."

His eyes wandered back toward the fire, but she reached up to his face, her fingers brushing over his beard as she turned his head back to her. "I want to help you put the pieces of your heart back together too."

When his eyes locked her gaze, he pleaded with her. "I don't want to be without you, Amalie, not for another day."

Slowly she lifted the bracelet and slid it over her wrist. Pulling her face close to his, he encircled her with his arms.

Shadows danced on the wall around them, the fire blazing in the hearth, but it was his kiss that warmed her this time, all the way down to her bare toes.

Epilogue

....

Amalie knelt down in front of the white tombstone and placed the wildflowers on Friedrich Vinzenz's grave. A spring breeze swept down Lookout Mountain and over the grassy hill that harbored the graves of the more than ten thousand Union soldiers who had died in battles around Chattanooga.

The chirping of birds replaced the fighting now, the creatures oblivious to the bloodshed that soaked these hills and scarred the town six years ago. Instead of sending troops to battle each other, the States were united again. They were trying to rebuild, but it would take many years for their country to heal from her many battle wounds.

Amalie ran her fingers over the etching of Friedrich's name and company on the tombstone. While she had long stopped wondering about his decision to fight, she often wondered if their country's leaders would have pursued this war if they had known they would lose 600,000 men. Even after the Union won the Battles for Chattanooga, the war raged on for another year and a half.

Matthias proposed to her right after he returned from Chattanooga, and they were married in March of 1864. The whole community, including Carl Vinzenz, celebrated their wedding with them. Matthias had loved her like he promised and helped piece her shattered heart back together until it finally felt whole once more.

His heart had healed slowly alongside hers, and they worked together to supply food and clothing to Union soldiers until Robert E.

Lee surrendered to General Grant at the Appomattox Court House the following spring. Thankfully, the war never came to Iowa, but families across their state were still hurting over the loss of their sons. She prayed their hearts would heal as well.

She wished she could tell Friedrich all that had happened since he left Amana, but perhaps he already knew. Niklas Keller finally married Friedrich's sister and they were expecting their first child. And months after Jonah Henson joined their society, he married Karoline.

"You should see Jonah," she whispered, as if Friedrich could hear her. His arm had healed, and now he and Niklas worked alongside Matthias as carpenters. It was as if Jonah had lived in their community his entire life.

Her gaze wandered beyond Friedrich's grave, up the crags of the mountain. The Kolonie hadn't changed much since his death but her people had changed. Amalie's parents arrived with the last group from Ebenezer in 1864, and they settled in High Amana. Her parents visited the first Sunday of each month, but Friedrich's parents had welcomed her into their family.

And then there was Sophia Paul.

After Christoph Faust traveled with Matthias to Chattanooga, he returned to Amana and visited Sophia in Henriette's kitchen. The last Amalie had heard, Sophia was cooking for Mr. Faust on a wagon train bound for Oregon.

"Are you all right, Mama?"

Amalie blinked and looked down at her son. He wrapped his arms around her, and she gave him a big hug. "I'm happy and sad at the same time."

He nodded like he understood, and at his sweet empathy, her tears began to pour.

"Don't cry," he begged.

1863

She wiped the tears off with her sleeves. They were a mixture of happiness and sadness. Sorrow and joy.

"Uncle Friedrich is with Jesus."

She kissed his forehead. "I know, *Schatz*."

Treasure.

He stepped away from her, calling over his shoulder. "She's crying again, Papa."

She turned and looked at Matthias, holding their three-month-old daughter close in his arms. Gratefulness filled her heart. Matthias not only loved her, but he had suggested they travel together to honor their friend, the man she almost married. She was blessed in abundance.

Concern filled Matthias's eyes as he walked toward her. "Are you all right?"

Amalie put her arm around his waist, and he held her close to his side as their son wrapped his arms around both of them. In the silence, she rejoiced at the joy God had given her in her husband and in her children.

"Uncle Friedrich was a brave man," Matthias told their son as he ruffled the boy's hair. "He gave up his life to help rescue people who weren't able to rescue themselves."

Amalie leaned down and handed her son the box she once thought Friedrich had made for her, the fragments of rose petals still inside, and he slowly walked it over to the tombstone. Matthias kissed her hair, and she clung to him as their son placed the small box by the fresh flowers.

She wished Carl and Louise could be there to see the child they called grandson honor their son.

"He should be here soon," Matthias whispered, and she nodded her head. Matthias took her hand, and together their family walked to the base of the hill to meet the man whom they had traveled eight hundred miles to see.

A carriage was waiting by the entrance to the cemetery. The door opened, and a handsome man stepped out of the carriage, dressed in a black suit and top hat, followed by a woman dressed in yards and yards of a vibrant green color, a newborn child secured in her arms.

The man took off his hat and stretched out his hand. "My name is Taylor," he said. "Taylor Barnes."

Matthias shook Taylor's hand and introduced Amalie and their baby daughter. Then he nudged their son forward.

"This is our son," Matthias said. "His name is Friedrich Roemig."

Tears damped Taylor's eyes. "It's a pleasure to meet you, son."

Friedrich placed his hands on his hips. "You don't look one bit like a Rebel."

Taylor laughed as he wiped his cheeks dry with a handkerchief. "What exactly does a Rebel look like?"

Amalie was horrified when Friedrich pulled his eyes back and crossed them.

"Stop that," she commanded.

Taylor laughed again, messing up Friedrich's hair. "I think your son is right, ma'am. A lot of Rebels looked exactly like that."

Amalie took a deep breath, relief washing through her. She'd been afraid her heart was still filled with hatred for the man in front of her, but God had replaced the hatred with love.

When Taylor introduced his wife, Udela Barnes held out her elegant glove to Amalie. "I am so grateful—" she began, but tears interrupted her words.

Matthias stepped forward again, speaking to Taylor as Udela wiped her tears. "We were surprised to get your letter."

"It took me a long time to find you, and then I didn't think you would want to meet me," Taylor said. "But over the past months, Udela and I, we felt like we were supposed to contact you."

Taylor took a book out of his pocket, and Amalie looked down to see the Gospel of John.

"I've had this since the battle." He handed the Gospel to Amalie and she opened the first page to read Friedrich Vinzenz's name. "I've taken good care of it for you."

"Thank you," she said, and then she leaned down and showed the Bible to her son. "Friedrich's parents will cherish it."

"Friedrich died a hero."

Amalie glanced over at Matthias, but instead of jealousy, she saw only kindness in his face. "He lived as a hero as well," she replied.

Tears filled Taylor's eyes once more.

"Please—please forgive me," Taylor asked of her.

She watched the young man, thinking for a moment that he was begging forgiveness for keeping Friedrich's book for so long, but then she realized what he was asking. He wanted her to forgive him for being alive.

Her gaze wandered from his tears to the eyes of his wife and then the face of his precious child. Friedrich wouldn't want him to carry this burden another day, and neither did she.

"It was God who rescued you, Taylor, and it was God who called Friedrich home. You did nothing wrong."

"Please—" the man begged again.

Amalie remembered the part of her that had blamed this man for Friedrich's death, a Confederate fighting to keep people enslaved. Friedrich had died for Taylor, and in her heart, she had hated the Rebel that he used to be. Yet God had redeemed her and her family, even with her hatred, and she knew He desired to not only rescue this man's life, but his soul as well.

She put one arm around Taylor Barnes and the other around his wife.

"You are forgiven," she whispered.

When she released the Barnes family, she heard little Friedrich behind her, cheering for them all.

Author's Note

....

It was such a pleasure for me to return to the Amana Colonies to write a story that takes place more than thirty years before my novel *Love Finds You in Homestead, Iowa*. The United States was in turmoil during the 1860s, but the Community of True Inspiration remained strong during the War Between the States. The Inspirationists' faith in God and pursuit of community was intertwined with their work and families and the building of their colony.

In spite of the community's beliefs regarding pacifism, eight men left the Amana Society to fight in the Civil War, though many of these soldiers returned to the Amana Colonies after the war ended and rejoined the Society. Adam Stahl, one of these Amana men, was a private with the 28th Iowa Infantry. Seventeen additional men from Amana were conscripted to join the Union Army, but after the elders paid commutation fees, these men were relieved of this duty.

The Amana community donated thirty thousand dollars (worth approximately half a million dollars today) to the war effort along with blankets, coats, and other supplies for the soldiers. And they continued to pray for peace in the States and petition the country's leaders to humble themselves and search for a peaceful resolution to the war that cost the lives of more than 600,000 men.

The Amana Colonies no longer operate as a commune, but their community is still vibrant along with the Amana Church (www.amana-church.org). Empowered by the Holy Spirit, Amana Church members guide and support each other in a relationship with Jesus Christ, and they recognize their obligation according to Scripture to pray on behalf of their civil government as well as be subject to its authority. Amana men served in both world wars and have fought in subsequent conflicts around the world.

Thank you to Peter Hoehnle (*The Amana People*), Brandi Jones, Emilie Hoppe (*Seasons of Plenty*), and other friends in the Amana Colonies for helping me learn about the rich history and spiritual vibrancy of the Inspirationists. Thank you, Peter, for your meticulous work checking my facts, coloring in the lines of this story, and providing me with the information to reflect the heart and heritage of the Amana Society and its people. Any errors in this novel are my fault.

A special thank you also to:

The incredibly talented team at Summerside Press—Carlton Garborg, Rachel Meisel, Ellen Tarver, Jason Rovenstine, and Suzi McDonough. Thank you for the opportunity to journey alongside you in telling the stories of small towns and communities across our great country. It is a pleasure working with each of you.

Pinn Crawford, a miracle worker of a librarian. I am continually amazed at the old books and articles you are able to locate. What would I do without you?

Sandra Bishop, my agent. Thank you for your constant friendship and direction.

Kelly Chang, Kimberly Felton, Leslie Gould, Jenna Thompson, and my sister, Christina Nunn—thank you all for your insight and expertise.

My parents and both friends and family members who continue to pray and encourage me as I write. I am thankful for each one of you.

Jon, Karly, and Kiki—I am blessed every day by your love and grace.

And, most of all, I am grateful to Jesus Christ who is the same yesterday, today, and forever.

"For the LORD is good and his love endures forever; his faithfulness continues through all generations" (Psalm 100:5 NIV).

Blessings,
Melanie Dobson
www.melaniedobson.com

About the Author

....

 Melanie Dobson is the award-winning author of eight historical and contemporary novels, including *Love Finds You in Homestead, Iowa* and *The Silent Order*. *Love Finds You in Liberty, Indiana* was chosen as the Best Book of Indiana (fiction) in 2010, and her suspense novel *The Black Cloister* received the Foreword Book of the Year award in 2009 for religious fiction.

Melanie is the former corporate publicity manager at Focus on the Family, and she worked in public relations for fifteen years before she began writing fiction full-time. She spent her high school years living in Iowa where she became intrigued by the Amana Colonies and Amana people, and she now resides with her family near Portland, Oregon.

www.melaniedobson.com

POST CARD
CARTE POSTALE
Love Finds You

Want a peek into local American life—past and present?
The *Love Finds You*™ series published by Summerside Press
features real towns and combines travel, romance,
and faith in one irresistible package!

The novels in the series—uniquely titled after American towns with romantic or intriguing names—inspire romance and fun. Each fictional story draws on the compelling history or the unique character of a real place. Stories center on romances kindled in small towns, old loves lost and found again on the high plains, and new loves discovered at exciting vacation getaways. Summerside Press plans to publish at least one novel set in each of the fifty states. Be sure to catch them all!

NOW AVAILABLE

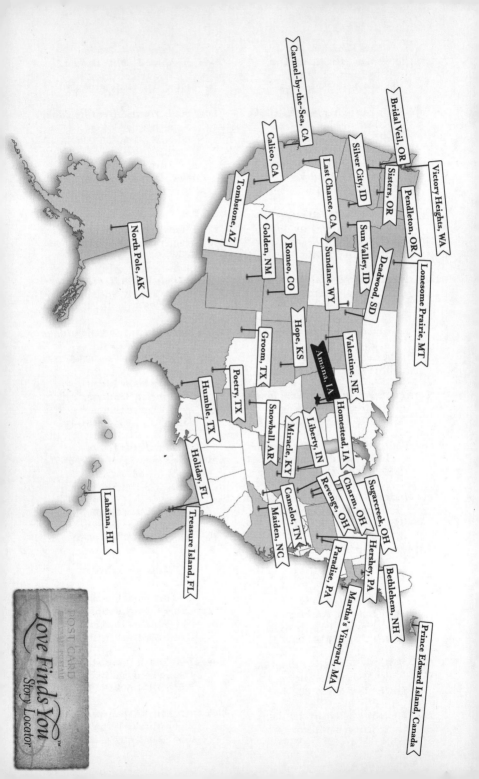